Adrift in the Middle Kingdom

Also published by Handheld Press

Adrift in the Middle Kingdom

by J Slauerhoff
translated by David McKay

with an introduction by Arie Pos and Wendy Gan

Handheld
Press

Handheld Classic 9

First published in The Netherlands in 1934 by Nijgh & Van Ditmar
as *Het leven op aarde*.

This edition published in 2019 by Handheld Press Ltd.
72 Warminster Road, Bath BA2 6RU, United Kingdom.
www.handheldpress.co.uk

ISBN 978-1-9999448-7-2

1 2 3 4 5 6 7 8 9 0

Series design by Nadja Guggi and typeset in Adobe Caslon Pro
and Open Sans.

Printed and bound in Great Britain by Short Run Press, Exeter.

This publication has been made possible with financial support
from the Dutch Foundation for Literature.

N ederlands
N letterenfonds
dutch foundation
for literature

Contents

Arie Pos has lectured on Dutch literature and culture at the universities of Coimbra, Lisbon and Oporto, and is a translator of Portuguese literature into Dutch and vice versa. As well as a Portuguese translation of *The Forbidden Kingdom* he has published many articles and several books on J Slauerhoff and his work.

Wendy Gan is Associate Professor of English at the University of Hong Kong and the author of *Fruit Chan's Durian Durian* (2005) and *Women, Privacy and Modernity in Early Twentieth-Century British Writing* (2009). Her latest book, *Comic China: Representing Common Ground, 1890–1945* (2018) examines Anglo-American representations of China and the politics of humour.

Introduction

Slauerhoff and the novel

BY ARIE POS

Jan Jacob Slauerhoff (1898–1936) is one of the most important writers of twentieth-century Dutch literature, and his poetry and prose continue to fascinate large numbers of readers. His short and troubled life was a restless quest for happiness, lasting love, a home and peace of mind, none of which he found. Born in Leeuwarden, the provincial capital of Friesland in the cold north of the Netherlands, he was asthmatic from an early age and could only breathe more freely during summer holidays on the island of Vlieland. The vitalising contact with the sea, the stories of seamen in his family and his passion for books about adventurous voyages and exotic cultures inspired a longing to travel and see the world.

He studied medicine at Amsterdam University from 1916 to 1923, and published his first poems in student magazines and literary reviews. After making sea trips to France and Portugal he decided to become a ship's doctor. It seemed a good choice to get away from the cold and wet Dutch climate and the petty bourgeois society that he despised. His first collection of poetry, *Archipel*, was published at the end of November 1923 and a week after he took his Hippocratic Oath. In early 1924 he was on his way to the Dutch East Indies (modern Indonesia) to start a floating doctor's life in the Far East. However, shortly before his arrival in Batavia (modern Jakarta) he suffered a lung haemorrhage, later diagnosed as a first sign of tuberculosis. He returned to the Netherlands to recover and worked for short periods as a locum before returning to Batavia, where he signed a contract with the Java-China-Japan Line in September 1925.

For two years he served as a doctor on the 'coolie boats' that transported Chinese plantation workers to and from Java and took other passengers and freight to Hong Kong and the ports on China's south and east coasts. The ports he visited most frequently on the twelve journeys he made before his return to Europe in October 1927 were Hong Kong, Amoy and Shanghai. On some journeys the route included extra stops in the Philippines, Korea or Japan. Slauerhoff was able to leave his ship and visit the city or make small excursions inland. He took notes, kept a diary and wrote poetry and travelogues. His years in the Far East formed a major inspiration for his literary work; as well as poetry he wrote short stories and two novels set in China, the country that fascinated him throughout his life.

From 1928 to 1931 Slauerhoff worked on the luxurious Royal Holland Lloyd ocean liners, sailing from their home port of Amsterdam to South America. On his return he often had to recuperate from illness, and on one of his sick leaves in Holland he met the dancer Darja Collin, whom he married in September 1930. During another sick leave Darja gave birth to a still-born son in April 1932, a tragic event which affected Slauerhoff deeply and destabilised their marriage. Half a year later he started the first of five voyages to Africa as a doctor for the Holland West Africa Line.

Because of his health problems he often thought of giving up his work at sea and he looked for places with a more stable, warm and dry climate where he could settle as a doctor or consul, but his inquiries about possibilities in Shanghai, Lisbon, Barcelona, South America and Persia came to nothing. In 1934 he set up a private medical practice in Tangier but after half a year he gave it up and went back to Holland where his divorce from Darja Collin was granted. He returned to sea and travelled to South America and then to Africa. In Mozambique he contracted a severe form of malaria which, in combination with his tuberculosis, proved fatal. After a year of vain hopes of recovery in convalescent homes in Italy, Switzerland and Holland, Slauerhoff died in Hilversum on

5 October 1936 at the age of 38, three months after the publication of his last collection of poetry, which was ominously entitled *An Honest Seaman's Grave* (Een eerlijk zeemansgraf). He published ten volumes of poetry, two collections of short stories, two novels and a play. A third novel appeared posthumously in 1937.

A large part of Slauerhoff's poetry and prose is dedicated to the sea and the seaman's life, situated in exotic settings, often featuring lonely wanderers trying to reach the unattainable on endless seas, in desolate deserts or amidst the ruins of a glorious past. Slauerhoff expressed his own romantic longing and disillusion with reality through transfigured images of pirates and desperados, and of explorers such as Christopher Columbus and the eighteenth-century Dutch explorer Jacob Roggeveen, military conquerors such as Genghis Khan and Napoleon, and the poets Baudelaire, Rimbaud, Verlaine, Corbière, Camões and Po chü-i. Taking liberties with biographical facts he recreated them as images of himself and his companions in misfortune. By inserting himself into the lineage of the French *poètes maudits* and of a Portuguese and a Chinese poet whom he pictured as equally doomed, unhappy wanderers and outsiders in a hostile world, he created his own many-faced muse whose inspiration was necessary but had to be carefully controlled to avoid his own identity being subsumed into those of his inspirations. This 'struggle with the demon' appears in many forms throughout Slauerhoff's work, often linked to the central motif of 'the hollow man' who is looking for a way to fill the emptiness of his seemingly meaningless existence. Although there is no proof that Slauerhoff was acquainted with T S Eliot's *The Hollow Men* and *The Waste Land* or Ezra Pound's *Personae*, or the heteronymous poems of Fernando Pessoa, Slauerhoff's handling of themes such as identity, alienation, depersonalisation and multiple personalities place him in the international tradition of modernism.

The same can be said of his pessimism about the future of Europe. Like many other authors and artists active after the First World War he felt that Western civilization was in decline and had lost its vital energy, becoming incapable of new achievements. This view was highly influenced by the compelling comparative study of cultures presented by the German philosopher of history Oswald Spengler in *The Decline of the West* (*Der Untergang des Abendlandes*, 1918–1922), which had become a widely read and much discussed international success. Spengler demonstrated that, like all living organisms, cultures were born, grew, flourished and, inevitably, declined. Spengler's intuitive and symbolic interpretations of historic events as expressions of the 'soul' of a culture in determined stages of its organic life met with heavy scholarly criticism but were especially appealing to writers and artists during the period between the two world wars.

Slauerhoff considered himself a late-born and weakened descendant of Western culture doomed to live in decadent, degenerating and self-destructive times. These ideas come together in his two 'China novels' *Het verboden rijk* (*The Forbidden Kingdom*, 1932) and its sequel *Het leven op aarde* (*Adrift in the Middle Kingdom*, 1934). Here, the hollowness is not just a metaphor for the poet's need for inspiration or an expression of romantic longing but an existential problem linked to the decline of Western culture. The main character in both novels is Cameron, a solitary man tired of his life as an outcast and hoping to free himself from his miserable self. He is a twentieth-century Irish-born ship's radio operator but is not considered to be a real Irishman because he is said to have Celtic or Iberian forefathers. He has lost contact with his family, has no friends, no steady relationships and lives an isolated life at sea.

In *The Forbidden Kingdom* he is nameless, and suffers a mental crisis after surviving a shipwreck off the east coast of southern France. He feels empty, and starts recovering strange memories from the Portuguese past. He goes back to sea to work on boats in the Far East where the strange memories become stronger. Unknowingly he travels to places in and around the Portuguese enclave of Macao where the exiled sixteenth-century Portuguese poet Camões once lived. Gradually the spirit of Camões takes control of Cameron, and the two characters merge when Cameron arrives at the location in the Chinese desert where Camões had supposedly died. Their merged personalities separate again after their return to Macao: Camões lives on in the past and Cameron awakes in the present in a dirty Chinese hotel. He realises that he can't escape from his fate by letting himself be demonised by a spirit from the past. He doesn't want to return to sea, and decides to penetrate deep into China to either lose himself in the delights of opium or become an enlightened soul.

Cameron's identity problem is set against the background of the cultural decline of Europe, Portugal and Macao in opposition to the unalterable immobility of ancient China. The struggle that he has with the spirit of Camões can be seen as a metaphor for the dangerous inspiration Slauerhoff sought through his identification with poets from the past.

In *Adrift in the Middle Kingdom* Cameron is identified by his name, suggesting that he has gained an identity. Why Slauerhoff gave him a Scottish rather than an Irish surname is not explained: he may have chosen Cameron because of its similarity to Camões. That he is Irish seems simply to have been due to Slauerhoff's encounter with an Irish ship's radio operator during his first visit to Macao around the New Year of 1927, where he made his first notes for *The Forbidden Kingdom* (Blok and Lekkerkerker 1985, 32–33). He also used Ireland's nickname 'the Emerald Isle' and the name of the small islet next to Macao, Ilha Verde (Green Island), to indicate a connection between the lives of Camões and Cameron.

Between 22 October 1925 and 1 September 1927 Slauerhoff visited Shanghai nine times and stayed there in total for around thirty days. He made some friends in the city, including the French harbour pilot Paul Fouletier, to whom *Adrift in the Middle Kingdom* is dedicated, and his wife Claire, who lent some traits to the character of Solange. Their house in the French concession with its opium room inspired the description of the house of Hsiu in Chapter 3. In his diary Slauerhoff recorded opium sessions in their house, where he met two other Frenchmen, Sylvain and Godet (Slauerhoff 2012, 137–138, 145–146). Characters with the same names appear in chapter 3 in passages adapted from his diary. Slauerhoff smoked opium but, because he was asthmatic, breathing difficulties and coughing seizures often ruined the effects.

In the first four chapters Slauerhoff used many personal observations and experiences from his life aboard ship and his visits to Amoy and Shanghai, but the rest of the book was set in parts of China he had not visited. He fitted in experiences from elsewhere in China and other information gathered from a variety of printed sources, but not with the intention of giving a topographically and geographically accurate description of a journey from Shanghai (Taihai in the novel) up the Yangtze River and over land to Chungking. He used his sources mainly to collect Chinese terms and local colour, and to get information about landscapes, vegetation, the climate, the population, housing and local customs. Much of what he describes is easily recognisable as being close to the China of his day, but many places passed by the expedition to Chungking are not where Slauerhoff describes them as being. The most remarkable case is Chungking which he moved far to the northwest of Chongqing, not on the Yangtze River but on the Yellow River (Huang He). Slauerhoff constructed his fictional city with elements from a description and a map of Chengdu from the *Géographie universelle* (1927, tome IX, première partie), to which he added some features of what seems to be Liangzhou (modern Wuwei), an important old international trade city on the Northern Silk Road (Blok and Lekkerkerker 1985, 117–120 and 164–165).

The obvious name change of Shanghai to Taihai is an early warning to the reader about the fictional character of Chinese space in the novel. Slauerhoff selected and manipulated elements from Chinese reality and history to construct a virtual China which provides the symbolic setting for Cameron's journey. His compact and terse style – considered edgy and unpolished but highly authentic by some of his critics – is charged with implicit meaning. Instead of telling and explaining Slauerhoff shows and suggests, creating a dream-like atmosphere where strong visual images of landscape and surroundings reflect Cameron's state of mind and the stages of his quest. A modernist use of symbolisation, metaphor and allegory adds an extra dimension to the narrative, cutting it loose from realism and turning China into a metaphor for the Unknown or the Void that Cameron is confronted with after losing his social, religious and philosophical certainties.

The story is narrated mainly from Cameron's first-person perspective, with the exception of the panoramic chapters 9, 11 and 16, the beginning of chapter 4 and Kia So's letter to Wan Chen in chapter 10. Alienated in the foreign Chinese environment Cameron doesn't have a clear view of the situations he is in or the people he meets; this causes his judgement to falter and raises doubts about his perception of reality. Despite his passive attitude his hope of finding a better life keeps him going, although he doesn't know where it will lead him. Slauerhoff confronts Cameron's existential hollowness and his struggle with emptiness with Buddhist views represented by Chinese characters who identify his attitude and facial features with those of oriental sages who live detached from the world. Kia So is frightened after seeing Cameron's photograph sent by Hsiu to Chungking. He recognises the features of an anchorite and fears that this foreigner will bring destruction to the city. The Tuchun, on the other hand, is favourably impressed when he meets Cameron, and the monk Wan Chen guides and protects this foreigner, unbeknown to Cameron himself.

Hints and allusions earlier in the book suggest that Cameron has experienced Buddhist influences ever since his arrival in Taihai. When Cameron visits Hsiu's house the Chinese merchant is pictured as 'a fat, burly Chinaman with a smooth, pudgy face and a receding forehead that merges with his shiny scalp' and later 'seated at a desk as massive and ornate as an altar': he looks like a statue of the Buddha (38 and 63). Hsiu is a criminal merchant but also, according to Solange, 'a wise man' who seems at home with Buddhist and Taoist wisdom and sends Cameron on a three months' pilgrimage to a remote shrine high up in the mountains of Shantung before their journey to the interior begins. This immoral bandit-sage seems to be beyond good and evil, a possible echo of one of Friedrich Nietzsche's thoughts about Buddhism that Slauerhoff – an interested and regular reader of his work – must have known: 'Buddhism already has – and this distinguishes it profoundly from Christianity – the self-deception of moral concepts behind it – it stands, in my language, beyond good and evil' (Nietzsche, 129). For Cameron the journey with Hsiu is a second stage on the Buddhist ladder after his friendship with Chu the watchmaker in the Taihai suburb, from whom he rented a room, and who believed life is continuous change ruled by the 'wheel of existence', the endless cycle of birth, life on earth, death and rebirth. That a person can free himself from this cycle and attain nirvana when they understand that mundane life is impermanent and that attachment to it is the cause of desire, suffering and pain, appears to be the message of the journey.

The expedition passes through a timeless China, through scenes of horror, ruin, death and decay. On Hsiu's junk they sail up the Yangtze River through its seasonal flooding, where people are starving and drowning. Hsiu mercilessly profits from the hungry by trading rice and beans against their last money and valuables. By forbidding Cameron to share his food with the desperate peasants, Hsiu teaches Cameron to detach himself from feeling pity. On the second part of the journey they travel by camel and on horseback through empty deserts where people live in holes in the ground and only an occasional ruined grave or house is to be seen. The expedition is surrounded by symbols of death and decay and seems to represent a passage through an inferno of human suffering meant to detach Cameron from life.

For a long time Cameron seems to succeed in freeing himself from his Western past and his attachment to life and worldly longings. When he arrives in Chungking his detachment and progress towards enlightenment are noted by Kia So and the Tuchun, and by Wan Chen whom Cameron sees when he is led before the Tuchun, though Wan Chen is invisible to others. Cameron is lodged in the house of the last descendant of Pedro Velho, a character from *The Forbidden Kingdom*, who lived in Macao in the time of Camões and moved to Chungking. The host and the house, with a room full of relics from the Portuguese past, are a threat Cameron is now able to resist. From his room he can see a 'serene white mountain top' in the distance that seems to attract him. The mountain is part of the Land of Snows in Tibet where Wan Chen and other Buddhist monks fight demons that obstruct the process of rebirth of the dying.

Cameron and his own past are activated when the Tuchun orders him to build a radio. Gaining freedom of movement in and around the city to search for materials he can use and fearing death if he fails, he feels an attachment to life again. During his explorations he notices that oil is seeping from excavations in the ground. When he demonstrates the radio the oil well erupts, flooding and destroying the city. Its yellow colour makes the Chinese think that the underworld (Yellow Springs) has opened and that they are all going to die because the radio experiment has angered the gods. An explosion follows and seems to kill Cameron.

In the Epilogue, however, he finds himself on the mountain top he had seen from Velho's house. Wan Chen beckons to him from the Land of Snows, but when Cameron tries to reach him he falls and enters the poppy fields of the 'western paradise' where he experiences perfect happiness smoking opium and endless pleasures with a woman who is 'more than all who preceded her'. But the paradise doesn't last and Wan Chen tells Cameron that he is not strong enough to come with him to the Land of Snows. Cameron returns to the Middle Kingdom to 'go on wandering without ever stopping, until the end, avoiding Europeans, no longer hoping for closer contact with the Chinese' (228). He takes no further part in life on earth. 'I had fulfilled life's meaning, largely in spite of myself, through the twists and turns of my fate, liberating myself from the conspiracy of lineage and menacing spirits, and conceiving the narrow remainder of my days. I would not have to destroy myself before my time' (228).

Cameron cannot enter the Land of Snows and does not reach nirvana because of his attachment to life. The Epilogue seems to describe a near-death experience and the episode in the western paradise is based on the description of the Fourth Day of the fourteen days of apparitions of seven peaceful and seven wrathful deities that the deceased will see from *The Tibetan Book of the Dead* (Blok and Lekkerkerker, 263–65). On that day the deceased should concentrate on the dazzlingly bright red light of the apparition of the Buddha Amitabha, the Light of Wisdom, and not on the dull red light of the Preta-loka that shines at the same time. Cameron, however, seems to follow the light of the Preta-loka and the passion of attachment, lust and feelings. He sees the red of the poppy fields and experiences the bliss of opium and bodily love with a woman instead of seeing Amitabha and the lake with the white lotus flowers of rebirth. Cameron indulges in an intensified form of the worldly pleasures he idealised earlier but never could enjoy fully. He chose the wrong red light and is not prepared to be reborn.

The main source for Slauerhoff's descriptions of Wan Chen and the Land of Snows was *Mystiques et magiciens du Tibet* (Paris 1929) by Alexandra David-Néel, from which he took many extraordinary details about the life and practices of Tibetan monks. The life story of All-But-One he adapted from a fragment from Sergej Tretyakov's 'bio-interview' *Den Schi-Chua* (Berlin 1932) (Blok and Lekkerkerker, 165–67; *A Chinese Testament: The Autobiography of Tan Shih-hua*, 1934). His sources and the Buddhist themes which Cameron responds to show that Slauerhoff wrote more than an exotic adventure or a work of fantasy. *Adrift in the Middle Kingdom* is an unconventional novel that is perhaps best characterised as an allegorical novel of ideas. Its modernist theme, techniques and multi-layered meanings made it unique in Dutch literature at the time and the early encounter between existentialist and Buddhist thought was decades ahead of Western interest in Zen and Buddhism.

Slauerhoff and China

BY WENDY GAN

The China of Slauerhoff's *Adrift in the Middle Kingdom* is an artful construction. This fact is easily forgotten, especially when the opening chapters overwhelm the reader with a documentary grittiness that was obviously drawn from his personal observations and experiences. As a ship's doctor working the China-Java-Japan route between 1925 and 1927, Slauerhoff had ample opportunity to explore the China coast, including the cities of Amoy and 'Taihai'. He also had occasion to observe the Chinese at close quarters – not just the Chinese sailors who would have been his shipmates but the numerous passengers that his ships transported between south-east Asia and China. All of this results in an introduction to China that is steeped in an earthy reality, reminiscent of Pearl S Buck's best-selling and groundbreaking novel *The Good Earth* (1931). Slauerhoff's China is not an exotic, romanticised world populated by the gracious sages and delicate maidens made familiar by chinoiserie. Instead, like Buck, he levels a non-judgmental eye at the underclasses, conscious of their poverty and what acts poverty drives them to – the emaciated and exploited tin-mine workers returning home with wealth earned at the cost of their health, the houseboat family willing to prostitute their daughter for a dollar.

It is an unsparing and unsentimental portrayal of China, and this downbeat approach extends even to his depiction of the most glamorous of Oriental cities, Shanghai.

That Slauerhoff chooses to call Shanghai Taihai is an important reminder that, in spite of the grim realism with which the novel begins, he is dealing with an imagined China. Yet Slauerhoff's intimate familiarity with Shanghai and its temptations makes it difficult to read Taihai as merely fantastical. Indeed Taihai is often nothing more than Shanghai with its cesspool aspects amplified, a surreal, sometimes nightmarish, locale for a protagonist on edge. An unpromising piece of territory ceded to foreign powers in the aftermath of the First Opium War, Shanghai had developed since its founding in 1842 into a financial and trading powerhouse. The treaty port consisted of the International concession, which was governed by the Shanghai Municipal Council (comprising mostly British and American residents with some representation from the Japanese), and the French concession, which lay next to it. Together, they formed International Shanghai, an extraterritorial haven where Chinese law did not apply and foreigners were free to recreate their home lives as they pleased. Though many a Shanghailander (as residents of International Shanghai were called) attempted to live in deliberate ignorance of the Chinese, this was clearly impossible. International Shanghai was dependent not only on Chinese servants for the smooth running of its households, but also on Chinese property owners who paid rates essential to the governance of the territory (certain sections of Chinese society – revolutionaries, the criminal element, the well-off – had discovered the advantages of having a residence outside Chinese legal jurisdiction and yet still within China). Furthermore, adjacent to International Shanghai was the teeming Chinese city of Shanghai itself. Shanghai was therefore a hybrid, cosmopolitan hub where the Orient and the Occident rubbed shoulders and, in that febrile atmosphere, it grew into a glittering example of an urbane, modern city combining the best (and worst) of East and West.

Shanghai had an underbelly and its centre was located in the French concession. Rue Chu Pao San, better known as Blood Alley, was where visitors seeking the pleasures of dance hostesses and alcohol in the nightspots that lined the street often came to a bloody end. There were also the temptations of opium, and the French concession was notorious not only for its opium dens but for its dealings with a Chinese crime syndicate, the infamous Green Gang, which was deeply involved in the smuggling and distribution of the drug. The leaders of the French concession and the Green Gang had come to a mutually pleasing arrangement where, as a reward for closing their eyes to the presence of opium within its territory, the French were given a cut of the gang's profits and also promised their assistance in policing the concession's Chinese populace (Wakeman 1995, 121). Corruption was widespread and it was common knowledge that key Chinese personnel in the French constabulary were also major figures in the Green Gang (Martin 2008, 68).

The French concession of Shanghai thus had a reputation for hedonism and criminality. Though the novel's depiction of Hsiu's private opium den and of Hsiu himself may seem outlandish, these were in fact quite true to life. Hsiu was likely modeled on a crime lord like Du Yue-sheng of the Green Gang, who had a finger in every kind of criminal racket there was, from opium smuggling to gambling to gun running (see Martin 2008). Yet he maintained a public persona as a respectable businessman and had considerable political clout in the interwar years. The exotic Frenchwoman Solange, who presides over Hsiu's opium den, is almost a stock character. One of the more sensational aspects of Shanghai for the visiting foreigner from the West was the shock of seeing white women, usually impoverished Russians in exile, becoming mistresses of Chinese tycoons or, worse, working as escorts and prostitutes for a Chinese clientele (Field 2010, 39–43). It was yet another indication of the territory's seedy decadence.

The Taihai sections of the novel are the most reminiscent of a modernist text – the city that induces states of anomie and alienation amongst its inhabitants. The rapidly modernising city dissolves all stable sense of self. Cameron wanders Taihai in a fashion that anticipates the Parisian meanderings of the dislocated Sasha in Jean Rhys's *Good Morning Midnight* (1939). Unlike Sasha, however, Cameron turns his back on the city, rejecting the dubious pleasures of expatriate Shanghai for a Chinese working-class suburb nearby.

Where in his first days the dank chaos of the Chinese city had overwhelmed Cameron, this section of native Shanghai now becomes a refuge for him as he comes closer to a nervous collapse. We move from the lurid excesses of International Shanghai, where Cameron is often at a loss, plagued by his insecurities and aware of his marginal status, and return to a quiet setting, viewed with a documentary-like gaze recording the neglected underclasses of China and their everyday life, with a new focus on the figure of Chu, Cameron's landlord. This stage of Cameron's life with Chu and his family on the outskirts of International Shanghai marks a rare representation in Western fiction of the changing fortunes of the urban Chinese working classes, with Pearl S Buck's *The Good Earth* being the other example. While this phase is a respite for Cameron, the lives of the Chinese poor are never untroubled and soon Slauerhoff details with convincing realism the devastating disruptions of war and disease on this neighbourhood.

Republican-era China was very unsettled, with warlords, battles, and banditry commonplace. The Manchu Qing dynasty had fallen in 1911, but hopes of replacing it with a more modern and democratic republican state faltered as former Qing generals began to seize territory and power for themselves. Thus began the warlord era and China remained decentralised and fractured as a nation until the Kuomintang (KMT), the political party of the father of modern China, Sun Yat-sen, ventured from their Southern base in Canton and began their Northern Expedition in an attempt to unify the country. Though Sun and the KMT had been crucial in toppling the Manchus, they had been outplayed in the aftermath of the revolution and it was not till 1926 that the party had gathered enough military strength to challenge the warlords. Sun had died in 1925 and the Northern Expedition was left in the hands of the extremely able military campaigner Chiang Kai-shek. By 1927, the KMT and its army was moving towards Shanghai, worrying not only the warlord in control of this region, Sun Chuan-fang, but also the leaders of International Shanghai, who were unsure if Chiang had designs only on Chinese Shanghai or also on the treaty port. The rise in anti-foreigner violence in the wake of the Northern Expedition and the growth of Chinese nationalism in other parts of China had driven a steady stream of Western refugees towards International Shanghai, so there was an understandable nervousness about Chiang and his army. International Shanghai, unsurprisingly, was in full defence mode. The upheavals of war had also brought an influx of Chinese refugees fleeing the fighting to the Chinese city as well. All of Shanghai was thus on edge.

After such an anxious build-up, the arrival of the KMT was an anti-climax. International Shanghai was not seriously threatened and the anticipated battles between the Northern Expedition army and Sun Chuan-Fang's troops were mostly avoided by last-minute defections to the KMT by Sun's generals. What little fighting there was took place in Chapei (Zhabei), a Chinese suburb to the north of International Shanghai, as troops loyal to Sun were making their escape, heading towards the train station located there. Fires created by falling shells destroyed nearly 3,000 homes (Jordan 1976, 116).

Slauerhoff depicts a version of this wartime scenario in Chapter 4, significantly not written from the perspective of anxious foreigners in the concessions but instead highlighting war and its effects on the Chinese. It is unlikely that Slauerhoff experienced the arrival of the KMT army in Shanghai in person as his visits to Shanghai in 1927 were in February, July, and August. He might however have felt and witnessed some of the tensions during his February visit. Our sympathies are drawn especially towards Chu and his little daughter dying of dysentery caused by poor wartime conditions. Yet for all of Cameron's interest in his Chinese environment and his sense of kinship with Chu, the novel is not ultimately focused on the state of China and the plight of the Chinese. Behind the grim realism and affection for Chu lies the exploration of an existential question that plagues Cameron: how to live? This is where an understanding of Slauerhoff's title in its original Dutch is essential. *Het Leven op Aarde* translated literally means 'life on earth'. The choice of 'life on earth' instead of 'life on land' suggests that the novel has a larger, more abstract purpose of understanding the meaning of life. Cameron's search for meaning takes place, of all the possible options in the world, in China and this choice of locale for such a quest gives us the clearest indication that Slauerhoff's interest in China and the Chinese is ultimately less ethnographic and more allegorical.

This agenda becomes more obvious as the action of the novel moves away from Taihai and into the Chinese interior. Slauerhoff could not rely on personal experience as he had not travelled inland before, but he did research it and the sections that detail Cameron's journey to Chungking as part of Hsiu's armament delivery entourage are a fascinating melange of fact and fiction. The boat journey, the accounts of the destruction of the floods, and the resulting famine in the countryside ring true (these were common-enough occurrences in China), but, as discussed above, the geography is completely awry.

Putting together an imaginary Chungking free from the strictures of reality allows Slauerhoff to show his hand more clearly, revealing that for him the value of China lies in its rejection of modernity. He creates a fictional history and geography for Chungking, defining its central characteristic as its independence from the rest of China, calling it 'the only free city in the great, fossilised empire' (118).

Chungking thus becomes a celebrated bastion of traditional, anti-modern China, static and unchanging, the 'immovable city' (201). At a time when the Manchu leaders of China were being forced to open up their empire to foreign trade as well as foreign missionaries, the novel's version of Chungking stays resolutely closed, rejecting even metals like steel, nickel, and aluminium. The arrival of the arms dealers, however, signals the beginning of Chungking's entry into the modern world and one that is deeply contested and feared, especially by the influential priest of the temple of war, Kia So.

The destruction of Chungking and its eventual transformation into an oil-extracting concession with a European and a Chinese city side by side suggest that China cannot escape modernity and exploitation. Even a stalwart city like Slauerhoff's imaginary Chungking cannot resist the winds of change. Yet China remains the space that will shelter Cameron because there are parts of China that cannot be sullied by European progress, especially its mystical and spiritual traditions. Kia So as a representative of this lineage does not fare well – he is the least likeable character in Chungking and dies an undignified death. But there is also Wan Chen, who makes occasional, enigmatic appearances in Chungking and is quietly interested in Cameron. After the explosion, waiting to die, Cameron is drawn towards the Land of Snows where he is certain that Wan Chen awaits him.

Thus begins the most enigmatic part of the novel: Cameron in trying to reach Wan Chen finds himself in a paradise of poppies and opium. Here he sheds his past and his memories and falls into an opium bliss that had always eluded him in the past. Opium in this space is not a drug to escape the world's ills. Neither is it one that lures and entraps addicts, like Sylvain, the French naval officer who smokes himself to death in Chungking. Instead, it is an experience akin to what Cameron had imagined early on in the novel as the true use of opium – 'a gift of the gods to humanity' not to be abused in seedy dens but smoked 'on the floor of a lofty temple at the edge of a bottomless ravine' (47). Paradise is where opium is used correctly.

The idea of a peaceful refuge located in the remote regions of Tibet is reminiscent of James Hilton's *Lost Horizon* (1933). Though Slauerhoff was probably unaware of Hilton's novel, the two works are uncannily similar in imagining a utopic space that is tied to the practices of Buddhism, as well as being located in the Land of Snows. Cameron is led there by Wan Chen, while Hilton's lamasery of Shangri-La is ruled benevolently by a particularly long-lived High Lama. Cameron's paradise is an opium haven; Shangri-La is more attuned to scholarly pursuits, with the additional benefits of up-to-date amenities such as central heating and modern bathrooms. Hilton's utopia also is imbued with a delicate air that enables its inhabitants to age very slowly.

Paradise in both novels has been stumbled upon by accident, but it is also easily lost. Hugh Conway, *Lost Horizon*'s protagonist, altruistically chooses to help his younger British colleague, Mallinson, who is immune to the pleasures of utopia, and a Manchu woman, a resident of Shangri-La in love with Mallinson, to leave. Without his mountaineering experience, they would not survive the harrowing journey back into the real world from the mountains. By the novel's end, it is understood that Conway will attempt to return to Shangri-La, but whether he will be able to find his way back is unclear. Paradise is not easily re-gained.

Similarly, Cameron steps out of his utopic space, though not by choice. Unfortunately for him, his paradise begins to disintegrate and as it does, Wan Chen meets him to instruct him on his future. Too weak to join Wan Chen and his monks in their spiritual battles against demons, Cameron is expelled from the mystical world. All that remains as a potential home is China, though not the China of modernity, progress, and Western influence. Wan Chen advises Cameron to live amongst the common folk of the Middle Kingdom, invoking the literal meaning of China's name and one more commonly used centuries ago. This choice is striking as it reminds the reader that beyond the treaty ports and foreign concessions, the teeming Chinese masses continue on unabated and unbothered by modernity, living lives much as they would have in the Middle Ages. The notion of an antiquated, unchanging China still stuck in its medieval past is a familiar trope, but Slauerhoff uses it not to denigrate but as a sign of enlightenment. Amidst natural disasters and other upheavals, the natives of the Middle Kingdom understand the fundamentals of existence: the conception and termination of life. For a dislocated individual like Cameron, the strife and strain of the masses in the Middle Kingdom will prove to be a haven, the 'surest distraction and strongest protection against the emptiness and the demons' (227). Life on earth is nothing more than a disinterested wandering in a land that bluntly accepts human existence as a constant struggle for survival.

Slauerhoff was not alone in preferring the lessons and values of old China over the more discomfiting visions of modern China. Though writers like Pearl S Buck and Nora Waln addressed the pain of the younger generations caught between tradition and change, their best works celebrate China's old ways. Buck exalts the land, the agricultural roots of the Chinese peasant, and Waln in *House of Exile* (1933) focuses on the charmingly archaic practices of a well-off rural Chinese family. Slauerhoff opts for China's mystical and religious traditions and the unchanging harshness of life for the underclass, but, in essence, he is like Buck and Waln, uncomfortable with and ambivalent about modern China. They all share in varying degrees an engagement with representing the everyday reality of the Chinese rather than that of the expatriate ensconced in a foreign concession, and ultimately all of them look backward at a China not quite gone yet but slowly disappearing.

Works cited

Blok, W and Lekkerkerker, K (eds), *Het China van Slauerhoff. Aantekeningen en ontwerpen voor de Cameron-romans*, Nederlands Letterkundig Museum en Documentatiecentrum, 1985.
[Slauerhoff's China: Notes and drafts for the Cameron novels]

Field, Andrew, *Shanghai's Dancing World: Cabaret Culture and Urban Politics, 1919–1954*, Chinese University Press, 2010.

Jordan, Donald A, *The Northern Expedition: China's National Revolution of 1926–1928*, University of Hawaii Press, 1976.

Martin, Brian G, 'Du Yuesheng, the French Concession, and Social Networks in Shanghai,' *At the Crossroads of Empires: Middlemen, Social Networks, and State-Building in Republican Shanghai*, Nara Dillon and Jean C Oi (eds), Stanford University Press, 2008, 65–86.

Slauerhoff, J, *Het heele leven is toch verloren. Gedichten, brieven, essays*, Arie Pos and Menno Voskuil (eds), Het Literatuurhuis, 2012.

Nietzsche, Friedrich, *Twilight of the Idols and The Anti-Christ*, translated by R J Hollingdale, Penguin, 1968.

Wakeman, Frederic, Jr, *Policing Shanghai 1927–1937*, University of California Press, 1995.

Works by J Slauerhoff

Poetry

Archipel, P N van Kampen & Zoon, Amsterdam, 1923.

Clair-obscur, Palladium, Haarlem, 1926.

Oost-Azië, De Gemeenschap, Utrecht, 1928.

Eldorado, Van Dishoeck, Bussum, 1928.

Fleurs de marécage (collection of French poems), A A M Stols, Brussels, 1929.

Saturnus, Hijman, Stenfert Kroese en Van der Zande, Arnhem, 1930.

Yoeng poe tsjoeng, A A M Stols, Maastricht/Brussels, 1930.

Serenade, The Halcyon Press (A A M Stols), Maastricht/Brussels, 1930.

Soleares, A A M Stols, Maastricht, 1933.

Een eerlijk zeemansgraf, Nijgh & Van Ditmar, Rotterdam, 1936.

Prose

Het lente-eiland (Kau-Lung-Seu) (short stories), A A M Stols, Maastricht/Brussels, 1930.

Schuim en asch (short stories), Van Dishoeck, Bussum, 1930.

Het verboden rijk (novel), Nijgh & Van Ditmar, Rotterdam, 1932.

Het leven op aarde (novel), Nijgh & Van Ditmar, Rotterdam, 1934.

De opstand van Guadalajara (novel), Nijgh & Van Ditmar, Rotterdam, 1937.

Theatre

Jan Pietersz. Coen (tragedy), A A M Stols, Maastricht/ Brussels, 1931

Modern editions

Alle romans [collected novels], Nijgh & Van Ditmar, 2004.

Alle verhalen [collected stories], Nijgh & Van Ditmar, 2010.

The Forbidden Kingdom, translated by Paul Vincent, Pushkin Press, 2012.

Een varend eiland. Brieven [letters], Hein Aalders (ed), De Arbeiderspers, 2016.

Jan Pietersz. Coen, Aspekt, 2016.

Verzamelde gedichten [collected poems], Hein Aalders and Menno Voskuil (eds), Nijgh & Van Ditmar, 2018.

Adrift in the Middle Kingdom

by J Slauerhoff

*Pour mon ami
le capitaine Paul F.*

Part One

Chapter 1

An old summer's day on the Chinese coast, where the grey rocks and cliffs and brown shores have been lapped and hollowed for so many centuries by the waves of the South Pacific. But the coastline has barely retreated. There is little movement besides the slow churn of the waves; the water swirls around the tongues of rock, the fishing fleets swarm down the coast in silence and the solitary cargo junks crawl from port to port as if lost in thought. European steamships scurry in and out, almost unnoticed, and in spite of them, everything stays the same.

One old summer's day like so many before it, the *Shu San* approaches the islands on which Amoy is built. She is an old steamer, painted black, and on the small side. Still, she brings fifteen hundred passengers back to their country: tycoons from Singapore; traders from Malacca and all the isles of the Dutch East Indies, returning after many years with their small fortunes and large households of wives, sons and daughters; coolies, who sold themselves for three years but were kept for five in toxic tin mines and sun-baked rubber plantations, now returning with withered muscles and sunken cheeks but also money belts stuffed with silver dollars. They are all jammed, stacked and jumbled together on the cramped lower deck and the scorching iron upper deck, wherever there's room between sloops, derricks and freight. There are newborn babies among them, chubby and soft as little molluscs, their big brown eyes wide open and mild in their tiny faces. There are also the ancient of days, their loose skin sagging over timeworn bones like an oversized garment, returning merely to die in the Middle Kingdom. Some have already died on board; the afterdeck is cluttered with as many coffins as sloops. They lie on layers of quicklime, the lids against their faces. But they will arrive at their destination. Merchants bear up their bulging bellies with pride, bodily proof of their prosperity. Opium-smokers sit in the corners like bundles of dry wood, deaf and blind to the world around them.

Yet all of them – children, invalids, and corpses; the elderly, the well-fed, and the wrecks – form a whole, a clump of humanity on its way to China. From the lower deck comes a rumble and scrape like the sawing sound of some giant insect; a stench rises from them all, hanging over the ship.

Amoy is in sight now: the rumbling grows louder as the lower deck empties out, save for trunks, berths, baskets and a few dying or dead travellers sprawled in their own filth. Many passengers now recognise the coast and the high, brown, rocky slope of Gulangyu Island. Others have never seen Amoy but recognise it all the same. Almost no one is planning to stay there; Amoy sucks migrants in and spits them out again, in and out, out and in.

An entire village is also on board, having left three years ago during the great famine. They laboured in mountainside plantations in Natuna; they stuck together, mostly; many died, many were born; and soon there will be a new village somewhere in the interior.

The ship weighs anchor far from the city in the pouring rain. But before long, the boats from the inns have arrived. Twenty or thirty large sampans surround the ship. The innkeepers toss up ropes and board like marauding pirates, their sticky feet pattering up the hull. At the same time, firecrackers go off everywhere in unpredictable bursts. So much for the silence out at sea, the monotonous rumble below. Shrill cries pierce the air. The innkeepers are dragging people off, hauling away luggage and lowering it into their boats. In this chaos, how many passengers will recover their possessions? As they board the sampans they seem bewildered, but not for long; soon they have resigned themselves to their boats and their fates. They descend the ladders from the decks in a constant stream. Very young children are wrapped in slings and carried on their hips, very old women on their backs. Their hair wound tight, their black tunics glistening in the rain, they grin, stump-toothed, at the sight of land.

Then the sampans sail off in an almost continuous chain, overloaded with passengers, like one great raft, no, like a piece of China. A piece that is joining the whole.

An hour after the ship's arrival, they have all been put up in musty hotels in alleys of footworn paving stones, back in a familiar stench and half-darkness. They have returned safely, but as little changed as if they'd never left. Others are already traveling on, with all their worldly goods on carrying poles, through the rice fields around Amoy towards the interior.

A little while later, a sampan at the stern is loaded with some twenty coffins: the last passengers to disembark.

I didn't get to know anyone on the ship, couldn't pick out even one person in the crowd. Fifteen hundred of them shared this small space with me for sixteen days without any real contact between us. The ship is empty and silent now that they're gone, and the smell is not as bad. That's all. And there are fifteen hundred more people in China, but no one will notice.

So what is the point of this voyage? We'll load and unload soon; nothing else will happen. Or yes, it will, but only after dark.

A few shrieks from the last sampans as they glide away: one woman was seated on the low edge, scooping water; another was hit by an oar; and a few children started crying at all the strangeness around them. Then a deathly silence fell over the ship like a large grey bird of prey that had hovered over it for hours waiting to strike. The heavy rain kept pouring down, the decks remained empty, and everything turned shiny and wet. No one had started unloading yet. The ship was utterly dead: first a cage for thousands, and now a huge, floating iron tomb for the few who remained. No one came on deck; they were all penned up in their cabins, alone or together, hiding from the rain.

I was no longer who I had been. Before, I would have surrendered to that temporary death, simply whiling away life in the absence of life's source: the crash of the sea and the breath of the wind.

Now I could go ashore if I wished.

How had it come about – after all the disasters at sea and on land in the pale course of the years that I spent almost constantly on board – that my desire had been rekindled to go on shore, and not only that, but to travel far inland and never see the sea again? It was not a ghost trying to possess me, but was this longing my own, or was it the pull of the great country beside that small, island-wreathed sea? In any case, this pull did not frighten me; it was of this earth, not from beyond. When would I give in to it?

Among all the Chinese passengers, the large families, the village, I hadn't got to know a single one, hadn't ever exchanged greetings or caught a smile in passing, let alone any words. At the start of the voyage, when boarding, I'd caught a glimpse of a young woman, barely more than a girl, her black waves of hair, her lovely figure – as far as I could make out through her black jacket and short blue trousers. It crossed my mind that I could ask her to come to my cabin. There was something wild about her as she boarded, like a young animal that has been free and is suddenly caged, wanting to pull free but too shy and gentle to do it. For five dollars, her parents would have agreed in a flash. But what then? She would have put up with my advances and gone her way. I never looked for her after that and never saw her by chance in the crowd.

Who else could I remember? A few especially charming, funny children with round bellies, jumping about like monkeys. A couple of centenarians, one always perched on the edge of a hatchway, reading, the other staring into space, doing nothing – the scholar and the sage. And a living corpse, an opium smoker; even the light in his eyes had died out. Other than that, they were all the same to me. Now I longed to be in the midst of that crowd, which had already scattered out into the much larger crowd in Amoy. I was now free of the fear that I would encounter the ghost which had once seized hold of me, but I was kept back by a premonition of the loneliness that would weigh on me in the middle of that crowd, all those people I could not reach with words or looks or gestures. Still, I was planning to leave the ship anyway as soon as I possibly could, so why not now? No one would notice until morning that I was gone. All right, then.

I called out softly to one of the sampans, which are always bobbing around the big ships day and night, but a larger vessel approached. Only after boarding did I realise it was a houseboat. The mother, the father and four children lived under a small awning and slept squatting. The parents and one daughter steered the vessel. The father sculled with one large oar over the stern, the mother managed the sail, and the daughter used a smaller oar at the bow, but I think that hardly made a difference. Besides, she seemed half-dazed for lack of sleep. I sat on a bench on a reed mat near the stern. Under the awning, where a small oil lamp was burning, I could see the other three children and a few piglets lying side by side. On a shelf were the household effects: a few dishes and bowls.

The houses close to the waterside were already in sight. I could even make out a lantern here and there, lighting up a piece of the outer wall or a few tall, gaping windows without glass, but everything else was shrouded in darkness; I was approaching a dead city. The boatman brought the sampan to a halt and pointed to his daughter. I didn't understand. He called her over; she came up to me and pressed herself against me. The father gestured. Why go into town? What I was looking for was here, and cheap: one Mexican dollar.

Here on this boat less than one yard across? Where six people lived, with their animals? I sat motionless on my bench, weighing my miserable fate against theirs. This was taken to show my consent. The sleeping children and pigs were laid out on the foredeck. One child woke up for a moment and began to cry softly but was soon silenced, I don't know how. A space was cleared under the awning, and the girl lay down there, her legs sticking out from underneath it. I went to her and looked at her by the smoky lamplight. She may have been fifteen years old and wore a long-suffering look. Her body was quite shapely. She made a few gestures of invitation, but when I kept my distance, she gave that up and lay still, coughing now and then.

I crawled out from under the awning, gave the father two dollars and told him to keep rowing. He made a regretful gesture but obeyed, and two minutes later I was on shore. I asked him to point me towards the quickest route out of town. He moored his boat and led the way, first over a mucky square and then through ever narrower alleys. Out of the houses came muffled groans or music. Amoy was a city of transients, many on their way home with their gains, and there were many houses of joy. Every time we passed one, my guide would stop for a moment, but I drove him on. Ten minutes later we were outside the city – before me a dark plain that smelled of salt, beyond it a white stripe of water, far in the distance a group of scattered lights. So this part of the city was built on an island. The city out there seemed larger. But maybe it was on an island too? I asked, and yes, that too was an island, with more water beyond it. Then came the mainland. I could have had him take me there. Now that the rain had stopped, the night was quiet; the waves were calm. But I gave up. Maybe it was cowardly. I had him bring me back to the ship. Disgust swept over me as I climbed the ladder and crept past the drowsy watchman across the dark ship to my cabin. There I was again.

But in a flash I understood: China itself now scared me, almost as much as the ghost that once threatened to overwhelm me. This land would shut me out at first and then absorb me – suddenly or gradually, but irresistibly – until nothing was left of me as I was now. How could I make the transition? Taihai came to mind again. I would stay there for a while to adjust before going further upstream. But even the ships on the wide rivers remained outside China, even if they went as far as Hankow or Ichang, thousands of miles away from the sea.

Not upstream. Taihai. That was as far as my thoughts would take me. I couldn't sleep and now wandered the passageways, sure that I wouldn't run into anyone. I ended up where I'd never gone before, below the poop deck. Near the propeller shaft I discovered a few small cabins. Who could live in such a place? The lowliest of the stokers. I smelled a sweet fragrance; I pushed a door open. On a bare couch lay Li Shen, a coal trimmer. The pipe lay next to him; the lamp was still lit. His eyes were wide open, seeing nothing. How far he must be from the ship, how vast the space in which he drifted, even as he lay in this scorching iron sty.

I took the pipe; there was still a crust of opium in it. I tried to take a few puffs over the lamp, but almost nothing came out. If anyone saw me now, a white officer, sneaking the remains of the lowest coolie's pipe – but no one saw. And my attempt to scavenge his leftover joy was another failure.

I turned to leave, but Li Shen was not as stupefied as I had thought. He grabbed me by the arm, ran his hand over mine, grinned, prepared a pipe with great agility and offered it to me with a bow. I was too ashamed to refuse. Without desire, I sucked in the smoke. Another one. Then another for Li Shen. Then another for me. I no longer felt abandoned. Li Shen, a Chinaman, was my brother after all. We did not speak. We smoked. I thought I had found my salvation.

The next day brought the wreck of reality. My head and stomach tormented me, but not as much as my embarrassment. I was a British subject. I loathed drunkards. And I myself took opium. I imagined that all the Chinamen I ran into on board were looking at me with covert mockery. The whole day was spent loading and unloading – fore, aft, amidships, everywhere. My head pounded and roared. I checked the ship's radio but could pick up almost nothing.

Worse than a prisoner – that was how I felt on the ship, a good-for-nothing. My escape had ended in failure, my opium dream in failure. What now? I could already see myself wandering the streets of Taihai. How would I find my way to a better life there?

Yet I longed to move on. So what to do?

By evening I'd calmed down a little. I knew that in spite of everything I would do it. Something would happen, something sudden to jolt me loose. It was time. This could go on no longer.

At six o'clock, even before darkness fell and the sun sank behind the houses of Amoy like a fat red ball, frenzied shouting echoed through the ship from fore to aft. The coolies put on their rags, scrambled down the ropes into their lighters and rowed away. A few boxes at the bottom of the hold had been exposed, destined for Taihai. From Hong Kong. They had forgotten to paint over the black letters. The Canton–Hong Kong boycott extended even as far as Amoy.

Nothing else could be unloaded from the ship unless some arrangement could be made. Money can still triumph over slogans. But that was for the next day.

Abrupt, dead silence fell. At the table, next to my transmitter, I fell asleep.

***

Night, hot, heavy, and starless, lies over land and sea. Engorged with heat that has no place to go – not on the scorched land, not at sea, still full of the heat of a long day – the dark air smothers life. Nothing moves. Facing each other, invisible, lie the ships with their triangles of red and green lanterns facing the city, which is likewise defined only by scattered lights in the darkness. The hulks against the wharf are dark, the warehouses black and dark. Scent, that is the only sign of life – the scent of rot from the alleys, of grain and tar from the warehouses.

It's as if death has come over the earth, as if the planet is once again as hot as it was before the stirring of the first germs of life, as if everything will suffocate in the smoke and the heat and by dawn the docks will be strewn with corpses, which, after briefly fouling the air, will vanish. Then there will be nothing left but stone and earth and sea.

On a night like this, living things long for destruction. All the same, a few stars come out. But they themselves have been dead for hundreds of light-years. So it remains for hours, hours without purpose, and even so, time passes. There are still living people lying awake, and they grow impatient.

***

A light beams up on the dark shore, frees itself, and drifts up and down in a slow nod, like a weary, swaying flower, as if it would like to move on but is too tired to leave its spot. Maybe it's a will-o'- the-wisp, risen from a grave, attached to the top of a stem that goes down to the dead man below.

Between the green and red lamps of a ship, another small light appears. It shuffles back and forth, never moving far, like a spark hopping to and fro between two carbon electrodes in very slow motion. Then at last the light on shore sets out, approaches, uncertain, meandering. Now the other one holds still and almost goes out. Then a brief wave of light passes over the bay – not a lightning flash, but a flicker of heat. For a moment, the city looks out over the graveyard of ships with its many square eyes.

A junk, the only moving thing in all that paralysis, searches its way through the dark. The light is by the paddle, moving up and down with the vessel. Another flicker, then it's dark again. From the city comes a cry. The death wail of a murder victim, a caught thief, a guest in a brothel putting up a fight, a rich man in his bed.

Or a signal.

The water rocks, languid as molten lead. Slowly but surely, the junk drifts towards the ship, which is lying out towards the rocky island, almost outside the bay. The lights move closer together and, both at once, go out.

***

What woke me? I was far gone, dreaming of an inn in Belfast with sand on the bare floor, half-darkness even by day, the lamp burning day and night in the winter, someone leaning on his elbows over a zinc bar with his glass close at hand, a woman behind the bar who would bend far forward when no one else was drinking and let you reach with your hand as far as you liked.

Tonight something is happening. I go to the upper deck, lie on my stomach, peer into the darkness. Nothing to see. But something bangs into the iron of the ship's side and I seem to hear ropes creak, then a sound like the lid of a petroleum barrel popping off. Without thinking, I run barefoot towards the sound, slam into a body, grab a bony arm, feel a linen suit, grab the suit.

Somebody else grabs me from behind. I kick and pull out my pocket torch. Li Shen, my companion from last night. Ho Kam Yong, the quartermaster.

No need to wonder what's in the package. Opium commands a good price here. A moment of indecision. Why don't they throw me overboard? Because I'm holding onto Ho Kam Yong so tightly? 'Let go,' says Li Shen. 'We tell captain you smoke opium.' I respond with a laugh.

'Let go or ...' A third form looms up with a knife. The deputy foreman of the stokers. I grab Ho Kam Yong by the throat and let out a warning cry, softly.

Li Shen lets go of me. I hold on to the quartermaster and take cover against the bulwark. The other two whisper. 'If you not tell, maybe tomorrow under pillow thousand dollar paper.'

I say, 'Now.'

'Now not as much.'

'Then I'll keep the opium. I know where the rest is too.' It's really no more than a hunch: in the corner with the bench and the lit lamp, cluttered by day with work and worthless rubbish. Number three slinks off and returns with six hundred-dollar bills.

'The rest tomorrow.'

'No need,' I say, letting Ho Kam Yong go. They whisper to each other. Do they think I'm a decent fellow, or a fool?

Li Shen says, 'Suppose you like smoke big pipe, come back night time, no tell other chief men.'

'No, Li Shen, I now have enough to live on for two months in Taihai. That's long enough. After that my dreams of bliss will show me the way.'

I stay to watch, and the men don't seem to mind. Twenty

packages are lowered into the junk, light shines for a moment, the junk pushes off, and all the lamps are put out. The two Chinamen return to their hot, airless quarters without a sound, near the propeller shaft under the poop deck. In a few years they will live in large country houses with plenty of wives and, above all, plenty to eat. Or else they'll have rotted away in some unknown prison.

The next day, the waiting goes on until noon. The conflict cannot be resolved. Maybe by now coolies one and two have both received their share, more than I got. Ho Kam Yong and Li Shen want to move on as fast as possible. And that is what determines this ship's fate. A scrawny quartermaster, a skeletal trimmer. Others, the captain and the Company, imagine that they, along with God, are the ship's masters.

She departs with two hundred tons of cargo still in the hold, gets stuck for a few hours on a bank she could otherwise have sailed over, finds herself caught in a storm because of the delay and finally reaches Ningpo two days behind schedule.

That evening, after the others have gone to bed early or to the dance halls for a simulacrum of love and joy, I disembark, leaving behind all the little that I possess, without signing off. Three days later, I board a ship to Taihai as a passenger, having kept hidden the whole time in Ningpo without ever leaving the harbour area.

Chapter 2

To me, Taihai was more mysterious than Mecca, Memphis and Atlantis put together, even if it was only a hundred miles upriver from a ship-ridden sea, even if I knew it from seamen's stories as a place where London's commercial districts and Paris's nocturnal pleasures combine to make life more intense, by day and by night – at least for those who see life as a series of major transactions and boundless extravagances – and yet a place as far removed from reality as market hubbub is from starry silence. To me, Taihai was something else: the last stage, the final hurdle before I could become my other self, fulfil my destiny, as I still too often doubted that I would, a destiny I feared as a poor man fears wealth, as a believer in predestination fears the hereafter, and often I yearned for the inescapable misery of the old days.

That old misery was still close enough, here on board. Every time I looked in the mirror, I flinched. I in no way resembled the man of decision going out to meet a higher fate. I was pale, poorly dressed, droopy and undernourished.

The other passengers were also my mirrors. They looked at me with contempt. My thought was always: just you wait, just you wait until I've become the man I must be. But those people would never know anything about that, and then it would occur to me how foolish it was to see those arrogant, fatuous creatures as connected to my destiny in any way.

My fellow travellers fell into two categories. The first was a bevy of girls, all with permanent waves over their smooth, pale yellow foreheads, under the supervision of a colossal old Cantonese lady, who turned her thick-lipped, black-toothed grin on everyone in a rictus of friendliness, and especially on the second category of passenger: the merchants.

As logic demanded, contact was quickly made between merchants and merchandise. All day and much of the night, the narrow deck saloon was both market and café at once. The slapping of thighs resounded louder and louder between the narrow walls; piercing shrieks and laughter whizzed through the low room like panicky insects in reckless flight. And that saloon was the only refuge on the ship.

By day the cabins were nearly dark; the portholes were small and could not be opened except on the calmest of seas, and the stench was unbearably foul to any waking person. After four hours of sleep, at most, you had to pace the deck for an hour in the wind and weather to recover. So I spent most of my time alone on the narrow black deck, searching for sheltered corners, and not much better off than I would have been with no cabin or bed at all. My new self-confidence sank by the day, and now there was no one to help me maintain it. It was like the old days – me alone among drunks, despising them, sometimes tempted to join them and despising myself for it – and it took more and more effort for me to go on believing in a better fate. Then the change in the outside world came, none too soon. The sea, which had been dark and drab for days, covered with waves that were not very large but freakish and violent, turned still and yellow and gently lapping; a mild wind blew over it, and on the horizon its turbid yellow surface made a vague transition to grey shores. For me, this was the wide entrance to the stifling world through which I'd have to travel to reach the life that awaited me.

The ship slowed down near a long, narrow white boat, as graceful and luxurious as an American yacht. But a squat rowing-boat came to meet us, and the pilot charged with bringing us into port was a gruff man, his head sunk deep in his heavy shoulders. His coat hung open and crooked around him, and a duffle bag swung back and forth on his back as he tugged himself up the rope ladder. Most of the passengers were out on deck, curious, and staring at him as if he were a being from another world. He pushed through the crowd to the bridge, shoving a couple of them aside, and shot me a look in passing that said, 'That one'll have a rough time of it, keeping his head above water in Taihai.'

As soon as he was on the bridge bells began ringing, down below where the machines were waiting, as if to summon us all to mass. The wheels were brought back to turning, rumbling life again, and the ship sailed on through water that grew ever murkier. I heard the pilot on deck, shouting orders, and compared his lot with mine. He went back and forth between city and sea, fullness and emptiness, noise and silence, and neither had a hold on him. He knew the dangerous spots on the river bottom and the tricks of the current, and he fought them; that strengthened him and kept him fit. He could take great pleasure in his nights on land, and no less in the days he spent waiting on his white pilot boat. The course of his life was always smooth, never stuck. And what about me? Slow and sluggish from my unrelieved years at sea, I would now, with no transition, have to beat a path across the land.

Why do the weakest so often bear the heaviest burden of fate? How is it possible that so many of them press on and see their journeys to an end – even if not a good end?

Now the shores were converging; in the pale meadows on either side stood the Woosung forts, greyish-white and rusty like neglected gas tanks. Farmhouses and clumps of trees under low skies. Now and then the sounds of the countryside found their way to the ship: cocks crowing, wagon wheels creaking. How frighteningly familiar the landscape was, especially now, before its inhabitants showed themselves. It was just like the green isle of Erin, which I would never see again as long as I lived but which for all that was still my homeland – except that this landscape was less marshy and misty, home to fewer birds and sheep and far too many people.

***

The ship moved faster now; the tide had turned, and it swung around a sharp bend. There lay the city in the distance; tall warehouses, wharves, and coal heaps filled the shores, and the low-lying land behind them had disappeared.

In the distance, in front of the tall row of emporiums and banks, the whirl of another life was visible. From here, it looked as if beads were rolling around each other in a dim cupboard, while above them the sun made the gold of the giant letters and symbolic forms on the rooftops glitter. Another sharp turn. Far in the distance junks were moored in midstream, packed close together like tangled plants past the house fronts and the ships' funnels. Their masts were like a forest of reeds in front of the city's immense piles of stone, and the sight made me think of the wide plain that must open out somewhere far beyond them. That was the only way forward that I could conceive.

The ship was moored far from the city, on the opposite shore, not along the shoreline but – after continual to-ing and fro-ing with the propellers to the creaking of stretched cables – against the edge of a kind of framework of free-floating wooden planks. No one came to welcome the new arrivals; everyone on board calmly prepared to disembark.

The merchants, oblivious to the girls now, packed up their wares. The girls were doing their faces, their squabbling and shrieking at an abrupt end. Almost conscious of their dignity, or at least of their market value, they sat on the red velvet couches of the saloon, constantly checking themselves in the mirror, adjusting their hair or their make-up. Once the ropes were secure and the gangplank was in place, a few men in uniform and a few others in long, dirty-grey smocks came striding across the coal-dusted yard between the landing stage and the warehouses, all wearing flat-topped caps with insignia.

***

Policemen and emigration officers were the only people who came to meet the *Chi Shang*. After a quick inspection, the merchants were allowed to leave the vessel and board a low launch that would bring them to the Bund. Two of the girls were turned away, owing to flagrant juvenility. The matron made a terrible fuss, backed up by her children's choir, until all of a sudden they too packed their things, stepped into sampans and calmly left the two tiny tots behind. Later that evening the two girls vanished without a trace. Were the immigration officers bribed, or did they take them for their own use? Did the children strike out on their own, to seek their fortune in the coolie district behind the docks?

I wasn't allowed on land either. I had more than twice the entry fee, but my papers left some doubt as to my nationality, and I couldn't show sufficient means of subsistence. The British consulate would decide the next day; I had to spend the night on board.

As dismayed as I was – yet another night, when I was determined to leave all things nautical behind me forever – in my heart I was grateful, because I feared the city, which presented a dark front behind its lights, its neon signs leaping about like fierce dragons as the wandering beams of searchlights blinded me.

The ship was gradually deserted; no work would be done that night. The warehouses stayed closed, the landing site empty and dark, a grey mass as evening fell. The officers were the first to disembark, in pairs or one by one, in creased, camphor-smelling uniforms they hadn't worn in a long time, with stiff felt hats and cherry-red or grass-green ties, most of them with a rigid expression of mandatory pleasure. They saw me standing there, passed and did not greet me.

Next were the Chinese, some in their blue smocks, others – numbers one, two and three and a few more whose smuggling had gone well – in more expensive fabrics than the officers. They were the gentlemen. They were at home here – even if the foreigners did, for now, possess the capital and the movable and immovable property. Later, after all, it would all belong to them – or to their descendants, which made no difference in their minds. They went forth with quiet confidence, proud and noble in their poverty. How unlike the Europeans, hounded and tormented by their own pleasure-seeking and grasping greed, with their loud voices, red faces, and jerky motions!

Sampan after sampan pushed off; a few, which had no passengers but expected them later that night, were still bobbing alongside the ship, or in the patches of open water between the planks. The officer on guard duty walked by on his round now and then and saw me sitting on the wooden bench by the stern post, and even that solitary man made no effort to start a conversation with me.

I tried to cloak myself in deep thought. Later, just before midnight, a small motorboat came alongside and the customs master jumped back onto the gangplank. For an instant, I wondered: had he come back to visit me?

The absurdity of the thought betrayed my deep sense of isolation, and, wrenching myself from those mental depths, I realised he must have lost something on board that he was attached to, or something of great value he wasn't comfortable leaving on the ship all night. My guess was right; I helped him search and soon found it: a cigarette case with two small portraits inside. He thanked me and gave me a cigarette, looking at me as if seeing me for the first time. No other human being had taken an interest in my situation in years, and I was ashamed and felt like walking off. Why? He could see the state I was in, of course, but was that so shameful? Besides, so many wrecks washed ashore in Taihai that he must have been used to the look of them.

'Taihai's not a city for men like you; you'll drown here. You must get out as fast as you can. Go to sea, whatever job they offer you.'

I told him that after years as a sailor, I had just turned my back on the sea for good. He took another look at me and seemed to ponder, as if he didn't believe my story and wanted to put me to the test. 'I could help you find a ship.'

I made a dismissive gesture and said, 'I don't want a ship and I don't want to stay in Taihai. I want to get as far away as I can, as fast as I can.'

'I can give you a temporary job as an assistant to my driver. You wouldn't have to drive me, just clean and look after the cars.' I stared in surprise, because his answer seemed to have so little to do with my words, but he interpreted my surprise differently.

'Yes, you must be asking yourself how a simple customs officer can afford more than one car, but in Taihai Europeans live a few classes higher than in their own country. There are customs officers here with three houses – a summer home in the concession, a winter home in the centre of town and a country home in the mountains – not to mention a yacht or even a private golf course. Tell me now you're still not tempted to try your luck in Taihai. A lot of people here started out with nothing.'

'No, less tempted than ever. I don't want cars and houses; I want space.'

'Good, at least you know what you want; you won't let

yourself be taken in. People here may earn ten times more than in Europe, but they spend it twenty times as fast and enjoy it a hundred times less. Everything's rushed and forced and always, always, blows apart into crude entertainments. I live in the midst of the uproar like a hermit. I have a little house with a big garden. But then again, I come from a place that gave me the strength of character to be myself wherever I go. Even during my long years at sea on small ships. I don't come from a port city or a fishing village, where the first step of your life is taken on board and it's easy to choose the sea, since there is no choice. I come from the highlands of the Pyrenees and found my way to the sea from there. Why shouldn't you find your way from the sea onto land?'

I so rarely encountered any real understanding that it took me by surprise, and I couldn't believe it. Imagining he was making fun of me, I kept my mouth shut.

'I lead a secluded life and never go to bars or clubs. I'm a member' – and now it was his turn to hesitate, as if he feared I would make fun of him – 'of the Theosophical Society. I can tell by looking at you that you have no roots, no social standing, nowhere to call home. Nothing to hold onto. Taihai will be your ruin, or you'll vanish into its underbelly forever. The ruler of Mongolia, the living Buddha, became a drunken swine in the space of a month here, after falling in with rich English louts. Fortunately for him, he was forcibly abducted, and now he reigns over his steppes again. The experience must have been good for him, since his country's now better than any other at resisting what they call peaceful penetration.'

The motorboat honked three times, sharp and shrill, the sign that it had been waiting for an hour. He produced a card and jotted a few quick characters on it.

'Show that to the officials tomorrow, and they'll let you

through in no time. I wrote that I vouch for you and I'll give you a job. And if you want, I will.'

'I'm much too afraid I'd get bogged down. How about instead you give me the address of a place where people are recruited for trips to the interior and dangerous ventures.'

He shrugged and mumbled that he didn't know much about that sort of thing, but then he scribbled something else on another card and said a hasty goodbye, with a hint of rancour, as if he regretted getting tangled up with me.

The motorboat crossed the water in brief spurts, and I was alone again on the ship, with the water sloshing around it, the sides scraping against the posts, and no other sound but the footsteps of the watchman on his rounds. One more night.

***

From the districts behind the warehouses, I could hear the noise of a night out, like a roaring sea behind tall black dikes. In front of the buildings was an empty black strip with piles of wood and coal. Between them, puddles of oil were scaled with unnatural colours in the moonlight. I would always be this way, at the edge of a void, where only filthy refuse or indifferent commodities could find a place, and where, behind a black wall, lay life, which I longed for even as I reviled it. Yes, I knew very well this life was nothing more than a wallow in the muck, whooping and shouting to drown out your own despair, your shame and your transgressions, for the sake of mere survival. And I knew this truth was especially vivid in ports, where life played out faster. I knew it was exposed still more starkly here in China's largest port, where out of three million at least two don't know if tomorrow they'll eat or die. Yet I longed to become part of it. Late that night, I tried to go ashore. But two soldiers by the gates, dozing in the huts on either side, suddenly dropped their guns in front of me like a

27

barrier. I turned back. The two windows of the saloon were still lit, but it looked to me as if they were spattered with soot. Insects from eddies and inlets swarmed towards the light and began colliding with my face. I tried to hunker down in a dark, hidden corner for a while, but the dirty white shade of my suit was like a lure, and in time I returned to the cabin, which I had to myself now. The fat merchant, who had fouled the air with his emanations, had left. The ship lay still, in the bend, in the windless night, between heaps of coal and the open, packed depots, as oppressive as if it would never leave that spot, any more than I would.

***

The next morning I woke with a start to distant shouting. After that night, I couldn't imagine what reason anyone might have to shout like that, and I went out on deck, curious.

The sun was already up, blurry-edged above the warehouses. Across the yard and over the pontoons, their gleaming yellow torsos partly or wholly bared, marched the coolies, letting out those shouts as they worked. Nowhere else have I ever heard labour accompanied that way. Some worked in pairs, toting their burdens – crates, sacks, or machine parts – on bamboo canes, which were deeply bent by the weight and on the verge of snapping. Sometimes four of them shared an especially heavy load. Many, moving a little faster but bowed deeper, were carrying coal back and forth in baskets on their shoulders or heads. The air was thick with a black powder. In the morning mist, it was almost dark. Yet the sun shone as hard and hot as if it was noon.

The rhythmic groaning of the men as they heaved and toiled was strangely like crickets chirping in a minor key, an accompaniment to the ruthless grind of the city consuming its people on the opposite shore. Later, the only other places I heard that same sound, but more delicate, were along the

Whangpoo and in a hairnet factory where six-year-old girls operate the looms and sometimes die at those looms like butterflies in a web that they, in their floundering, have spun. This time it filled me with courage and hatred of the city. I would have to listen to it for hours more.

The immigration officers never came. So I'd been forgotten on board? The day progressed; the first, jellyfish sun was now a hard, glaring disc. I wandered around the yard, half-aimless, and gave in to the urge to hold out a dollar to a coolie. With difficulty, he removed one hand from his pole and took the coin. I expected him to throw down his load and run off, but he slid it into his braided hair, giving me a sidelong glance – no gratitude, nor even surprise was visible in his eyes. His head was close to mine; it looked like a camel's, which has the same expression, resigned to its burdens and staring out onto an empty plain without end. Nor did the other carrier give any signal of desire. They were, after all, one pack animal together, the front and back legs of a load-bearing machine. Together they faltered forward, step by step; together they kept up the call-and-response of their groans, the pitch rising and falling with the rhythmic swing of the carrying pole. They moved on.

Yet my uncalculated act had an effect. One of the guards at the gate came up behind me and held out his hand, half a question but more a threat. I took out a dollar but held him off, pointing at the opposite shore. He nodded and returned a half-hour later with a low-ranking immigration officer. I showed him my card; he inspected my papers, held them up to the light and made a couple of scratches on them with his pencil. This cost five dollars, and two hours later I was dropped off on the far shore, suddenly in the middle of town.

I took my money to a bank, kept a hundred dollars on me, and spent three full days roaming the city searching for a place to stay for the time being. Where could I go? I had planned to take a room in one of the Palace hotels so that I could make contacts. But I never managed it. One afternoon I entered the lobby and found myself in a thick clot of the *crème de la crème*, but a gap opened up around me. I couldn't reach the hotel office and was back out on the street a minute later.

I rebounded straight into the Chinese city across the road, a hundred metres away. It was a shock, as if I'd fallen a thousand metres deep and ended up in another world, even though all I'd done was cross a wide boulevard and pass through a gate.

My memories of Amoy, the city of deepest darkness, now seemed bright and airy. The alleys, narrow and stinking like small intestines, teemed with a race of jostling parasites. Parasitic on what? On each other, on the houses, on something underground. Though none of those creatures meant anything to me, I had the feeling that all together they were killing me, simply by being there where I couldn't be, yet was. I wanted to turn back but could no longer find the way out of the labyrinth. I'd heard that in the centre of the Chinese city there was a pagoda thirty-five storeys high. Just as an explorer lost in the jungle climbs a tall palm tree to regain the view, I climbed the spiral stairs of the pagoda, which rose high and pure from the heart of the filth. From the uppermost balcony I hoped to see the sky. It wasn't there. The Chinese city lay small and round in the depths, surrounded not by high ramparts but by the smoke and fumes of factories like an impenetrable wall. I could make out nothing of the city I was looking down on. It most resembled a dense overgrowth of coarse plants with chewed-up rotten leaves of a toxic green-brown hue. But even all the way up there, the street noise rose like bubbling gases through a decaying surface.

Wearier than ever, I circled back down the stairs and crossed the swaying bridge. A rickshaw was waiting there, having brought a foreign passenger. Since I couldn't persuade the runner to point the way for me, I lingered until the foreigner came back out. At my request, he kindly agreed to go slowly enough for me to follow the rickshaw back. It wasn't far. A minute and a half later, I was back on the boulevard I'd left hours earlier, hours spent in that other world. That very instant, my fellow European and guide brought the runner to a trot with his cane without another look back at me. There I was, abandoned again.

I hadn't yet decided to take the card to the address I'd been given. Instead, I tried to make my own way. I spent another day wandering around the concessions of the great powers: France, America, Japan. There, behind tall fences or whitewashed walls at the ends of broad avenues, lay their houses and mansions like royal palaces, some larger, some smaller, but even the smallest one larger than a thousand Chinese houses put together. Yet I knew these were the homes of merchants, often less cultured than the poorest Chinaman, but living there all the same, occupying the territory, which is why the people who came from this country were packed into their besieged, stifling ghetto.

Chapter 3

Like a piece of wood on the high seas, rolled and tossed by the waves and never carried to the coast – that's how I was those first three days in Taihai. In all that time, I never exchanged a greeting or spoke a word to another Westerner. I went to the races and placed bets; I went to the bars and drank. The only thing they wanted from me was my money: for drink, for food, for tickets, for lodging.

I hadn't needed lodging the first night. Until four in the morning, I'd loitered in a dance parlour, hoping I could buy something resembling tenderness. They'd gone to great lengths to make it look like a party, with garlands and streamers, mood music, and dancing girls in fancy dresses covered with stars and spangles, but the only time they smiled was when someone invited them to dance with a bump or a nudge. At other moments they stared out ahead of them, some rigidly, some sadly, and all the visitors at their tables around the railing or under the palm trees, except for those in a drunken haze, looked grim and dejected.

I spent the rest of the night walking along the riverbank. It wasn't a peaceful morning walk. I had my work cut out for me fending off the Russian beggars of both sexes. When the day began, I bought myself a suit and moved into a big Chinese hotel. I received a courteous welcome there, with plenty of bowing, after I'd paid in advance. On Saturday afternoon I went to the races, and after that my evening and Sunday were completely blank. I stayed in the hot hotel all morning, warring with my thoughts; some time that afternoon I gave up, put on the expensive suit and took a rickshaw to the address the customs master had given me. It felt like a defeat, but what else could I do? I didn't think I could go on living without spending at least a few moments in human company, however dubious.

I stood at the edge of the international concession in a blazing hot street where the close-packed houses were barely separated by scraggy. gardens. I found the house number, went up the front steps, and rang the bell. It was a blocky, medium-sized house with very few windows. After three or four minutes, the flat, yellow, expressionless face of a sleepy house boy appeared behind the barred window. I held the card out in front of his eyes. The window slid half-open, and he thrust his hand out. No, I was not about to part with my only means of entry into human society. 'Call your master.'

The window closed again, for another few sweltering minutes. It was as if I could feel time trickling through an hourglass, grain by grain, while I myself, caught in the narrow neck, held back its progress.

What was I doing here? Well, I had to be somewhere in the world. Here, as always, I was in search of the place where I was meant to be. Maybe there were thousands of other places like this, where I would pass my days waiting, waiting for what I did not know. Now the door swung open a little. I was let inside and it was shut at once behind me. I stood in a small entrance hall, every bit as crammed with luxury goods as the Chinese city with people. Panel paintings, candelabra, jade objects in cabinets, miniatures, and so many cushions that the floor looked like a hilly landscape. Chinese, Indian, Arabic, European, all jumbled together, styles that clashed and competed for air. I looked all around and tried to focus on something beautiful, something familiar, but there was no escaping the sheer extravagance of it all. The hall was filled with a heat even more oppressive than out in the city, and feeling myself grow dizzy, I staggered and groped for a chair. But there were no chairs, only cushions. I lowered myself onto one, sunk away inside it, had to pull up my tight trousers over my sharp knees, and rose again a moment later, struggling with my constricting new clothes.

Just then a rattling curtain of beads fell aside to reveal, not my one acquaintance in Taihai, as I had expected, but a woman, Chinese – no, European, but in a close-fitting Chinese gown. Her limbs were slender, her face and bosom full. She looked like an overloaded fruit tree. Flowers twined across her garment. She held the card like a magnifying glass through which she was scrutinising me, and when I asked whether Monsieur Jourdan was out and I had the honour of speaking to his wife, she laughed scornfully and said, 'No, this is the home of Monsieur Jourdan's great friend Mr Hsiu.'

She went on, 'I see from this card that you are the man who will stop at nothing to enter inland China.' As she said this, she eyed me again, thinking, *He doesn't look the part.*

I told her that was true. Anything that would free me from my solitude and get me away from the coast, as far away as possible – I would do it.

'Do you smoke the long pipe?' she asked, still staring at me. The last time I'd smoked had been ages ago, before leaving the *Shu San*, and I longed to do it again. I couldn't understand why I hadn't got round to it yet, but after poking my head into the dens in Thibet Road, I'd hurried out again. I had no interest in smoking a pipe which thousands of other mouths had touched, and I gave her an honest answer, 'I've done it once, a while back. I never had the chance to do it again.'

'Then you have a lot of smoking to do before you can be sure you fear nothing, no matter how brave you may be. Shall we start straight away?' She made a friendly, hospitable gesture.

Straight away! Could any invitation be more appealing, on this parched, scorching afternoon in this unfamiliar city of dusty streets and burning sun, than to let all my troubles go up in smoke? But I hesitated, the way you might if you strayed into a house of ill repute when you'd thought you were visiting a museum. I don't mean she reminded me of the hostess at that sort of place. But the way her face was made up, she hardly looked European. A layer like the glaze on porcelain covered her face, her eyes were narrow, and a wave of hair swirled over her forehead. There was something calm and confident about her whole way of being, as if she were the daughter of a long-established French family, of a banker or sub-prefect from some provincial town. But what did it mean that I'd been welcomed not by the stiff, tanned official I knew, but instead by this woman, who seemed only conceivable in the close atmosphere of reception rooms, luxury cars and cigar lounges, between lacquered or upholstered walls, surrounded by *objets d'art*. She was already steering me through a corridor into a small room with a wide but uncovered couch, where behind a curtain hung six cotton kimonos, all alike, dark blue.

'How do you like it here?'

I stared at her and gave no answer.

'The least little surprise seems to scare you off.'

I replied that I was overwhelmed by all her hospitality. And by all her charms, I meant to add, but before I had the chance she slipped away behind a screen.

'Ring the bell whenever you're ready and the boy will show you the way,' she said as she left the room.

I hurriedly asked, 'Whose house is this?'

'Mine', was her simple answer, as she slid the door shut.

While I made myself physically comfortable, I was tormented by questions to which I had no answers. This reception was too luxurious – sooner or later, I'd be expected to pay the price. What would it be? Maybe they expected things of me I'd be unwilling to do. Acts not of courage but of cowardice: assassination or theft.

My first thought was that the sleeve of my kimono would

be the best place to hide the small revolver I always carry, but I realised it would take me a few seconds to retrieve it from there. So I used a shoelace to tie it under one arm, where I could reach it with my opposite hand. I had scarcely finished when the door opened and a portly man with thin sideburns and a brick-red face entered the room. You could see straight away that this man went through life with a minimum of effort and a minimum of gesture. Later I learned that the same was true of his words and thoughts. He looked at me without surprise, gave a curt military bow, and said his name, which he probably used only in this house: Sylvain. Not concerning himself with me any further, he made himself comfortable, sitting down on the edge of the couch to remove his shoes and producing a pair of slippers from underneath it.

The door opened again. I admitted to myself that if I had known how many strangers I'd meet, all at once, in this situation, I would certainly never have come.

The new arrival looked somewhat different from Sylvain. He had a child's face, a boy's body and a girl's prissy manner.

He introduced himself at greater length than Sylvain: 'Godet, first lieutenant in the Colonial Army, *Officier de la Légion*.' Turning away from me and towards Sylvain, he launched into an ode to Tonkinese opium and its superiority to the Shantung variety. Sylvain said nothing at first and shrugged his shoulders. After some time, he replied, 'What are you doing here, then? Should've stayed in Tonkin.' I silently agreed; this milksop would be more at home in Tonkin or Annam, where even the old men have a quality of character halfway between an ape and a weedy daytime maid, than he was among the large frames of the northern Chinese and the Europeans generally found in Taihai: coarse, robust businessmen, living for profit and for binges. In spite of their strong difference of opinion about opium, Godet and Sylvain rinsed off fraternally together in the shower. Sylvain had a package with him, wrapped in brown paper, which he now unrolled: a pair of pyjamas with crude red-and-black stripes. Wearing it, he looked more like a galley prisoner than an officer. 'Twenty-five francs at the Wing On department store, no joke! Half a dozen for a hundred francs.'

Godet raised his eyebrows in contempt and unfolded his own garment, a thin, rose-coloured silk kimono embroidered with a flock of herons. He seemed offended.

'People like you are a disgrace to the French officer corps. You shouldn't smoke. Why smoke when you can get absinthe? That's the intoxicant for people like you.'

Sylvain merely shrugged, but Godet went on insulting him. They talked as freely as if I wasn't in the room, assuming I spoke only English. It was a perfectly reasonable assumption. If my previous duties hadn't required it, I wouldn't have spoken a word of their foreign tongue. I kept my mouth shut, huddled on the edge of the couch. Soon the officers would find out I spoke French and think I'd pulled one over on them, but I didn't care. The hope of learning more about my hostess and the obscure Mr Hsiu kept me from betraying my comprehension of what they were saying. But I learned nothing. Opium was their only theme.

**

'Shall we go upstairs?' It seems they know the way. I follow them. Sylvain waves me ahead, but Godet pulls his kimono tight and hurries on.

In the room we enter, I at first see nothing but heads and shoulders, grouped around three small lamps that give no real light. A faint glow comes from above. Then a switch is turned and a table lamp lights the room. Our hostess comes up to us. Sylvain and Godet greet her. After a few moments,

I can make out three groups of people. Without hesitating, Sylvain joins one of them: three women and two men on a large divan around one of the lamps. One of these guests, having just drained the pipe, hands it to Sylvain and sinks back into the cushions. Sylvain sits with his legs outspread and prepares a fresh pipe.

At the other lamp are two men. One looks Moorish, with a crooked nose, small downy moustache, and narrow, bony face. The other is a fat, burly Chinaman with a smooth, pudgy face and a receding forehead that merges with his shiny scalp. While all the others are reclining on their elbows, he squats among the cushions, as if his ponderous figure were one with them. And while all the others barely favour me with a nod, he struggles to his feet, extends a short, plump arm and shakes my hand. Despite this friendly gesture, I feel an urge to wrestle him to the ground. I can only assume he's the host, since he's welcoming me.

So a fat, repulsive Chinese man possesses a European woman of rather extraordinary beauty. It feels like an insult to my race. But what do I care – that same race has cast me out, and the urge soon passes. It's none of my business, anyway; what are these people to me but means of reaching my goal, of getting away from here and into the interior? I shake his fat hand but, tongue-tied, do not answer his polite questions or even apologise. I am still the outcast.

But they don't make things difficult for me. The hostess prepares a pipe and hands it to me, and I realise I'm not even much of an opium-smoker. While the others drain their pipes in one long pull, as if out of sheer pleasure, I take short, awkward puffs. I watch Godet, who has brought his own pipe, a long slender one which he holds with grace. With small, self-assured movements he rolls a pill on the point of his needle, holds it over the lamp, lets it cook there for a while, and with a flick of the needle packs it into the bowl. The bubble is instantly pierced, and in a breath, Godet inhales the smoke. Here in this setting I admire and envy him. Anywhere else I would probably have despised him.

It goes on that way, pipe after pipe. I too greedily take what I am offered. A few hours of relief from the consciousness of existence seems to me like absolute bliss.

Sylvain alone not only smokes but also drinks many glasses of absinthe, set down beside him at regular intervals. So Godet was right about him. Now and then, he smokes some kind of cigarette with a sharp scent that pierces the sweet, heavy air. He must have built up a high tolerance to stimulants.

After the third pipe, Hsiu asks me if I am the man who will stop at nothing.

'Yes, what do you want from me?'

He makes a dismissive, flattering gesture. 'No so fast, Mr Cameron! We do not speak of such things here. Another time. We are here to smoke and get to know each other.'

But after another pipe, he begins to explain. It's an easy job, not even all that dangerous; what he needs is a person no one in Taihai knows. No one knows me, do they? He peers suspiciously out of the corner of his eyes.

No, I can put him at ease on that score. No one in Taihai knows me. Not one of its millions of Chinese inhabitants, not one of the thousands of Europeans.

'Well,' he says, 'that's the main thing, and to keep it that way, you'll have to be my guest for a few days, and not leave this house.'

To my own amazement, I refuse. To stay in a luxurious house with one of Taihai's wealthiest inhabitants – isn't that the most a stranded man could wish for?

The next to speak is Mrs Hsiu – whose name turns out to be Solange, a name that since then I have always remembered (since it suited her as well as it suits a flower of night). Solange too insists. She clasps my hand and sprawls next to me, forcing me to hold an arm out to support her. Soon, she has laid her head down and is gazing up at me.

I wonder what role they want me to play. Am I supposed to pretend to be Hsiu, sit in a car, ride down a road where bandits are lying in wait for him and be taken hostage in his place? My build makes me a less-than-ideal impersonator, it seems to me. So what do they have in mind? I give up thinking about it. I can feel Solange still reclining against me and have a powerful desire to shake her off, but it might look like I'm scared of Hsiu, and then they'd start to wonder whether I'm really the man who stops at nothing. But Hsiu's not looking at me. He's sitting in the light of a lamp on the far side of the room, with another Chinese man, who I didn't even notice when he came in, and who looks as if he must be skeletal under his long, lustrous black robe. His face is a dented triangle, his eyes so deep-set they're almost hidden. Strange, since the eyes of the Chinese usually lie in their faces like water in the lowlands, level with the ground and not set off by any slope.

He too has laid down his bony form on a heap of cushions; the two of them have no smoking kit and appear to be deep in conversation. The other group is lost in collective ecstasy, its members using each other as pillows. Only Sylvain sits some distance away, smoking cigarettes again and scraping his throat harshly. I long to untangle myself from Solange and go talk to him. How can I be the only one who still feels uneasy, with a vague cramp in my arms and legs, troubled by unsatisfied longing and a disgust that cannot find expression, while all the others, at least for a few hours, are tasting heavenly bliss or annihilation? And not believing in the first, no one could long for the second as much as I.

Solange must have noticed my state of mind; her eyes show pity and contempt. 'Poor man, you don't know how to smoke yet, you're not used to good opium either, you're not used to anything good, you can't even take a long, deep breath. Here, let's practice.' She presses her mouth against mine and gives me a long kiss, which I first resist, then tolerate and finally return. And afterwards, I'm astonished to realise I'm not winded at all – more astonished than happy – and I notice to my surprise that I can now easily finish a pipe in one go, a feat that seemed beyond me only an hour ago. Yet I still can't help glancing over at Hsiu's corner once in a while. She notices and thinks she's guessed my thoughts.

'I'm not his, never his, to him I'm one of his valuables, and not even the one he treasures most. I swear, he loves that sculpture, or that jade flute, more than he loves me. It's just that I'm alive, I can welcome his guests and lighten his mood. That's the only thing that sets me apart.'

'But he gets to see you, doesn't he? He has you near him!'

'Can't others say the same? You, for instance, right now?'

'I would despise myself if I ran around with a Chinese woman ... the opposite is all the worse, a white woman with a Chinese man.'

'*Pauvre petit*. Hsiu is better than a thousand Europeans who think they're civilised because they've picked up a few notions about morality and decency, which they throw off anyway as soon as they get the chance.'

But this is my own opinion, which I held long before tonight, or so I believe. Considering the mutual contempt that my fellow Europeans and I feel for one another, why shouldn't I ally myself with Hsiu and his like? Yet now that she's spoken that thought aloud, I feel myself turn against it, and it enrages me that a woman in her position dares to have the same thoughts and express them more clearly and distinctly than I ever have. Or is it the instinct of my race, do I belong with them as even a pariah belongs to the community that casts him out and confines him to his caste?

'What you're saying is true, but you'd only have the right to judge others if you had saved yourself and not given yourself up in exchange for ...'

'A life without any form of dependence except on a man, a wise man who hardly cares what I do.'

Again, she looks at me in pity and triumph. Her face comes dangerously close. Her brown eyes are wide open; despite a fixed look around the pupils, their wet gleam makes them seem so large that I grow dizzy and almost give in. I push her away. Why? Then again, why not? For anyone in my position, especially after so many years at sea, wouldn't this be a long-cherished, long-suppressed dream come true? Yet I don't want to. I don't want to lose my self straight away again here, not after it's taken me so long to seize hold of it.

Now she thinks, I believe, that I see her as a lure held out by Hsiu. She slides away, with studied indignation, and says, 'Hsiu is powerful. Many people envy him. Many dream of taking his place. Once in a while, one of them disappears forever in the streets of Taihai. Even the most powerful, most heavily guarded man can vanish without a trace one day, not into the mud of the Yangtze, not into one of the cellars of the Chinese city, but without drowning, without dying – merely erased, lacking any memory of himself. One day, long, long afterwards, he is rediscovered in the shadowy zones around the city or in a rickshaw behind a garden wall. Not a hair on his head has been harmed, there is not a scratch on him, no injuries, he hasn't lost weight, his old clothes still fit, but he no longer has any power, not even the power of thought.

'Others *are* kidnapped, by bandits, and taken to some remote corner of the mountains or held captive on an island, ringed by swamps and shallows. They demand the ransom in dollars, millions, and torture him daily. He writes letters pleading for help, friends and relatives scrape the money together, and in the end he's released, dropped off on a sandbank or along the railway. He lives until he dies, as hollow as a cast-off shell.

'Or even simpler: a conspiracy is formed to make him lose face in front of a large crowd. It happens again and again, until he can't show his face anywhere. That last method is the most elegant.'

'And Hsiu himself, isn't he an object of ridicule in the world's eyes?'

'No,' Solange replied. 'I take care of that.'

'So everyone thinks you're his wife, period?'

'Yes, and more than that, his slave, his plaything.'

'And that doesn't bother you?'

'No, that doesn't bother me. A woman's dignity and self-worth are built on other foundations and other territory than a man's.'

***

I lose the ground of my existence, which I have just reached. I drift away on who knows what current, and Solange's calm, self-satisfied face, as close as it is to mine, seems a sphinx that stares at me from every far horizon, solving riddles and posing new ones. In desperation, I scan the room for Sylvain, the only ordinary mortal in this nest of opiomaniacs and soul merchants. But he too has now drifted off to sleep, emitting soft, regular snores with his head tipped back, his taut Adam's apple and chin like the two unequal summits of a mountain, his sideburns framing his face like rough vegetation on a mountain slope.

Hsiu and his friend are asleep now too. Through the skylight falls the pale grey shine of the dawning day. This is a battlefield, and Solange is the only one keeping watch.

'Smoke!' she says. 'That's more than enough talk.' I refuse the pipe and she takes it herself, with derisive, overconfident laughter. Then another. 'Now I'm almost asleep,' she says. 'Now it's all the same to me, even the strange drifter, the outcast, the man I offered myself to, the man who refused me. Could any humiliation be deeper? Does he want me now?'

Why not? Maybe Hsiu will wake in the middle of it – so much the better if he does. All the same, I hurry. Solange gives no hint of whether any desire of hers is being satisfied, or whether at least she's secretly proud to have broken down my resistance. Once she too is sleeping I take the pipe, twice, three times, and finally reach a level of dense blue bliss. But one excruciating thought still shines like a final star on a pitch-black night over hopeless worlds of stony deserts on which swarms of meteors are raining down.

A star or a thought?

Then even that star sets ...

***

I see Sylvain stand up. Sylvain, in his black-and-red striped pyjamas, is suddenly an all-knowing oracle to me. I must seek his advice before daybreak. He leaves the room and returns. I want to clamp onto him but can't move a muscle, can't speak a word, and the sense of belonging in warm, deep, thick blue grows stronger and overwhelms me.

I wake up an hour or so later with a head like a stone, gasping for breath. I want air; there is none. The room is filled with the exhalations of the sleeping and the opium fumes, but I see Sylvain in his pyjamas again, as I did when falling asleep, preparing another pipe without a sound. I crawl towards him on my hands and feet; he sees my condition and says in a laconic tone, 'Yes, I always have a pipe instead of a *petit déjeuner*. I'll be done in a moment, and if you're ready to go, you can come with me.' Has he taken a large enough portion to last him all day, or is Sylvain as short of breath as I am? In any case, it takes him four or five puffs to finish the pipe. Then he rushes out of the room, with me at his heels. We don't look back at the sleepers, though I notice that Hsiu and Solange are both gone.

After strong coffee, served to us by a drowsy boy, we leave the house. It is six o'clock. No whites are out yet, but in the morning mist the streets are already bustling with coolies running errands and going to work. Many others lie sleeping along the edges of the footpaths and between the houses, in all imaginable positions; now and then a Sikh constable on patrol kicks at one of them, but sometimes the sleeper won't budge – that means he died during the night. The streets begin to fill with vehicles: large, wide-bodied lorries, small, fast luxury automobiles and creaky, awkward wheelbarrows with four or six girls on either side of the large wheel, trundled forward by a servant. Sylvain is in a hurry.

'Come on, come on! We'll have half an hour longer at the jetty if we catch the six-thirty bus.'

We barely make it. For another half hour, I have to put up with the press of human bodies on all sides, and then it's over. In a small teahouse on the landing stage with the turbid river flowing underneath it, I sit with Sylvain. The far bank of the river is out of view. Side by side in the current, like churches with towers and crosses of different heights, lie the battle cruisers.

Sylvain now points to one of the largest ones: 'That one's mine. In half an hour, the launch will pick me up, along with the others who spent the night in town. So you have until then to ask whatever you want to know.'

At that instant, raspy bugles blow on almost all the ships. You wouldn't call the sound triumphant. It's like the desperate cries of large animals driven into a corner. Yet any one of these ships, with one shot from its big guns, could send the whole city into a panic, just one of them using its full artillery could destroy a district, and a few hours of continuous fire from all their guns could turn Taihai into a heap of rubble. But it would be their undoing too: the rubble would fill the riverbed – no, not fill it, but obstruct it – and they would be trapped as if in a bottle, with no way of returning to sea. The red of the sun breaks through. The ships turn vaguer and greyer than they looked in the predawn darkness. I have a strong premonition that this mutual destruction will break loose.

Sylvain and I sit on the black landing stage, which shudders whenever a departing or arriving motorboat bumps into it, as if on a raft between two worlds. He doesn't seem to realise; he's waiting for his launch, now and then scraping his throat. In a dry, monotonous voice, he tells me what I want to know.

'They're very hospitable. They both like officers as guests, but everyone is welcome. It's a fine place to go now and then, except that it's much too crowded and there's too much talking, and then those women and all their fuss and nonsense ... If you want to smoke in peace, wait for me here. Thursday evening at six-thirty. The opium is not as good at Lu Tung's place, but it's quieter there. No unwelcome conversations.'

This leaves me not much the wiser, so I put the question to him straight: what kind of people are Hsiu and his wife?

'She's half Marseillaise and has some yellow in her family tree, and he's a man who deals in everything, without exception: money, opium, arms, soy, humans, you name it.'

He seems to think that says it all, and I stop asking questions. In a flash, I've decided not to see any of these people ever again, even if that means losing the connection I hope to find and returning to what I was before: a wanderer of the seas, on shore a stranger to everyone, who must find his own path and can't ask anyone the way. A drifter unaccustomed to traveling on land, who must nonetheless make this longest, hardest journey.

The large launch moors among many other ships. Sylvain shakes my hand. He is completely burnt out, his hand sapped of all its force, his eyes of their shine. He will do today's work like an automaton and return to life with his first pipe. Is this the liberating and uplifting power of opium, sole gift of the gods to humanity? No, not as it's used here by Hsiu and Solange and Lu Tung, but on the floor of a lofty temple at the edge of a bottomless ravine, where the blue smoke mingles with the fine mists that float along the cliffsides – it would be different there than it is here, where the soiled souls of the businesspeople drift through the ether like a rain of soot.

Chapter 4

The launch with its load of sleeping officers puttered away towards the waiting ships. Coming alongside the *Lannes*, Sylvain swung himself languorously out onto the grand accommodation ladder and ascended, stopping twice along the way. After a hurried breakfast in the garishly lit but unheated officers' mess, he went to the battery to supervise the disassembly of a cannon. Fortunately, the sailors had plenty of experience and admired the serenity he brought to his duties. While the other senior officers now and then, or quite often, interfered with the men's work, wanting to show that they still understood the practical side of their profession, Sylvain rarely did, if ever. If he had to, of course, he could aim and shoot and calculate trajectories. Beyond that, he merely provided his physical presence and never carried out the required inspections alone. But as he entered the turret that morning, he was met by worried faces, and his direct subordinate, who had been on the launch with him, coming back from a different party, made a beeline for him and took him aside.

'We've been summoned by the commander.'

The two of them went down the low, narrow corridor from the guns to the command bridge to receive what was probably their final warning.

***

As I stood on the landing stage watching the ships, I suspected none of this. I envied the two of them, imagining how good they had it. Nights on land, days on board, and now and then a mission on a fast-moving, well-maintained vessel that never had to load or unload. Such were my jealous daydreams. After a while, I turned away. Knowing what I had to avoid, I no longer set foot in the international concessions. Along this bank of the river – unlike on the far side, strewn with coal and trash, where I had arrived in the city – processions of cars advanced over the asphalt, carrying traders to their offices. The din of their horns was punctuated now and then by a brief silence. After eight o'clock it would be one continuous shriek.

I took a seat next to the machinery casing on one of the small harbour boats that went from wharf to wharf, and disembarked once we'd reached a calm stretch of the riverbank and were well away from the city. Or so I thought. But after a walk past warehouses, many deserted, and something resembling a large Chinese fishing village, I again found myself in an offshoot of one of the concessions I'd wandered around earlier. I walked on, sometimes slowly, sometimes even stopping, making a constant effort not to doze off against a fence, and by late afternoon I had reached the outer edge. A few low farmhouses were scattered here and there. Then I came to the end of those too. The Chinese city started up again, with its tight-packed houses that barely left room for the narrow alleys. The light was already fading, and the heat growing more oppressive, as I stood by a muddy streambed where flat-bottomed junks lay stranded in front of a wooden temple that looked old and dilapidated. The stream must have dried up one long summer twenty or thirty years earlier, and the winter rains had never refilled the bed. The boats had been left there and later claimed as dwellings by the lowest of the homeless. Boards lay spread across the mud in all directions between the hulks and the shore, and people, most of them either grey-headed or toddlers, were crossing them without a single false step, rarely treading on the muddy ground. They lived as monkeys live, walking back and forth on branches or resting on a gnarl in the trunk.

Along the stream and on some of the vessels were shops,

largely stocked with goods I couldn't identify. And beyond the temple, in the distance, lay a row of delicate houses with slender roofs and beams, lit up from the inside, now that night had fallen, like huge lanterns with shadow-plays along their walls. At a sharp angle to them was a regular row of stone Chinese houses. It was as if the city, having decided to stop here at last, had decided to correct its zigzags, twists and outgrowths and draw a firm line through the plan that could not be completed. Yet even this was not the end. Although rice fields stretched to the horizon in misty tranquillity, the green dome of the southern railway station also rose there, wide and podgy, and you could just hear the trains as they blew their whistles and thundered away.

But here, where everything, the people, the houses, the junks, had strayed onto dry land and decided to stay, I too could remain as long as I wished, more easily than in the larger Taihai, the city that had risen to power over the past fifty years and would not last a century, no matter how hard the banks tried to look like indestructible pyramids, with their concrete walls, marble lobbies, granite staircases, and lead roofs.

Night was falling, and I had to find shelter. I headed for the temple. Out in front were two monks selling imitations of jade carvings. I bought them. Inside the temple, I was offered incense sticks. I bought those too and left the temple on the other side. A gang of monks, dirty and ragged, sat squatting around a large, bubbling stone pot. At my request, I was shown to a cell where I could sleep. The stone was hard and bare. They found a wooden pallet for me but not a cover. It was a cool place to sleep, and I spent a better night in that unfurnished cell than the one before, suffocated by excess and human luxury. Even if I was moving in circles and detours, wasn't it possible I was drifting towards my goal?

Had the drifting itself become my goal, or was I merely on the run from emptiness?

I left the temple late in the morning; by that time I no longer attracted anyone's interest. In one of the shops I saw a light and, curious about who was trying to perpetuate the night, I looked inside and, in the distance, under the lamp that hung from the low ceiling, saw Chu seated at his workbench. He greeted me like an old acquaintance. I went into the shop and found myself surrounded by rings, bracelets, watches and pearl necklaces, hung from the ceiling and laid out on stands. Chu bowed and asked what I was looking for. A watch, I told him, but I could choose one later, I was in no hurry. He had tea brought to us and placed a box with a collection of watches beside me, so that I could select one whenever I wished. I stayed in my seat as people went in and out, and it struck me that not many of them were customers. Most passed down the small aisle alongside the workbench, said hello to Chu, and disappeared into the back of the building. When I asked, Chu told me they were relatives and a few lodgers. Could I stay there too? Bowing his assent, he said it would be an honour for his house and his family. Then he led me down the narrow aisle. On the far side of the yard behind the shop was a row of buildings of various sizes, without any windows except for slits above the doors. He opened one door and I saw the interior of a cell like the monks', a bit larger, a bit less dirty, and a bit more furnished, with a jug, a chair, a portrait of Sun Yat-sen and a vase.

I stayed there a long time but never met all the members of the Chu family. There were ancient women who sat on a stone in a corner all day, except on the rare occasions when they did laundry. There were middle-aged men, Chu's brothers or sons, who tilled the poor soil in the shadow of Taihai's walls; there was a gaggle of little girls who worked in the cotton factories, leaving early in the morning – I never saw them go – and returning late in the evening, pale and wobbly, while the boys, far fewer in number, went to school, and one of them, sixteen years old, well-dressed but as hungry and scrawny as all the others, was studying for his exams. Late at night he often used the lamp, after Chu had cleared his cogs and tools off the bench.

Soon Chu had taken me into confidence and told me of his great tragedy: he always had daughters, never sons. After five daughters – three had died young – a son was born, the boy who was now a student. Then came another five daughters in quick succession; his wife died giving birth to the last. Chu's mother, a fat old woman, was always strutting about in a glossy black smock, tight blue trousers, and high-heeled, open-backed shoes, never doing any work herself, always squawking at all the women and most of the men, holding sway and commanding obedience.

No one but Chu spoke to me. I tried to talk to the student, but he turned out to know nothing beyond the Chinese classics and outdated concepts of physics and metaphysics. He had learned Sun Yat-sen's doctrines by heart but had no idea what they meant. He said he would just wait and see.

Once a month a large meal with twenty dishes was made for the whole family and all the guests, and sometimes there was a cockfight in the courtyard. Not only the Chu family but also neighbours from near and far would sit hunched around it, making bets and cheering on the gamecocks.

They worked from early in the morning until late at night – I don't know what they all did. Yet there were always a couple of groups in one corner of the yard, playing fan-tan or betting on anything and everything: whether a bird would swerve left or right, or whether a withered leaf on a tree would fall or not. I enjoyed looking on, and once in a while they would even let me join them for fan-tan when they were short of players. The rest of the time, I would walk around the streambed or sit in the temple, or out in the sun, or in the light of Chu's lamp. He never took part in any games or festivities, except for the meals, where he was expected to play host. He was as solemn as a judge, never smoked a pipe, and had clear eyes with wide, darting pupils. His tools and cogs were scattered all around him, an unbelievable mess, but his hand always went straight to whatever he needed. When customers came in, he would set his work aside, put on a different pair of spectacles, and approach with a bow. Many customers refused to pay; others cursed him; some came to borrow money or sell watches, after endless negotiation. But Chu himself never lost his temper and, through patience, always got his way. Even the robbery later on, which turned most of his life upside down, failed to upset him. His outlook was childish and simple: the wheel of existence would have to turn for countless centuries before Heaven would take pity on Earth and make everything flow together. It should have happened long ago, he told me, but there was always another war breaking out, another cog gone missing. When I replied that there would be no end to war, he said no, one day the world would keep ticking without it. I thought his ideas were naive, but spending time with him did me good. I would sit in the workshop for hours without saying a word. Outside, the sun shone or the rain fell. It made little difference, there in the shop in the light of his lamp. Sometimes the street life swirled inside in the form of a customer, but there were also times when we sat for hours alone.

He told me what he'd been in the course of his life: a factory worker, a merchant and a member of the Hong, a sect that sought peace but incited riots. He'd lost everything he owned three times; what could happen to him how? Good fortune or disaster, it was all the same. He was certain the life that mattered would not begin until he lay in his carefully lacquered coffin, which he had shown me with pride. That was the only time I ever saw him show any emotion, except once, beside another, smaller coffin, months later.

When a horde of refugees, set in motion by the victorious armies in the south, fleeing from the defeated, mutinous troops of the Manchu generals, began flooding into the outlying districts in search of refuge and ran up against the closed walls of the city, most of the neighbourhood's residents shut their doors and gates, even though no refugee would dare remain long in such an undefended place, surrounded on all sides by mud and marshes, so close to the borders of the concession that it was exposed to every sort of danger. A few of the locals also seemed aware of the danger, or else they were infected by the panic from afar. They hurriedly gathered up a few household items, grabbed their children, and ran for it. Most of them, however, were loth to abandon their homes, however decrepit, and their belongings. There was also a flurry of activity in and around the houseboats. Hopeless attempts were made to barricade the doors, the gaps between houses were filled with stones, and the city gates, which had always been open and seemed to me like holes in the wall, closed their double doors with great creaking, banging and clouds of dust or, if they refused to budge, were nailed shut. The people on the houseboats had pulled in the planks and no longer came ashore. It was as if the whole world, expecting a typhoon, was digging in and holding tight, all the while secretly knowing it wouldn't help when the storm struck. Even the house pets, which wandered freely among the chickens and the pigs, were kept inside and sought out their corners. The children stopped playing, stood in a cluster and pointed south. 'That's where the great dragon will come from.'

The river of refugees crashed into the barbed-wire fences and was channelled around the city to the southern plain, where they went on starving. Then it was calm for a time. Doors and windows were half opened. But the barricades remained, and more were built.

It grew hotter and hotter as we moved deeper into the summer. The sky stayed cloudless. The marshes around us bred parasites and decay, and the well water stank. The water from further away, sold in barrels, was too expensive for most people. Children and the elderly were the hardest hit by diarrhoea and dysentery. They lay all over but preferred the small slivers of shade under the trees in the courtyard. They were unwelcome indoors, in the small, hot rooms; the ones who wouldn't leave on their own were carried out. No one disposed of their excrement; the children who were still healthy played around it, soiling and infecting themselves.

How can it be that I witnessed all this and did not become sick with distress, or walk away? I didn't know where to go and felt more at home there each day. At the time, I might add, there was no other place for me. I wouldn't have been allowed into the city, nor into the war-torn, pillaged countryside around it.

Then the second wave arrived: the defeated armies of the north, who had driven the refugees out ahead and were now being chased themselves, like dust before the storm. They did not reach the streambed, but we saw fighting around the station in the distance. They tried to climb on top of the trains; sometimes grenades went off; and once an engine escaped with a few wagons, whistling and screeching like a banshee and, half a mile later, rolling off the rails. The cries, which rose up ever louder, confirmed that the people crushed in the accident were being slaughtered.

The firefights continued day and night, and even the Japanese concession was attacked by one desperate, determined band, supposedly because its defences were weakest, even though the secret reason for their aggression, as they knew very well, was race hatred against their fellow Asians. The killing there went on for a day. Small groups of fighters used long ladders to reach the most outlying Japanese streets, which burned like vulcanised rubber. The despairing residents roasted in the ashes. In the evening, a sudden silence fell. The next day, pits were dug, human remains shovelled together, and already the slats and bamboo canes were being reassembled into houses, as if after an earthquake.

Now the southern troops were expected. The entrances to the city were completely blocked. The barbed wire grew thicker by the day and you could barely see the soldiers behind it, except for the Japanese, who were closest, and whose fence was not as tight-meshed. They seemed to spurn the idea of cocooning themselves in completely; there were so many of them, milling around in dense masses, making camp around the outermost houses, while the Americans, British, and French were never seen in groups of more than twelve or twenty at a time. So I felt like Gulliver, suspended between Lilliput and Brobdingnag, after he freed himself from both the fine-spun ligatures of the former and the heavy chains of the latter.

And seeing the soldiers in the distance, behind their bristly webs, became a habit and a minor source of amusement. Sometimes we got a closer look at them. A patrol came to check the perimeter of our area, but they never set up a post there. The children followed the soldiers around. Evidently they never considered it worth the effort to occupy this patch of slum in the middle of the battlefield, and after a few days the visits stopped.

A cacophony of signals and fanfares blared every morning and every evening, but no shots were fired. The days seemed so calm, so ordinary. Yet each one could bring our doom. But the victors never came any closer. They seemed to be sparing Taihai, the city they longed to possess, perhaps torn between taking only the poor Chinese city and making a play for greater Taihai and all the wealth and power it would bring, power over the territory of central China, over trade, finance, transport. They had to be there somewhere, beyond the hills in the distance. Sometimes a shot was heard there. Sometimes an aeroplane took off. That was all.

In our neighbourhood, the slow creep of dysentery now seemed relatively harmless, having been supplanted by outbreaks of severe, malignant typhus. In Chu's densely populated house, many were sick. They lay outstretched in all the rooms and corridors, wherever they could find shelter, because it was raining almost daily now, heavy showers that flattened everything. The courtyard was deserted, the dry trees engorged with water – some even sprouted a leaf or two.

In the back of the workshop, protruding from underneath Chu's table, lay a child six or ten years old, his youngest daughter, staying home from the factory. Chu himself tended to her. His mother looked in now and then but never laid a finger on her. She was too dignified to touch the child of a woman she hardly knew, who wasn't even her daughter. Chu didn't have much work at the time, and often sat with the girl. I too overcame my initial fear, and we continued our low conversations over her plank bed. The talking didn't seem to do her any harm, but she was scared of being left alone. If both of us left her side, she would scream and cry. Otherwise, she lay still, her eyes on us, mostly unconscious. Despite my warnings, Chu gave her a taste of every dish and, all in all, a lot to eat – including even the spiciest foods.

'It won't cure her, but it won't kill her either, and she's never eaten adult food. Let her at least taste it before she dies. It'll be a long time before she's reborn.'

That was the only time, in the face of death, that he felt anything like what we tend to refer to as love. Gone was his wisdom and equanimity. His grief was not effusive, but the day she died he sat with her for hours and was still there when the women arrived to prepare the corpse. Her narrow little coffin was placed in the workshop where her bed had been. Chu would lay aside his work many times a day to sit and look at her.

Relatives and children also came to see her and left toys and other gifts. She was much better off than she'd ever been in life, when she'd had to produce a hundred hair nets a day and came home in the evening with a few coppers clenched in her hand. Now she lay in her best frock, colourful and stiff with embroidery.

She had been so thin and emaciated, yet in time the air under the table, and then in the back of the workshop, and then throughout the workshop, was filled with corpse stench, and one day I went to Chu to tell him so. But he had such a look in his eyes that instead I stood by the coffin with him for a moment and said she was still so pretty, and did not speak of her removal. What I said was true; her mouth still looked so alive in her narrow face, so red from the cosmetics. Only the eyelids were turning a little green and purple.

***

The next day, however, the coffin was gone and Chu was engrossed in his work again, his lamp glaring. He said hello when he heard my step, without lifting his head, and the day after that, again, he did not speak to me. That was when I decided it was time for me to move on again. Chu, the only one I'd really known, was drowning in his sorrow and would never resurface. But I couldn't leave yet; the fighting had broken out again, just when no one had expected it any longer.

After all that time, the southern army came out in the open and advanced in a broad, deep front. Straight away, they came under intense fire from the concessions. But there were few casualties, and the soldiers soon came to a halt. Shots went back and forth through the air for a while, without touching either side, but grenades from both directions dropped onto the long-spared district, destroying what had already been so close to falling apart. Chu's workshop was spared, but most of the houses in the row behind it were blown to pieces, leaving us all homeless (except for Chu's immediate family, who slept in the workshop). We lived in the yard amid the mud and wreckage and could no longer wash ourselves.

The next day the occupation ended. The five-coloured flag of the Republic was raised beside those of the foreign powers, but the victorious army marched off in a wide arc. The next day, the city was reopened, and many people who had been trapped inside for months came swarming out over the fields and in all directions.

We found grubby printed proclamations declaring that Taihai had been polluted by foreigners for too long to serve as capital of the new, purged state. It had been left to choke on its own filth. Only Nanking, the old capital, was worthy to house the new regime. Everyone knew that no one would contest Nanking. It was an empty expanse with walls around it and sparse grass, with here and there a house or a rubbish heap. They would be safer there than in Taihai, which was prized by all.

The great campaign was over. A sense of disappointment remained that there'd been no great battle, even though the district had been razed to the ground. The ruins were tidied up, and houses were rebuilt where necessary – so many people had died.

The Chu family seemed small now, despite its more than thirty surviving members. Chu's mother had grown thin, and her authority seemed to have waned. I never heard her screeching orders anymore. And Chu? Well, the customers returned, he slipped out from behind his table and bowed, but he no longer seemed to see me, and, in truth, I believe he drew some connection between his child's death and the foreigner, who had arrived just before the great disasters began. Why not blame it on the dirt and the poor diet and the gruelling work he had made her do, or on the age in which he lived? Why on me? Yet I lingered, content with whatever I got, eating what Chu's mother served me or shoved at me, sleeping in any convenient corner. But fortunately, Chu himself came to me one day to say it would be better for me to go live among my own people. Otherwise sheer sloth might have kept me from ever leaving. I would eventually have married one of Chu's daughters, slowly dissolved into the family despite their resistance, and closed off the possibility of ever leaving. I, already considered a degenerate by my compatriots back home, would have faded bit by bit into my new surroundings, and my existence would have melted away after all. Yes, without the blockade, without Chu's daughter falling ill from a poor diet and contaminated water, and without her death, this would have come to pass. Great events condescended to influence my insignificant life. Maybe later I would be the grain of sand that would bring mighty machinations grinding to a halt.

Where would I go? The station was in ruins. No trains passed through it. But in any case, I would have been afraid to avail myself of a means of transport that even the most backward Chinaman takes for granted. I would never have dared to buy a ticket, board a carriage, take a seat like anybody else. And the land beyond was as empty and grey as nothingness itself, the nothingness for which I was not yet ripe.

When the city was reopened, the blockades removed, and the curfew lifted, when lights winked on all around until Taihai, like an enormous meteor in constant flames, gnawing its way into the earth, was visible from the edge of the plain, I felt drawn to the city again, secretly glad to be drawn towards anything at all. It was hard, even so, to prise myself loose from the place that had offered some semblance of a quiet life in the midst of the upheaval and the troubles. I didn't have the courage to say goodbye. I left most of my things behind and laid the money I owed on a crate. Looking back at Chu's lamp, still burning in the workshop, I crept along the row of houses, crossed the plain, passed without incident through the few guard posts that hadn't yet been dismantled and, in the late darkness before the morning mist, arrived in the city.

Chapter 5

This time I did not let myself drift on the currents of life in Taihai. Again, I went in search of Hsiu, resigning myself to the fact that he would decide my fate. But when I rang the bell of his house, which I'd hoped I'd never see again, no one opened the door. It had been evacuated during the troubles; a few windows were shattered. I walked around it, looked inside, but saw no signs of life. Standing in front of that empty house, I was gripped with fear. Would I have to keep roaming Taihai, follow the river again, try to find a ship, return to my old life? Slowly, glancing back over my shoulder, I wandered away, found myself in the business district, and decided to search for Hsiu there. In the phone book I found a series of forty Hsiu's, and I didn't know his two other names. On the phone, I would never manage to puzzle out whether I was talking to the right one, so I visited their offices in person – six, eight, ten stories up. Sometimes there was a lift; other times I had to climb the winding stairs, arriving faint and dizzy. But luck was on my side this time; the fifth Hsiu was the man I was looking for.

Still, I had to wait for hours on the sixth floor of a building on Shensi Road before he would see me. I sat out on the landing at first, on a bare bench between two tall, pot-bellied vases, and then in a dim waiting room, surrounded by plants and ceramic figurines, each with its own stale odour. I was swooning with hunger and thirst but had no intention of leaving. I would never have the courage to walk up to this floor a second time and wait again; if I walked out, I would never escape Taihai, but would live as a stranger there until I died. I went to the window and peered through the venetian blinds. Had these tall grey buildings really shot up from the hovels there below? I pushed one of the slats open to let in the light and was startled to find I wasn't alone in the waiting room. Four others had already been there when I came in, motionless in their seats, their hands on their knees, their eyes closed or slitted. Not one of them spoke a word or made a motion for the rest of the time that we waited there together. The boy came in. One of them followed him out with listless steps; the others remained as motionless as ever. Meanwhile, I sat and smoked, leafed through a book I'd found there, and returned to the window, until at last I sunk down beside them, too discouraged to stand up again. My ears were ringing and my vision flickering.

But my turn did come. I stood stiffly and followed through two other dim rooms full of scents and shadows. Then, in a flash, I was opposite Hsiu, who was seated at a desk as massive and ornate as an altar. I almost recoiled, but faster than I'd ever seen him move, he leapt up and extended his hand, which I took – his plump, fleshy hand, like a lifebuoy. If Hsiu had not noticed the state I was in, then he certainly felt it when our hands met. 'Sit down and eat first, then we'll talk.'

The boy who had showed me in now led me to a corner and brought me one dish after another, and I ate and drank while Hsiu talked on the phone, took notes and received other visitors, all without even glancing at me, until finally I rose and stood in front of his desk. Going on with his phone conversation, he gave me the once-over. He must have decided I was the right tool for the job, or at least, he told me he had something for me – not in Taihai anymore, unfortunately, I had let that opportunity slip away. 'Business in Taihai has been languishing ever since the siege,' he said in a tone of regret.

I told him I'd rather get as far away as possible. 'Our first destination is Hupeh, then maybe Szechwan – we'll see how long you last. But don't you Europeans carry that disease in your blood, especially the sailors?' he said, with a mocking look. 'Shouldn't we have Dr Chen test your blood first, three storeys down?' He reached for the bell. I shot to my feet, determined to leave after all, but he stopped me. 'No, don't worry. I'm well within my rights to ask for a blood test, but I won't insist. Still, you will need to get a series of photos taken by the photographer four storeys down. What? Not even that? Fine, I'll do it myself.' And before I knew it, he had snapped my picture – twice, three times – with a small handheld camera, all from his seat behind his desk. 'And would you read this for me?'

Hsiu handed me something that looked like a pocket diary, with a floral pattern on the cover. I took it, couldn't open it, it was a plate, my fingerprints were on it. All this happened in a matter of seconds. I was dumbfounded. Hsiu was already turning me into his underling.

'Now at least they'll know when you get there that you're the right man. See, I'm not going with you, or at least not all the way.'

'There was no need for all that. I told you I was prepared to do anything. And I suppose once you've had enough of me, it'll be easy enough to turn me over to the courts or have me bumped off.'

'No, that's not the plan,' Hsiu said in a placating tone, raising his hands in front of him. 'If we get mixed up with the courts, we'll be in it together, I guarantee you. But I'm sure it won't come to that. Your barbarian tongue has a charming word: "loophole". We have very large loopholes in this country. Even chubby old Hsiu can fit through them easily, so I'm sure the slender Mr Cameron can do the same. And by the by, there are no courts here really, except in a couple of places, and they're no match for Hsiu's money. This is just for convenience, believe me, so when you arrive there won't be any doubt that the man I've sent is the one they expected. There are so many cases of mistaken identity in this country. The distances are so great that along the way a person can change beyond recognition, become many years older or disappear completely, and someone else may play out his role. Such measures are unavoidable. Now I'll send a photo and fingerprint to Szechwan, four times at fourteen-day intervals. One of the four is certain to arrive. Once I've received confirmation, our journey can begin.' His eyes bored into mine for a moment. 'Well, that's decided, then. We leave in three months.'

'In three months?'

He saw the beggarly look in my eyes. My distress must have been written all over my face. Another three months! The hot summer in a city built for winter, without any shade or grass, aside from the footworn patches in the public gardens. Summer in Taihai, where people hurry past in the streets with towels to wipe the streaming sweat off their faces. 'Where am I supposed to go in the meantime? Surely you can see I have no money, I can't wait that long.'

'Can't wait that long? Tai Tung sat still and waited all his life, until he reached the age of seventy. Only then did he meet the ruler who sought his advice on governing the country, giving Tai Tung the chance to prevent its downfall again.'

'What did he do all those years?'

'He sat on the banks of the Wei, fishing. What's to stop you from doing the same on the banks of the Yangtze? And Lao Tzu, the old man, waited all his life for nothing, and only then noticed there was nothing he'd waited for.'

Hsiu was not the man to take ancient philosophers seriously, so I understood he was cruelly mocking me. I growled that his own life seemed far removed from all those wise teachings. This almost seemed to anger him.

'Who knows what my real life is, who knows! Perhaps at this very moment I am a just judge in the afterlife, and my identity as a shady dealer and swindler in Taihai is merely a cover.'

'That could very well be, but I need food for the next three months.'

'Then I'll give you a paying job to see you through. Just one thing: it won't be consistent with your religion. Hsiu is kindly, noble and trusting. He gives advances. You can pick up one hundred dollars at the Hong Kong–Shanghai bank.' He signed a cheque. 'Then go on a three-month pilgrimage to the Chusan Archipelago. Pray to all the gods there are – and there are many – for the success of our trip.'

I felt a surge of gratitude towards Hsiu, in spite of hating him as much as ever. At least this assignment would get me out of Taihai. At first I'd been afraid of the three months ahead. Now, all of a sudden, they felt like too short an interlude. The only problem, I realised with a start, was that I'd have to cross the sea again, to return to the element I hated with such a passion I would have preferred the thirsty deserts. I had no fear of the river. The prospect of sailing on it, watching the banks draw ever closer together, hearing the rapids in the distance, being towed through them, and watching the stream grow narrower still with each descent – a gradual transition from water to land – very much appealed to me. But I did not want to see the sea again.

'Does Mr Hsiu really believe good spirits will favour an enterprise that he himself admits is base in character, and lacking any higher purpose?'

'So many offerings have been made, including some very rich ones, that they're bound to have drawn some spirits – even some good ones – to the vicinity of the temple. Surely we're not to believe that the creatures of heaven, whose intelligence is so much greater and keener than ours, would overlook this opportunity?'

'But I could be stranded out there on the Chusan islands by

a blockade or a new war with Japan. Then I wouldn't be able to join your expedition, and your hundred dollars would have been spent in vain.'

Hsiu looked irritated.

'You're better at thinking up obstacles than you are at overcoming them.'

'Don't the gods in Shantung have much more influence over the interior than the ones on the remote, wave-battered, typhoon-swept Chusan islands?'

'I would almost think you had Chinese ancestors. Yes, there is one god in Shantung who has more influence than all the gods of the Chusan Archipelago between them. But his shrine is in an uncongenial place: the cave of the heavy westward-drifting clouds. There's no path leading there, no well nearby for drinking water, and no company but a few old stone-deaf hermits, and the god demands such intense prayer that you'll have no time for scenic walks in the countryside.'

Hsiu cocked his head, imagining this would put me off. But I took the job.

***

The cave of the westward-drifting clouds, not a temple but a hole in the rock that I reached after weeks of climbing, once a dwelling for hermits but now unoccupied, helped me more than living beings ever did, and more than the gods to whom I prayed. I saw nothing but the two hermits living in tents at the edge of the ravine. From time to time, one of them would bring some little offering to the idol and tell me I was wrong not to do the same, after coming all the way there. I never got round to it. But I did converse with it on long evenings, after the brief twilight, when the cave was dark.

That cave was a resting place. I had no desire to remain there, and none to leave. But when the messenger came to fetch me, I felt light enough to traverse great distances, hollow enough to take in great dangers without reluctance or fear. I never saw Taihai again, except far in the distance. We cut straight across the landscape – mountainous at first, then hilly, then levelling off – to the shore of an inlet, stopping beside an enormous haystack covered with reeds. It was already winter in the mountains, but down on the plains, it was still autumn. Great flocks of geese passed overhead, and at night the northeast wind blew straight through our thin clothing. The charcoal fire was not strong enough to keep the cold at bay. We took hay and reeds from the stack to cover ourselves at night, and revealed a large craft, lying half on land and half in the water.

One especially clear day I spotted Taihai in the distance, the first cloud in an otherwise clear sky. The smoke and fumes above it never blew away. Beyond the masts of the junks, factory chimneys rose to the skies like the trunks of great trees blackened by fire. Beyond that lay the Bund, like an immense basalt rock studded with crystals.

Utter silence hung over the land, until one evening the wind brought a confused murmur, in which I seemed to recognise everything: the thrumming of the looms, the pounding of machines, the groaning of coolies as they slaved away and the occasional shipment of coal hitting the bottom of some deep shaft. I did not think of the suffering. I thought of the time when all that would stand still, and of what would remain after the cataclysm: piles of rock and rubble, or a horde of low huts spread out over the ruins. But where steel and stone once flourished, no life will ever germinate again. I felt great satisfaction at the thought of the dark age to come.

'Wouldn't you like to visit just once more, to spend one last night in the places you so despise?'

Hsiu was standing next to me, having skimmed over to us noiselessly in his sampan, where he'd squatted for hours under the thatched roof. He looked like a peasant come straight from ploughing and seemed terrified that his enemies had followed him. He ducked behind the haystack, and when I suggested we travel on together, he didn't even mock me. But as soon he saw we'd half-exposed the large vessel, he lost his temper, even though there was no chance anyone would see us. The whole area was completely uninhabited; it was too marshy there to graze livestock or grow crops, and the small path by which I had come was known only to my guide. But Hsiu made us cover everything up again anyway, and we slept on the bare ground that night, shivering and half-covered with blankets, a mile away from the craft. Fighting wakefulness, I almost regretted shrugging off Hsiu's suggestion of one last night in Taihai. The bars and dance halls I'd detested were now visions of warmth and comfort, of civilisation.

I also began to have serious doubts about whether Hsiu's business empire was as vast as I'd imagined. If so, would he really be spending the night in the middle of the countryside without anyone to tend to his needs? I couldn't believe these were all precautionary measures, just to rule out any possibility of being spied on or shadowed. But before long my doubts were dispelled. Before first light he woke me, and as I rose to my feet, I saw him and two unfamiliar men, who must have arrived in the night, clearing away the hay and reeds to uncover a door. We entered a square room that was dark and musty, because Hsiu closed the door behind us and kept it shut. Then, with a sudden, heavy thud, the walls and floor of the hut were tilted. A continuous rocking followed; the vessel had been launched. She soon lay calm. On the bank, the men were hard at work, turning the heap of reeds and hay into a hollow mound that looked more or less as it had before. It was clear how anxious Hsiu was not to leave a trace. Maybe he was being watched from far away, through binoculars.

I briefly returned to the bank for a better view of the whole craft. I hadn't expected anything presentable to be hidden in that haystack, but she impressed me. Her prow was wide and solid and decorated not with the usual dragon carvings, but with ponderous arabesques. Her imposing deck seemed to have four sections; there were four doors on one side and three windows on the other. Though I knew she wasn't yet loaded, she was fairly low in the water, and I worried about how we would get her out of the shallow stream.

For the next three days, after we dragged her from the stream to the river, a small tugboat towed her to a place where she could join a train of barges. All that time, Hsiu hadn't shown his face. He probably had company in his spacious forecabin; many times I heard laughter, and the light burned late into the night. But no one ever came out; the vessel moved onward and Hsiu's servants were the only people I saw for those first few days. If he didn't want to be spotted, then it was certainly wise of him to stay inside; I've never seen such a packed waterway. It put the Thames and the Elbe to shame. No big steamers came in sight, but we saw all the more small ships with powerful engines, passenger vessels with flat decks and large paddle boxes, and between them innumerable junks with large families on board, where always, every hour of the day and night, children scrambled about and food was cooked. They had stoves on the fore and aft decks, heedless of the danger, and at night you could often see small accidental fires being put out. Howling dogs, squealing pigs, the penetrating odour of garlic and oil – we heard and smelled it all, as if we were sailing through city streets. I was often reminded of my time in Chu's neighbourhood, but felt no nostalgia. The first four days of the voyage were uninterrupted. Then the junk left the train to dock at a city that resembled Taihai from a distance but had much smaller factories and fewer warehouses and sheds along the wharves. Five crates were brought on board there, the size and shape of coffins. Since this is common practice on Chinese vessels setting out on a long voyage, it probably didn't occur to anyone that they might already be full, or intended for different contents.

The next evening, when the city was almost out of sight, Hsiu came out again; he stood on deck for a while, enjoying the peace and quiet. The junk had slowed down and was being propelled with four oars. When she could, she sailed a little way upstream; even this far inland, she was affected by the tide. Although I still loathed Hsiu, I was happy to see him again. I had grown accustomed to the river views, and the crewmen manoeuvred the ship without the quickness and rhythmic shanties with which mariners almost always accompany their work, and which might otherwise have kept my spirits up. They handled the tackle and sails like farm labourers, with slow, broad gestures, using much more strength than necessary. At first they treated me with deference; they must have thought of me as their master's friend. But their respect diminished by the day as they realised I was always alone and never joined Hsiu in his cabin. Now he was out in the open again and asked how I liked being a guest on his junk.

'It's better than all my previous ships, but still not what I'm looking for. I'm itching to go on land and begin our journey.'

'The journey began days ago,' Hsiu said. 'We'll be travelling *over* land soon enough, but we won't be *on* land for a while.'

I could tell he was hinting at something that wasn't yet clear to me, but I made no reply and stared out at the riverbank. Hsiu stayed at my side; he too said nothing, now and then breaking the silence by clearing his throat. Then, in a friendly tone, he asked whether I would join him in a glass of whisky. In the same breath, he called for the boy to put the carafe and glasses on the aft hatch. I guess he was looking for company too; perhaps he had finally tired of the goings-on in his cabin.

'Do you ever long for the pipe, Mr Cameron?' he asked, in a friendly tone.

'Not as long as we're on this expedition. After that, who knows?'

'After that, something even better may come along, right? Life imprisonment or a Chinese dungeon or death by torture, for instance, if our venture fails. Or would you rather be buried in your own country's soil? In that case, it might be best if you turned back.'

I told him the truth: it didn't make a whit of difference to me, but I would rather die in the field or kill myself than fall into the hands of his countrymen.

'You don't have much feeling for artistry,' Hsiu said. 'Otherwise you wouldn't begrudge our torturers the chance to test their refined techniques on an exotic foreigner. Well, let's cross that bridge when we come to it.'

He drained his glass and crept into his cabin, closing the door as far as his girth permitted, making sure I couldn't see inside.

Out on deck, alone, I spent a long time contemplating the pleasures of opium. I'd never taken it again. I finally concluded it was better to wait and not start until I was certain I'd never have to stop.

Chapter 6

The next evening before sunset, as Hsiu had predicted with such accuracy, I saw Minyang lying close to the riverbank, at the foot of a steep, massive hill that shouldered the river aside. The city presented the usual view of roofs, crags and woods with pagodas of many colours scattered pell-mell. But near the bank lay a couple of especially big ships with tall, sharp, red-painted prows the likes of which I'd never seen, and on the slopes above the city were numerous forts, their rounded walls half-buried in the soil of the hills.

Minyang appeared to be heavily defended. When I pointed out the forts to Hsiu, he told me that a few years earlier the city had been besieged by the Black Flags, a gang of bandits who normally plied the river in small black junks, pillaging vessels by night when too many of the crew were sleeping. After a lean period, they had decided to try their luck on land. 'Just like you,' he said, with a friendly slap on the shoulder. 'But they were unsuccessful. Minyang withstood the siege. A couple of cruisers chased them down the river and captured most of them.'

I asked him to tell me more about Minyang and said the location seemed favourable enough.

'Couldn't be worse,' he said. 'It borders on three provinces and gets tangled up in every war and border dispute, and not one of the three governors will ever lift a finger to help it, because everyone knows perfectly well that Minyang is always the first place to be captured and the first to be surrendered.'

At the bend in the river before we reached the city, the men slowly rowed the junk straight across the water. Once we rounded the sharp curve, the current was much weaker. The sun had come down so far that the city was bathed in its last, horizontal, fading light. And now I could see that the big ships down there in the floodplain were long, low temples, their roofs extending beyond the outer walls so sharply that I'd mistaken them for ships' prows. The domed forts did not reflect any light; they were great tombs crowded together, not glaring out at some distant enemy, but waiting patiently for the city's inhabitants, looming over them all their lives.

The city itself, between the tombs and the temples, seemed gloomy, downcast and deserted. The only activity was on the low riverbank around the temples and on or alongside the clustered ships at anchor. But it was silent and vacant compared to the waterside in Taihai. All we could hear were shrieks of prayer from one of the temples under the low, heavy roofs, accompanied by droning volleys from gongs and flutes. I saw shimmers and shadows come and go, rise and fall, and sometimes a garishly painted mask emerged, grinning, from the dark multitude. One adjacent temple was also lit, by a lamp in front of a dark stone sculpture embellished with glittering metal, before which a bald-headed priest was kneeling in a golden yellow robe. Serenity paying homage to serenity. But then a shadow fell, and I saw nothing but a deformed monster; my eyes fled back to the other temple, where the many people distracted my attention. And between the two, the crowd thronged together, thicker than ever. Although I couldn't see it, I knew that there in the jostling mass, a man was being put to death. His horror of the multitude closing in on him must have outweighed his fear of death, which drew closer like a small cloud over the current and would surely collide with the junk as it slowly neared the bank. I instinctively ducked behind the mast.

But the cool, sharp sword must have delivered quick relief. I thought I saw a ripple in the water, and then it was all over. I looked back at the riverbank. The people from the first temple and the place of execution were ascending in thin columns to the city above, and the bank was left empty and full of shadows. Then the junk slid up against the outer edge of the mass of ships and was tied to the others. A few minutes later it was flanked in turn by a ship arriving on the open side, and its assimilation into the mass was complete. Tomorrow the whole mess would have to be untangled, with endless cursing and scraping and trouble. But until then, peace and quiet would prevail. Hsiu now seemed to feel completely secure and at ease. He was wearing a grey cotton robe, an over-jacket of smooth taut silk and a close-fitting cap and looked every inch an ordinary travelling salesman. He slid his arms into the wide sleeves, the way nuns do, and smirked, which led me to conclude that he must have reached some kind of provisional goal. He wanted to go on land with me after one last whisky, but in his eagerness, it went down the wrong way, and he could hardly stop coughing as the two of us jumped and stumbled from one vessel to the next on our way to the riverside. Once we were on solid ground, he seemed even less comfortable, but he headed straight for the temple to his left and paused in its shadow. The moon had risen and was lighting up the interior, which was open on all sides and surrounded by columns. No lights were burning in there. No trace of the priest with a flickering lamp in front of his idol. Then Hsiu asked me, 'Don't you hear anything, from up there?'

And yes, it was as if I heard a confused sound, something like music but also like the grinding of circular saws.

'Yes, I think I hear a barrel organ.'

He pulled me after him, leaving the temple behind, and running his hand over the steep embankment that led to the city, found a stairway, half-embedded in the earth. We climbed the stairs as fast as we could, now and then bumping into a late water-carrier, whose water would slosh out of the metal jug and onto the stones. At the top, we arrived in a square, long and narrow with a gentle upward slope. There was the crowd that had filled the low riverbank, now heaped together. Hsiu, who despite his paunch was much quicker than I was, cleared a path through the crowd, shouting as he went. Against the rear of a building, in the light of six or seven torches stuck in the wall about ten feet up, was the shabbiest fair I'd ever seen. The organ-grinder was cranking, stalls lit by burning wood chips were selling refreshments, and a kind of horror story – twenty scenes painted on a board – was being explained. In a tent, you could see a giant spider with a child's head, and in front of the entrance, a monkey and a bear were forced to run in circles on short chains. That was everything.

Hsiu and I stopped to gaze at it all and adjust to the half-darkness. The bear-leader approached as if he recognised us. But after Hsiu waved him away, he waited until a small circle had formed around him and tugged on the chains. The bear kneeled; the monkey climbed onto his head and danced; they tumbled over each other a couple of times; and then the monkey was set loose with a copper bowl in his hand to make the rounds. Now the man passed Hsiu, pausing for a moment as if he expected a tip. Hsiu pretended to search his robe for a coin, meanwhile whispering, 'Board with the others here. Have tomorrow night's shipment sent on to Nanku Point.'

The bear leader nodded and moved on. Hsiu and I watched the bear a little longer as it went on dancing to the rhythm of a barrel organ played by a tall, thin man. Though his silvery-grey caftan was torn and sagging, he had a kind of dignity, even as he cranked. He did not once turn his head our way, but kept it as close as possible to the organ case, in the shadows. Was he ashamed?

The old street tunes disgorged by the organ cut through my flesh and bone. They were English, French and Chinese, all mixed together. It seemed that along with the turning barrel everything wheeled around me: Europe, Asia, past, future, humanity, beastliness, tenderness, the raw urge for destruction. We walked on. Then the man raised his head from the side of the organ and exchanged a knowing look with Hsiu. Did my employer know everyone, everywhere? Or had he organised this fair as a gruesome joke, for no reason, or with some intention I couldn't fathom? We drank a few cups of warm wine at a stall. 'I thought your countrymen loved a good fair,' Hsiu said. 'Yet even now, you're as glum as ever. I understand why you were miserable on that slow junk, but why here?'

I didn't respond to his ridicule, but for an instant I was almost homesick at the thought of an Irish fair: lights everywhere, noise, fumes, dancing and fighting, and the next morning's mass, full of light, fumes, music and prayer. But I'd never joined in.

Now we reached the tale of murder. The woman, swinging her cane, towered on a stool beside it, sometimes drowning out the organ with her husky voice. They were scenes from the mid-nineteenth century, battles with soldiers and generals in colourful uniforms and a boxy train about to run over a woman tied to the tracks. The next picture showed the two bleeding halves on either side as the train dwindled into the distance under a plume of smoke. In the next scene the true culprit, one of the generals, was locked in a big cage.

The woman was a gifted storyteller and had drawn a larger crowd than all the other attractions put together. The European element of her narrative seemed to appeal to her xenophobic audience. I could see her only from the waist up, but she looked large and statuesque, and her face, which I caught only in profile at first, was more beautiful than any I'd seen in a long while. It was a perfect oval. Her chin was round and firm, her nose not flat with open nostrils but slightly curved, her eyes like almonds in shape. She never looked in my direction but seemed to focus on something in the distance as her mouth bellowed. I saw her that way for a few seconds perhaps, in sheer delight. Then she turned her head from the board to point out to the audience just how horrible something was, gesturing with cupped hands as if to gather in their pity, and I saw the true horror: on the cheek under her left eye was a rough red bulge crusted with pus. While the sight suited the carnival atmosphere, it didn't suit her as I'd imagined her a moment earlier. It was somehow both vile and sad, and I was torn between revulsion and pity. Maybe it was a good thing she was hideous; otherwise she would never have been left alone for long on her travels in the Chinese interior.

She went on, slamming her rod into the sad, blood-soaked scenes, started collecting money with her other hand, and kicked the board with one foot as a warning to the onlookers. I couldn't take my eyes off her.

Then a hand tugged at my wrist, and Hsiu pulled me out of the throng. Once we were outside the circle of listeners, he hissed, 'Are you out of your mind? You were staring at her like a fool for five minutes straight. We're attracting all kinds of attention, and there are spies everywhere. Are you trying to spoil the whole thing before it begins? You'll have plenty of time to gawk at her, months and months.'

So she was coming with us, and the entire fair had been set up to bring together the members of the expedition, in disguise, in a prearranged spot. Hsiu certainly took precautions.

We went down an alley leading away from the square. I longed to crush him against one of the sharp corners of the buildings, so hard that his putrid body would be cut in half. I felt like pushing him into a cellar. But maybe I wouldn't have to. I had a strong feeling that Hsiu was more a figment of my imagination than anything else and would vanish like a ghost once I was ready to take him on. He was not the middleman between the Chinese interior and me, the washed-up castaway; he was the cloud that kept me from seeing the country as it really was. His shadow made it look freakish and terrifying, when in fact it might be a good place: comforting, vast and easeful.

But I didn't dare to liberate myself; instead, I clung ever tighter to him, following him meekly and wordlessly. From one moment to the next, his jeers and rebukes had stopped, as if he were afraid I might not put up with them much longer. On the riverbank, he pointed the way back to the junk. Then he slipped off, swallowed up in the crowd.

I stumbled back over the vessels, where smoking night lanterns lit up family scenes that even the Chinese, who don't have much sense of privacy, would normally keep out of their neighbour's sight. I tripped over a hook, nearly fell in the water – was it those few glasses of wine that had thrown me off balance, or the experience of being on solid ground again? – and finally reached our junk. I noticed that I had to step down from the deck of the neighbouring craft; when going ashore, I had also stepped down. The junk lay at least a metre deeper. So while we were on land, it had been loaded, probably from the next vessel, since the river was already blanketed in silence. The charcoal stove in the aft deckhouse was still smouldering, and I managed to reheat a pot of cold tea to an adequate degree of warmth.

Sounds of staggering over the boats warned me someone was approaching. They were probably arriving one by one; Hsiu was sure to stay out all night. This must be the bear leader. It would be strange for him without his animals on the junk, which would soon fill up with the members of the expedition. He was naturally drawn to the glow of the stove, the only sign of life on board. I downed a last large gulp of tea and slid the bowl towards him as he entered. Without a second thought, he took it and drank, and we had our first close look at each other.

I wanted to spare him the embarrassment of recognition; he had changed enough for that. Since our previous encounter, he must have sunk fast to end up at my level. My pretended ignorance would have been plausible enough; the room was dark, and even if it hadn't been, I could have insisted I didn't know him. There was no need for me to ask him any other questions either. There was nothing else I wished to know about that whole business in Taihai, and I felt sure he knew as little about our present mission as I did. But he didn't seem embarrassed and calmly shook my hand. 'When was the last time we met?'

'On the landing stage one early morning before the siege, after a night at Hsiu's, my first and last.'

'Oh, yes. Well, you must want to know what happened. It wasn't long afterwards. Despite having been warned, I turned up one more time unfit for duty, not because I'd been smoking but because I'd been abstaining. It was too dangerous to smoke on board, and early in the siege we were stuck on the ship for three weeks. I held out for eight days and then collapsed. The doctor tried laudanum to keep me on my feet, but that didn't work for long. One morning during a drill I fainted onto a gun as I was aiming it, I was reported, and at the end of the siege, after ten days of confinement to my cabin, the worst days of my life, I left the navy, along with seven other men. Hsiu fought for me for quite a while, and now he's got me, every fibre of me. He's promised me my daily ration of pipes – not many, but enough – for the rest of this expedition and afterwards, as long as I go on serving him, and I suppose I shall. Until we arrive, he doesn't have much use for me. All I have to do is keep up with the group. I guess he had less trouble getting to you? Though to look at you now, I'd say you're in better shape than you were.'

'I could hardly be in worse.'

'True,' he conceded. 'But these past months can't have been easy for you. When did you sell yourself to Hsiu?'

'Three months ago, soon after the end of the siege.'

'And while you were waiting, did he put you up in a good hotel?'

'No, in a windy mountain cave on a vegetarian diet.'

'That's just like him. He made me roam about with those animals for three months. But quiet, there she comes, the princess!'

I looked outside: it was raining, and I saw a figure climbing over the vessels in a cloak of woven straw so broad it extended far beyond her shoulders. I waited in suspense to see her at close quarters. She joined us, cast off her straw cover and stood there in ordinary Chinese clothing: a jacket and trousers. The bulge on her cheek was bright red like a carbuncle. Seeing her face up closer, I could find no other flaws. On the contrary, now it was no longer twisted into a constant shout, it had perfect, even noble features. Sylvain greeted her with a curt grunt. I couldn't work out whether they had travelled together or met for the first time at the fair.

'Is there any more hot water?'

I pointed to the pot on the stove and was about to rinse out the bowl for her, but she stopped me, produced a bundle of herbs from some inner pocket, tossed it into the bowl and drank. Then, with confidence, as if already at home on the junk, she went to the middle cabin, opened the door and disappeared inside.

'Who is she?'

Sylvain shrugged.

'Damned if I know! The first time I set eyes on her was a few days ago. She showed me a letter from Hsiu that said her name was Fong Shen and we were to travel together to Minyang, and even better, that she had some opium with her.

I was in a bad way. It's as if that devil Hsiu keeps trying to drive me to the brink of despair, giving me as little as he can. He's always dangling a carrot in front of me but hardly ever lets me have it. Oh, if I had the guts ... Do you still smoke?'

'Not any more. I'm waiting until this is over, so I don't have to limit myself and can just keep going.'

'Good idea, but not everyone can get by without it. I used to be held back by my sense of dignity as a French officer, but now that I've overcome that foolish prejudice, I'm on rations, and maybe I always will be from now on. When I have it, I put off smoking it, and when I don't have it, I crave it.'

He stared into the glow of the fire.

'Why wouldn't she have that ugly blemish removed in Taihai? It wouldn't cost more than ten dollars there – and even less here.'

'I don't know. Maybe it's too risky. Maybe it's easier for her this way – less unwanted attention from enterprising men. Now will you stop bringing up that woman?'

That woman? Had we spoken of her before?

But with a sweep of his arm that seemed to say the subject was exhausted for all eternity, on earth and in the hereafter, he turned to the door and asked me where he was supposed to sleep. I brought him to the room where I'd taken the uppermost of the three berths. He settled for the lowest, which was also the dampest, but at least he could roll straight into it, since it was practically at floor level, and that was a considerable advantage for him. Who would claim the empty berth between us? The old man we'd seen playing the barrel organ? I wanted to stay awake, but sleep took hold. The last thought in my mind was that I'd been reunited with an old friend. That had never happened in all my years at sea. Still, it hardly seemed to matter. Sylvain and his opium were inseparable; there was no place in his heart for any human connection.

Chapter 7

When I woke up the next morning, I realised that the junk was already moving. In the middle berth I saw, not the elderly organ-grinder, but a man's back and a head of tousled black hair. He couldn't be very old. Was this Hsiu's guest from the past nights, now traded in for the beauty from the fair, or had Hsiu been his guest on land? Sylvain was still sleeping. The junk was already midstream and the crew were rowing her slowly upriver; sometimes they were able to use the broad sail. Hsiu was in the best of moods now, especially when we sailed past a tall rock and a few more packages were lowered onto the deck. Now his ship was fully loaded.

The woman and the old man, if he was with us, stayed out of sight. The man in the middle berth rolled out of it when the sun was high in the sky and burst into uproarious laughter at the sight of us. Sylvain made a stiff military bow and left the cabin at once, and I went with him. A while later the new arrival, dressed in a white suit covered with large stains and a wide-open shirt, came after me on deck, said his name these days was Godunov, and asked who I and the retired officer were. I mumbled something like, 'Been sailing a long time, thought I'd try my luck on land.'

'A long time? Not as long as I walked, I bet: from Chengtu to Ichang.'

So he knew things about the area where we were headed. I blurted out, 'What's the landscape like there?'

'Not very different from here. Away from the coast, everything is the same. I wanted to ask you what it's like at sea. I've never seen it.'

He'd never seen the sea! I stared at him as if he were the most wondrous creature I'd ever met and was about to describe to him what the sea is like, but he stopped me and burst into laughter again, his large teeth showing, his shoulders heaving, and the whole of his strong, lean figure shaking.

'Save your breath, I know what water is. I've crossed Lake Baikal. In the middle of it, you can't see any shoreline, there are big storms, and plenty of ships are wrecked. It must be more or less the same.'

Sooner than we'd expected, our river views came to an end. A few hours later, the placid waterway was starting to look like a sea. First the air turned brown and dirty and the water started flowing faster. The junk couldn't go any further upstream and was pushed back. Hsiu had the crew moor her on the riverside, behind a large rock thrusting out of the water, like the one from which the packages had been lowered. All around us, we saw ships drifting downstream or, if they could, making a dash for the riverbank. All the sails had been taken in; the water was empty and ominous.

No storm came, but the water rose to tremendous heights; one great swell after another surged past. The rock towered over us at first; the next day, we were level with it, and another day later, we stuck out above it, waiting anxiously to see whether it would go all the way under, leaving us to be swept up by the current and dragged all the way back to Minyang, or still further. But the flood stopped in time. The water was no longer turbulent now the wind had veered to the west, and for the first time on our trip, the crew could hoist the sail and make headway without the oars. The flood waters had run into a narrow stretch further downstream, around Minyang, and were backed up there, blocking the current for a while. We had to seize this opportunity to move ahead. I was frustrated that our progress was so slow and that the crew manoeuvred so awkwardly. But why? I didn't know where we were headed; if I had, I wouldn't have been in such a hurry. Then my thoughts went back to Minyang, which I'd seen only by night, and which was now menaced by the river again. Minyang, place of calamities, was never left in peace. The temples, which had looked so much like ships on the low riverbank, must now be underwater, the waves climbing slowly, step by step, up the stone stairways.

The river grew broader and broader. The banks receded, but far in the distance there were still green fields, and here and there a farm with a thatched roof and mud walls, already soaked through. Closer to us was a line of willows and a wood of mulberry trees, both old and almost leafless, hazy as the ghosts of trees. Then all this was wiped away, not by a mist that had crept up unnoticed – the horizon was as clear and sharp as ever – but by the rising waters. The landscape was engulfed; the river burst its banks, becoming a wide, whirling mass of water and then a still lake.

The junk headed straight across it, using the oars on the bow side. Scraping over a dike a few times, it glided ahead over the still water, and just below the surface I could now see thatched roofs, which before the flood had dotted the land by the riverbanks. Further along, they resurfaced like the backs of large, lean oxen, with knobbly backbones and steep flanks; in the night, we moored alongside one of them. By daylight, we sailed on, surrounded by countless little islands, some of which disappeared or surfaced as the waters rose or fell.

Houses stood huddled together on some of those islands, as if they had fled to the top of a mound for safety. One was covered only with fallen boards and lumps of mud wall. Either there had been a fire, or the inhabitants had pulled down their own house and fled. This was a suitable spot for us – that is, for Hsiu to carry out his plans. The junk was moored to the house's foundations with four long ropes. There we could wait out the rising and falling of the flood, which had barely begun. If anything happened to the junk, then we could take refuge on the island. Then it was time to bring out the supplies. A hatch was opened amidships, between Hsiu's quarters and the other cabins, and a small two-inch cannon and a machine gun were hoisted up and mounted on the stern and bow. Then crates were brought up from the hold and their contents – millet, rice, beans and peas – divided into small packages. The river kept rising, transforming the large plain into an empire of islands that Japan might envy. Only the temples and monasteries were still fairly far above water. We sailed past them. Either they had stockpiled food of their own, or else the monks traded with the locals, as Hsiu had begun to do. We also avoided a few large, very remote villages; the population there was large and utterly famished and we didn't have enough ammunition to keep them away from our food. The surviving third or quarter of the farmers would have overpowered us. Isolated farms and the smallest hamlets made the best customers for us. We would come to a halt there – no need to lay anchor; once the junk ran into the branches of a bamboo or thuja grove, it stopped on its own.

Sometimes Hsiu raised a flag that announced in blood-red characters, *Rice for sale*. But that wasn't usually necessary; as soon as we lay still, small boats and rafts would row towards us from all sides. Then Hsiu would give a handful of rice or millet to the first to reach the junk. He would refuse even to bargain with the vessels that followed, closing the portholes and hatches and ordering them all to keep their distance. Their threats and insults would gradually turn into pleas, and eventually they would produce their last few coins from rags between their clothing and their skin. Sometimes they offered us art objects, but Hsiu tended to turn those down. He would accept only the ones that appealed to him personally, adding them to the collection in his suite. I saw him refuse the most exquisite jades – pendant earrings, flutes, perfume bottles – and even ancient treasures, simply because he already owned one or more similar pieces. A number of peasants must have starved to death for that reason. But people have died of less significant causes. In truth, we were all opposed to this kind of trade: Fong Shen thought it was tedious; Godunov despised it because it was non-violent and not dangerous enough; the old man, All-But-One, felt that any form of work was beneath his dignity; and I was ashamed to see the starving people surrender their money and valuables, the last barriers between them and starvation, into Hsiu's greedy hands. He fed on that flood of desperation like a giant fungus on a waterlogged, inundated field. We could express our disapproval to each other only by gestures and the looks on our faces. It wasn't until much later that we worked out a kind of lingua franca of Chinese, English and a few Mongolian words. Not knowing, back then, that we would be together for a long time to come, we didn't make much effort to understand one another. Even Fong Shen and All-But-One had no common language. She came from Hunan, he from Shantung; she, a woman of the people, did not speak Mandarin, and he didn't speak her dialect.

Maybe it was the impossibility of communicating with each other in those early days that made us, in spite of our disgust, meekly follow Hsiu's instructions. He had armed us with staffs that had sharp points and edges. When the peasants became too insistent, we pushed them away. It was dangerous work. Sometimes dense crowds surrounded the stationary junk and the people who were pushed away, wounded and roaring with anger and pain, urged the others to seize our supplies, which were there for the taking, by force. But it never came to that. They were timid, slavish creatures, accustomed to extortion and oppression. When the mood turned threatening, Hsiu and Fong Shen would open their outer robes to reveal the sickle and arrows embroidered in red on their black garments. As soon as the peasants saw the emblems of the most dreaded robbers' guild, they would give up the fight. The foolhardy peasants who had climbed onto the ship would jump overboard, never to be fished out of the water. And this only happened a few times in any case. Our affiliation with that secret society soon became common knowledge in the area, and the starving peasants threw themselves on our mercy. Women held their children high for us to see, their upper bodies bare, the hollows between their ribs so deep that their chests looked like cages in which only the hearts were still alive, fluttering without will, just as their eyes were the only living parts of their fleshless faces. Their mouths had slumped into loose, half-open grins.

For a long time, I could not eat. Everything I put in my mouth turned into a reproach that I was feeding myself even though I had no love of life as long as the people out there, stripped of every possession but life, were losing that too for lack of nourishment. At first I saved some of my own food and gave it away, but Hsiu noticed and forbade me to do it; it was bad for business. By then I was past pity anyway, and no longer feeling generous, because our rations were kept very scanty. Only Hsiu ate course after course; but since I was in disgrace, I never joined him, while the others were invited to his quarters one by one. It made no difference to me, and I eventually became blind to the starving people, however close they came, in rows on the benches of their boats, holding out their hands to us with despairing grimaces, as if rejected by the underworld and doomed to an eternity on earth, begging the living for pity and food. But this was unreal and untrue; there was nothing but the great grey water. What did it matter that birds landed there and took off again, fish sometimes leapt into the air, people fell out of boats or washed out of houses and floated away, sinking into the silt somewhere or getting tangled in the trees? Generations came and went; the people remained, multiplying in times of plenty, shrinking in times of want. Whether the plain was brown and arid or muddy and swamped, overcropped or neglected, it always endured. Sometimes the river changed its course, bursting its banks. A few months later, it had carved itself a new bed and laid waste to a region.

The only thing I had left was a desire, which sometimes arose irresistibly, to buy one of the little girls held out to us in the raised arms of parents who had no more money to offer. But what would I do with her? Wasn't my own fate miserable enough? But to those people, it must have seemed enviable; after all, I had food and would someday leave the famine-struck area. Sometimes I couldn't resist taking one of the wrinkled brown creatures in my arms for a moment; then I would return her and give her parents alms. Their faces would crease with disappointment, if they were still capable of expression.

Hsiu rarely showed himself. When he came on deck, he would sit in a heavy chair, his flabby figure wrapped in a loose robe, and even then he would act as if nothing was any of his concern. And yet it was he who arranged everything, down to the slightest details: the route, the prices, the quantities for sale. One day he was suddenly full of life, carrying on a long, excited conversation with the skipper as he scanned the horizon line with his binoculars. Then he handed them to me and asked me to tell him what I saw. In the distance, the water ran, carrying branches and leaves along with it, and for the first time in a long while I saw something other than roofs: here and there, the top of a windowpane was already surfacing. I told Hsiu what I had seen. He called out to the skipper. The dinghy was hoisted in, and straight away, the crew tried to set us in motion. But we'd been at rest there for many days, and she'd sunk into the mire. When at last we freed ourselves, it was dead calm. The east wind had gone elsewhere. The large reed sail didn't help; they fetched the big oars, but none of those were very strong, so even All-But-One and Hsiu had to help out, which they did, with a great show of contempt. Eventually, the skipper's strength and Hsiu's weight prevailed. But the original riverbed, which we were trying to reach, was still far away, and by the time darkness fell the junk was grounded again.

Now the water began to move. Branches, roofs, objects from houses, all sorts of things floated past us, singly or in dark clumps underwater. Sometimes a hand, foot or twig broke the surface. But as the moon rose there came a stasis so complete that the water no longer rippled. Then it flowed back in the other direction a little. Hsiu became hopeful again, puffed thick clouds of smoke out of his pipe and had wine served to us for the first time since Minyang. The water stilled again, the dirt settled and then we saw the reflection of the moon, dull at first, but shining brighter as time went on, appearing to us at a depth the water did not have. Then the night sky also grew clear, the stars took their places, and the earth was reduced to a level surface in which nothing could be discerned but lighter and darker strips and shades of grey.

We stayed out on deck until late, and for the first time since we'd been together we enjoyed each other's company. Hsiu recited a poem:

> *The world is hidden under water*
> *The ripe moon sees its own countenance*
> *The wheel of existence has turned onwards ...*

He repeated it several times with scarcely detectable variations; only the moon kept its place in the rhythm of the verse. Then Fong Shen sang a sad, droning tune. All-But-One told a story in which spirits of people and flowers kept taking on new guises, falling into each other's arms and fleeing again. Sylvain sat still and silent, and Godunov now and then let out his booming laugh.

All of a sudden flocks of birds came out; some landed on treetops rising from the water. Others went on circling high in the sky. They were vultures, and an hour later the wind rose and the water started to flow again. When the birds had arrived, everyone had started preparing for departure. Hsiu ordered one hatch opened, a couple of heavy crates were brought up from below and, with our combined strength, we shifted them out onto the roof of the deserted farmhouse next to us. Then we heaved our last bags of rice overboard – their market value had dropped anyway as the water had risen – and at last our vessel was fully afloat. The current had grown stronger, drawing the water back to the old riverbed, and the junk was carried along. There was no need for the oars; a couple of crewmen kept watch with fishing spears to push away dangerous driftwood, and the skipper and a few other men leaned on the steering oar. Once we had almost reached the old riverbanks, we heard grinding and creaking underneath the vessel; large branches whipped upward, making the water splash and fly all around us. Again the junk came to a standstill; this time she was immovable.

Morning came, grey and wan. It seemed that the water was no longer flowing back towards the river, but hanging over the plain in a mist. The branches of the driftwood kept reaching further and higher over the deck; caught in a tangle of trees and a bed of silt, we could forget about breaking free. I was curious how Hsiu would get himself out of this; I imagined he would take off in the shore boat with his profits, leaving us to our fate. After all, we could find our own way back to dry land. Godunov and All-But-One seemed to have the same suspicions; one of them was always on deck and close to Hsiu. He made no attempt to get away, and we later realised he had no intention of leaving. He acted just as if there were no trees and branches sticking up out of the water all around us, as if the junk were not sinking ever further into a watery jungle; he sauntered to and fro, spoke casually and smoked his pipe. I couldn't resist discussing his inexplicable serenity with the others, and that meant Godunov, because All-But-One and Fong Shen were just as indifferent as Hsiu to our plight.

'Why hasn't Hsiu abandoned us here and gone on to Lanchow?'

As usual, it took a while before Godunov replied. He first had to recover his breath after one of his convulsive fits of laughter. Then finally he answered, 'Don't you know that for Hsiu the main event has just begun? Did you think he left his office in Taihai to sell rice? That was another masquerade, like the fair in Minyang.'

'So what does he have planned?'

'Now he intends to take the guns and ammunition to Chungking. The first and second acts are over now; the third and most important act is beginning.'

'But how will we fetch those crates from the farmhouse?'

Laughter seized him again. 'Did you think Hsiu would mount an entire expedition for the sake of two crates of guns? Those were ballast, that's all. The bulk of the shipment is making its way along the river embankments. We have to wait for it here.'

Then I asked him if he was going to Chungking too.

'Who else could teach the civilised slant-eyes how to use their weapons?'

'Well, Sylvain, for instance.'

'Sylvain? Sylvain is always sleeping, and when he wakes up, it's just so that he can go back to sleep, deeper than ever. Not that it matters. As soon as we make our getaway, the weapons will be ruined again anyway.'

'Who else is going?'

'Not Hsiu. He has other business to attend to, and he'll be

careful not to get too close to Chungking. Otherwise he'd wind up a hostage.'

'Then which of the two of us will lead the operation?'

A new fit of laughter began, but this time astonishment won out, and then derision.

'Which of the two of us? Hsiu needs you here. With your experience as a sailor, he'll want you to keep an eye on the grounded junk and get her out of the river safely next time it floods – a few years from now, no doubt.'

The prospect of spending years here on this flooded plain while the others went ever deeper into the interior was so distressing that I didn't stop to ask myself whether Godunov's story was plausible. Besides, I felt there was no other way for me to preserve my dignity – so I attacked him. He was much shorter, but tougher and more muscular than I was. He grabbed me with his long gorilla arms and squeezed the breath out of me, and in my confusion I did something desperate, forcing him to the edge of the deck with the last of my strength and almost sending us both tumbling overboard. But at the final instant, he let go of me, overcome by yet another fit of laughter. At first I thought it was a response to my fighting technique, but he pointed behind me and muttered, 'His name means "Son of the Turtle", but he should be called "Son of the Jellyfish".' I turned around and saw Hsiu standing in the moonlight. He had crept up on us as we stumbled around the deck, dressed only in wide-legged trousers with one leg rolled up. His flabby upper body quivered like shark's-fin or bird's-nest soup with every movement he made. He was furious and told us we both could have drowned. He must have felt we had some value after all, although probably of a very transient nature; in six months, he might wish us all the torments of the underworld, and do his best to dispatch us there.

When he heard what we were fighting about, his astonishment knew no bounds. I don't know whether it was sincere or feigned.

'So the barbarians think they will command my operations? If I decide to leave you, All-But-One will carry out my will, and if he dies, I would rather appoint Fong Shen to replace him, even if she is a woman, than either you or Sylvain.'

Godunov exploded again. 'How I'd love to bow down before the princess with the carbuncle on her face!'

Hsiu did not deign to reply, crept back into his quarters, and the two of us had nothing else to say to each other. We were equals again: the hirelings of a Chinaman we both despised, each just as deeply humiliated in the other's presence.

It was hard for us to keep out of each other's way. I stared inland and Godunov took the river side. The water level kept dropping, now exposing the rotting leaves of the bushes, tangled with algae and hung with dead fish and birds, all looking equally desolate. Then came the long-anticipated moment when the top of the embankment emerged above the water. Even the boat could no longer go anywhere; there may have been a foot of water left. The lightest of our party, All-But-One, was sent off on a light raft. He had just reached the dike when the waterlogged structure fell to pieces. He pulled himself up the slope, his long robe clinging to his body, and, probing out ahead of him with his cane, headed towards Lanchow. His silhouette was like a withered branch against the soot-grey sky, unbroken by any house or hilltop. No ship sailed along any visible horizon, and suddenly he had disappeared as if into dead endlessness. None of us thought we would ever see him again.

***

But he returned, though not alone. On the afternoon of the third day after his departure, far beyond the dike, which now rose half a yard above the water, a long line of porters made their way toward us, preceded by what looked like a shuffling row of grey and brown hillocks.

The camels' arrival in this waterlogged landscape, perhaps from the stony deserts of Central Asia, made me sad. I greeted them as exiles from the other side, and for the first time I sensed for a moment what I sought, which—though my doubt outweighed my faith—surely had to exist, somewhere far away, but not beyond reach. Later, too, once the heavy crates were resting against their ungainly flanks on both sides of the humps, I held onto that sense and that memory. Running my fingers over their hide, or walking alongside them for a while, in the same slow plod, was enough to bring it back.

All-But-One, the porters and the drivers remained on the dike. Six of the camels, the foremost bearing a Mongol herdsman, cautiously descended the slope and lumbered towards us, their sluggish legs sinking into the boggy soil with every step. One of them could not free itself. Its mournful face stayed above water for a long time, writhing back and forth on its curved neck and staring at us accusingly, like a great dying swan.

The others completed the difficult crossing to the side of the junk and were loaded, like lighter barges, with crates and sacks holding everything Hsiu wanted to salvage. On their final trip, they carried us to the dike. We arrived safely to find All-But-One and, some distance away, a group of coolies resting in the mud. They took some of the sacks and led the way. Then the camel drivers went to work, and the convoy set off, at a lethargic pace, towards Lanzhou. We remained in sight of the walls of Lanzhou for seven days, probably waiting for part of the company to join us, but they never did, and finally Hsiu gave orders to move on.

Chapter 8

Hsiu, Godunov and All-But-One usually headed the caravan, with Fong Shen not far behind, and Sylvain and I lagged to the rear as the day went on.

We passed through rice paddies at first, and later through fields where cogon grass rose metres high. Then without warning the steppe lay ahead, rough country and seemingly deserted – the locals dwelt in caves and hollows in the side walls of the many shallow ravines. Looking down the steep slopes from the path, we sometimes caught a glimpse inside, where they swarmed like bees on a honeycomb. Viewed from a distance, that landscape was nothing but a wide, wrinkled expanse of yellow. I did not look back once; I tried not to think of the past any longer, still afraid that the spectre of that past would catch up with me here, but that fear diminished by the day. I was escaping – for good, I thought. Still, I didn't expect to find a different future beyond the horizon; instead, it was as if we were on our way back, leaving the near past behind and riding out to meet the other, greater past of the country, open only to the sea, closed and hardened in the middle, between the salt lakes, the mountain ranges, and the stony deserts. This mesmerising monotony remained unchanged for the rest of the journey, even though the obstacles we encountered and the incidents we stumbled into were hard and complicated enough. The journey itself resembled the shifting of a glacier, invisible and inevitable. The disasters rolled across it like loose boulders, leaving deep tracks and wreckage behind them, but without ever slowing the shifting mass.

At first each day was like the last, grey and dusty and soundless. Not a cart drove through the landscape, not a farmer worked the dry fields, not a cloud crossed the sky. Crumbling old gravestones sometimes bore witness to past life, with half-eroded characters and dry, greyish-white bones scattered around them. The rivers and lakes were unrippled by currents or vessels; the reed marshes were sometimes home to roving bands of reed-cutters and weavers, driven to that miserable occupation by the flood.

As far as I was concerned, the journey could have lasted the rest of my life. I had never known so much peace, so much space. I stayed in the rear, not hurrying the camels or their drivers, but making sure they kept a steady pace. The others were usually towards the front of the caravan, but their murmurs about the dry climate, our slow progress, and the uncertain reward that awaited us reached my ears all the same. They kept trying to draw me into their griping, but I kept my distance, as did Sylvain. Fong Shen usually shared a camel with Hsiu, and we only ever saw and heard them some evenings by the tents.

So I had found what I'd sought: a trek over land that seemed certain never to end, so slow was our progress, so numerous the possible detours, digressions, delays and setbacks. Even so, I tried to persuade All-But-One to tell me how much further we had to go and where we were headed, and in truth I was relieved when he answered my questions and my pointing into the distance with the words, 'Not nearly there. In three months, if winter doesn't come early, and otherwise next year.'

If we spent the winter in that wasteland, we were likely to die, but that didn't seem to trouble him.

I picked up some of the language from him along the way. It seemed an impossible task at first, because he spoke no English, but when people spend a long time together in isolation, I believe they become infected with each other's languages – or rather, the oldest, toughest, strongest language forces its way into the brain of the one who belongs to the newer race, a process that cannot be traced step by step. The infection lies dormant until one day it breaks out. And the moment came when I noticed that All-But-One and I were simply talking.

After a while, he began to tell me about his life, and because I could easily imagine and relive it, my knowledge of the language continued to grow. Even though the whole story was set in an unfamiliar region and country, even though the sorrow of a man belonging to a mongrel race was wholly alien to him, even though he had never laid eyes on the sea, I saw a similarity between our lives. While the course of his destiny had sometimes brought him close to success and perfect happiness, while mine had kept me on the brink of utter doom, in fact our situations had led to the same outcome: we were strangers wherever we went, cast out of every sphere of life and thrown back on our own shabby selves. That was how both of us had become tangled up in smuggling, which we both despised, and why the desert and its perfect desolation, which would have seemed like an airless void to anybody else, brought us such peace. Sometimes I entertained the thought that in our next lives, All-But-One and I (who might just as well be called 'Hardly-At-All'), could form a symbiosis, a complete being, but then with a shock I would realise I was wishing for what I'd once fled, half-crazed with fear: I once again ran the risk that someone else would take possession of my being. Then I'd take another look at All-But-One and feel reassured. I had nothing to fear from this final scion of four hundred lineages, for whom life had become a formula, not a magical formula but a solved one, a question answered once and for all with a platitude. And the clearer that fact became to me, the more the sight of him soothed me. So a person could go that far in life without dying of it. At the same time, I realised that to find the same peace that had been gathered in and baled for him by countless earlier generations, I would first have to go through desperate and agonising struggles.

But such peace did exist, and in a different form than that known by the ever-industrious, ever-toiling watchmaker, the man who not so long ago had seemed to me the height of earthly contentment.

In this way, without a word, without requiring any help from external conditions (dangers, in this case), I solved my relationship with All-But-One. He was an example and a beacon to me, nothing more. As for him, he seemed unaware of this evolution. He was grateful to me for little kindnesses: when I laid out his bedding, tied up his horse, or warmed a cup of wine for him after we stopped for the night. And when a few days passed without these little attentions, the expression on his face never changed, any more than it did on the days when my fear of spirit possession returned and I avoided him completely.

Meanwhile, Godunov and Fong Shen seemed to have found each other, without any objections from Hsiu. They were always together and almost always seemed to disagree. Sometimes he would lash her with the reins, but every evening — after a quick dinner with the rest of us, where they would pick out the choicest titbits for each other — they would withdraw into a black felt tent, block the entrance, and not show themselves until morning. One night I woke up and found the place next to mine empty. Sylvain was in a deep sleep, as usual, having smoked a few pipes one after another; Hsiu had gradually increased his ration. All-But-One was missing. It wasn't the first time he'd gone out at night, but I lay awake for a while and he didn't come back. So I, in turn, crept outside, looked around in the darkness and found him with his face pressed up to the felt tent. I tugged at his shoulder, and he impatiently pulled free and motioned for me to be still. In this quiet space, far from the anthills where humanity jostles and mates, exterminates and multiplies, that near-dead man was still possessed by the same thoughts as all the rest. A melancholy took hold of me that I could not shake off by gazing at the stars or strolling by the place where the camels slept, kneeling or leaning against one another, and the worst of it was that there were moments when I too yearned to join All-But-One in spying on what was happening in that cramped, sultry tent. Those moments passed, but my sense of space did not return. In its place was a longing at last to reach the big city where we were headed and lose myself in the crowd there. That was better than the clammy desire that had first taken hold of me, but I still felt degraded. I had thought that this spacious life would have been enough for me from now on, and instead I had fallen back into being human.

When All-But-One finally returned, I vented my anger on him, asking if the wisdom he claimed to possess had inspired his shameful spying. But he answered calmly, 'When you are as old as I am, you too will have to make do with little pleasures, you'll see. And if I were you, I would make an exception in this case and have a look inside. See how different she is when she's laid aside her baubles – not all but one, but every single one.'

Then I threatened to reveal what he'd done, and he cringed with fear.

'Don't do it, they'll drive me away. And what about you? You'll be left alone here. Who will help you with the language then? Who will tell you about the city where you hope to stay and where otherwise you'll never feel you've truly arrived?'

'So you're familiar with Chungking, All-But-One? Have you been there, have you lived there? Why didn't you ever tell me that before?'

'When you've lived as long as I have, there are parts of your life you'd rather keep hidden from everyone, and which you even forget yourself in the end. I held a high office in Chungking, but was banished for unbecoming conduct.'

'Aren't you afraid you'll be recognised?'

'It was too long ago, and there's nothing left of me now.'

'Don't you have any hopes of making something of yourself again?'

He gave no reply. I took a good look at him. In his dingy robe, with his little pigtail, his patchy stubble, his eyes deep-set for a Chinaman, he looked a proper wreck. Yet there was something in that man that might yet be reborn – what, I do not know, but I had the feeling his slumped back could suddenly become straight and supple, his drowsy voice full and commanding, his slack features eloquent and resolute, if only ... What? Every one of us awaits the event that will bring him to himself or lift him above himself, but it usually doesn't come, and we forget or make the best of things. That was what had happened to All-But-One, and that was what would happen to me. Over the next few days, I also felt that my satisfaction with the sense of space was a thing of the past. It had been a brief repose on a higher, but empty, plane. Now I hoped the event that would bring me to myself would take place in Chungking.

We continued our procession in the same order. Hsiu was said to be growing weary. Now and then he'd considered returning while we went on, but each time he'd changed his mind. Fong Shen, in contrast, grew more and more brash, hardly taking notice of Hsiu. She, who had once feared All-But-One, now laughed in his face and was no longer bashful with me, but provocative. She sometimes brought her mount alongside mine, but I did not pay her the least attention. When she stayed away from Godunov too long, he would fetch her back, and *him* she still obeyed. He seemed pleased with me for not making the slightest effort to speak to Fong Shen or make any form of contact with her. Why he was so fond of her, I do not know. She did look fresher and stronger than at the start of the trip, but the bulge on her cheek spoiled her beauty so radically that no thought of her ever crossed my mind. Many nights I saw All-But-One slip out to her tent. In return for my silence, I made him tell story after story of Chungking, and I imagined I knew the city more precisely than any place I'd ever been, that I could find my way around from the very first day, that I'd recognise the layout of the squares, never lose my way in the labyrinth of streets, and even know who to approach and who to shun. This confidence came not only from All-But-One's stories, but also from my growing certainty that Chungking must be my destination. Only in my dreams at night was I lost again, blown back to Taihai.

The journey became more dangerous; the areas through which we passed were often terrorised by bandit armies. But I, normally the most fearful of all, now strode ahead with greater confidence than anyone else, save All-But-One – whatever happened, it was all the same to him. I had expected to become better acquainted with Sylvain, but he kept himself more and more aloof. He was usually trailing after Hsiu as if he hoped for a sudden invitation to smoke an extra pipe—but that never happened. Nothing else interested him. Utterly extinguished he went on, and I sometimes expected to come upon him alongside the road one day, like a termite mound.

All-But-One, on the other hand, was becoming a little more energetic, and once when I asked him about the source of his renewed vitality and whether it was the scenes in the tent that had revived him, he admitted, after long hesitation, that the prospect of seeing Chungking again, without being seen himself, was the first thing in years that had brought him any satisfaction. He had given up hope that it would ever happen and felt indebted to Hsiu, even though he hated the man as much as I did. He had less interest in what would become of him after we arrived in Chungking. They could kill him as soon as he passed through the city walls, as long as they didn't toss him out again but buried him there straight away, in a coffin if possible or a rolled-up mat if necessary. He confessed to me that this outcome seemed likely, since the outrages for which he'd been banished were nothing short of dreadful. That naturally led him to tell me his life story. There, in the middle of the desert, it was the first sign of life China had sent me. Until then, there had been nothing but seeing and suffering.

Then I heard he had another name, a real one, but no longer wished to use it. For most people, it was like a half-death in life to lose one's ancestral name, but he'd grown accustomed to it over the years, and now preferred it that way. He came from a large family, which had been prosperous until a lawsuit – in which his father had become entangled because of the accusations of a dismissed manservant – had, after years of litigation, ruined them completely, aside from a little currency that his mother, showing greater foresight than his father (who always returned to the subject of the suit, despairing of an equitable remedy), had buried deep in the soil of their courtyard. It must still be there, All-But-One told me, but he felt absolutely no urge to go looking for it. Houses had probably been built on top of it by now. Once the family had been reduced to penury, they were banished from the city. They had gone to Pahsi; some had died on the way, but his grandfather, carried on his father's shoulders, had survived, despite their hopes. In Pahsi his father – who had been a merchant until his misfortune had sapped him of all his self-confidence and insight, but not of his brute strength – hired himself out to a sawmill. He worked as a scribe there, but also as a labourer, pulling the slow saw, which can take days to cut a log lengthwise. The boy's elder sister became a prostitute; his younger sister sold dried cherries on sticks, and she too soon earned a little extra on the side. He and his two brothers did nothing in particular, roaming the city all day, working only when the opportunity forced itself on them. But they usually brought something home with them: food, fruit or crumpled silk or cotton cloths, snatched from a display and tucked into their tunics. Once, caught on a roof, he was punished with fifty strokes of the cane, and when he got home his parents gave him fifty more. They had never done that when he brought things home for them. His father was always going on about how unfair people were, and now the boy had experienced that for himself at his father's own hands. It was a great source of amusement to their neighbours, who all laughed and made fun of him, at first behind his back and later to his face. His sister, too, was beaten whenever her customers walked off without paying, as they quite often did in the early days. He tried to talk to her about the injustice of their lot, but her expression remained as it was.

Yet better years came. Bit by bit, his father returned to his senses. He stopped fretting about an abstract idea, became a harsh taskmaster to the workers under him and was promoted to number three in the sawmill. He was entrusted with the complex administration of planks and boards and had the income to keep his daughters at home and later marry them off. The boy's brothers went to work with their father at the sawmill, but he had to go to school, because he was too feeble and coughed when he breathed in sawdust, and his family had given up hope of seeing him die young. In the stuffy schoolroom, he felt even unhappier than in the bustling streets around the market squares, but he learned faster than all the others, and when the criers shouted in the streets that the Hao Yan had come from the capital to hold the examinations for the lowest rank of scholar-officials, he presented himself.

After the first round, his family and personal names were

written on the large board outside the fenced-off examination site, with those of less than a quarter of the candidates. He made it through the second round as well. His father was already visiting friends to brag about his son, who rushed after him asking him to keep quiet until after the third and final round, but to no avail. His father kept shouting, 'You're almost done now – all but one!' And wherever he went he had to drink with them – warm yellow wine – and eat much too much food, more than he'd ever drunk and eaten before. He showed up for the third exam with a pounding headache and spent the whole day in his cell. The assignment was an essay, at least five hundred characters long, on the meaning of a passage by Confucius. He couldn't come to grips with it. He was still one hundred characters short when time was called and the examiners made their rounds, placing their stamps at the ends of the last lines.

He passed the following days in fear and uncertainty, walking in countless circles around the examination building. When the list finally came – twenty-six of the five hundred names – his own was not among them. Again, he had a great deal to endure: his father's regret about his premature boasts, which he took out on his son, and the mockery of his friends and neighbours.

A year later, he had to try again. This time the examinations were in Lengchi, four days' journey away. They hung a few strands of copper coins around his neck, shoved a few pieces of silver into his bag, and sent him off with a silk caravan. Again, he passed the first two examinations with ease, but then his money ran out. He had used the last of it to buy paper for writing the assignments. He asked the innkeeper to let him stay and sent a messenger home for more money. The third exam was still three weeks away. The examiners were old and slow and had many banquets with the local authorities to digest. The innkeeper put up with him for another week and then made him sleep by the courtyard palisade and eat the kitchen scraps, finally chasing him away when no money was sent.

He spent the last few days wandering the city and arrived at the examination ragged, dirty, and famished. He was admitted, because he had passed the first and second exams, but the invigilators shot contemptuous looks at him. In his dull, dizzy state he couldn't finish his work, an essay about poverty as the supreme virtue and the sage's only joy. Too bitter to approach the topic with sufficient reverence, he turned in his work early and wandered off indifferent. As soon as he was outside the wall, he collapsed. When the examiners saw him lying there, they thought he must be drunk, and drunks are not allowed to join the ranks of the civil service, no matter how intelligent they may seem. They noted on their lists that he was never to be admitted as a candidate again, that year or any other. Once they had posted the list, he came skulking by to look for his name but did not find it there. By then, he had deluded himself that his essay had really been quite excellent, and he consoled himself with the thought that he must have been disqualified for fainting by the wall. He went home alone, on foot, looking so piteous that no one bothered him on the road. When he arrived, he started to rebuke his father for the lack of money that had led to his downfall, and he mentioned how well he had done in the first two rounds, but his father cut him off: 'All-But-One again, I knew it from the start.'

Since then, everyone had called him by that name. The spoiled food he had eaten left him with a lingering illness, and once he had recovered, he fled the city and joined one of the armies of hirelings that roved the plains. There were many educated men in the army, because a person who has studied and expended his will on learning wise sayings and writing compositions on dead sages is forever unsuited to working with his hands and learning a trade. If he does not pass, he has nothing left but the most despicable choice.

The half- or near-scholars are easy to recruit, and are sometimes advanced to the rank of officer from one day to the next, if their force has suffered great losses and defeats. When their fortune turns again and it's easier to find recruits, they are sent back to the rank and file or expelled from the force. Yet he remained an officer there for a long while. Determined never to forget that his family's decline, poverty, and injustice were the causes of his ruination – since after all, there had been nothing wrong with his examination essays – he decided to keep the name 'All-But-One'.

After this story, All-But-One remained silent for a long time and avoided my company, as if he regretted having revealed his secrets. No matter how I urged him, never once would he relate how he had made his way back to Chungking and been exiled from there as well. He had probably been given another chance there and failed again, or entered under a different name and later been recognised and expelled for earlier crimes. But I couldn't be sure.

Near Lengchi, two men joined us. All we ever learned about them was that they were Buryats, herdsmen who doubled as soldiers. They were quick to do what we asked, rode far ahead, went hunting, and kept their quarry for themselves. Hsiu strove to maintain the appearance of authority, commanding them to keep an eye on particular coolies he distrusted and to inspect and oil various firearms, but they ambled along beside us as if they hadn't heard a thing, their rifles on their backs and staves in their hands. And after a while they were the true commanders. The coolies obeyed us because they had seen Hsiu assign us certain responsibilities. They obeyed the Buryats because they were awed by their domineering manner and physical presence. Peace-loving themselves, and more prone to whine and protest than to turn violent, they came under the influence of those men, larger in stature than any of us. While the Buryats did not boast bellies the size of Hsiu's, they had massive arms and shoulders. Their weight seemed to overwhelm the horses that carried them, and they often walked. They could easily match the coolies' pace, even on foot; the rest of us could not keep that up for long. You could see that all their lives they had done nothing but drive herds and fight as irregulars in the borderlands of Mongolia, Turkestan, and Tibet.

All-But-One and I could not compete with them. Even so, they treated us with some respect, occasionally gave us some of their game and helped us break camp. Godunov tried to maintain his authority against them, and it was clear that conflict would erupt before we reached Chungking.

The elder herdsman had returned injured from a late-night pleasure trip to a neighbouring village and demanded a few days' rest. But we broke camp and left him where he lay, at Godunov's insistence. Then the other one galloped out ahead of the caravan and waited for us where the road ran through a narrow cleft that permitted no other way forward. He stood in the path with his rifle lengthwise in front of him, barring the way like a half-living, half-metal cross. As soon as the coolies caught sight of him, they came to a halt and cast down their loads. Godunov made futile attempts to drive them onwards; a few followed him but soon ran back up to join the others, leaving him alone in the cleft in the face of the enemy. They sat along the edges of the cleft, a few metres above the level of the road, so as not to miss a moment of the spectacle. But before it was too late, Godunov conceded. He spoke to his adversary, rode back, and ordered the coolies to prepare a stretcher. He had avoided defeat but his authority was gone. He had lost Fong Shen too. She'd had second thoughts well before then, selecting the taller herdsman, who did not spurn her but haughtily accepted her reverence and services.

And as we approached Chungking, we became strangers to each other again, each of us riding alone among the mass of coolies. I barely exchanged another word with All-But-One. The desolation around us, the nearness of our goal, the danger we all faced, instead of bringing us together, threw us back on our solitary selves. Seeing as there was no way back, we all longed to arrive in Chungking and hoped to find a little happiness there. How we would find it was a question that probably no one considered. I knew that for Fong Shen and the herdsmen it wouldn't be so hard, and for me almost impossible.

The landscape began to change. We noticed we were approaching the outskirts of a large, isolated city. Yet for days we caught no glimpse of the city itself. Behind us were the arid plains, dotted only with a few houses and graves. Ahead, trees rose from the moist soil of the lower-lying land. Willows grew by the still ponds, and the caravan had to make large detours to avoid sinking into the marshy earth. Later the ground became firmer, but for now, jungles of bamboo blocked the way, bamboo larger than anyone had ever seen before. Some stalks had reached the height and thickness of an ancient oak.

Like all China, this region had hardly any animals, only large flocks of birds like herons but squat and black. Every time we drew near they would fly off towards the horizon, as if they were scouts reporting our approach. Maybe they really had been trained for that purpose. One evening Hsiu had a long, intense conversation with Godunov, and then with the two herdsmen. The next morning he had vanished. Godunov relayed to us that Hsiu had begun his journey back and placed him in charge of the rest of the expedition. A few moments later, the elder herdsman told us the same thing. It made no difference to us, of course, which one was telling the truth, especially since the very next day we noticed we were surrounded. In the distance, on all sides, were small groups that never came closer and never dwindled out of sight, obviously trailing us. In the evenings six or seven fires burned along with ours in the haze of the humid night.

Godunov now deigned to confer with us – that is, with All-But-One, Sylvain, and me. He feared that Hsiu had received the money and delivered us into the hands of this army, sent from Chungking to subdue us, take the weapons and force us to return without payment, or else imprison us for life. He proposed that we take cover behind two hills, bury the weapons in the dark of night, and go no further until they guaranteed our safe conduct and paid us half in advance. It was understood between us that what mattered most was not the money, but the chance to remain in Chungking. And it would be better to enter the city not as captives, but as men whose terms had been accepted. But how could we survive, out on that plain, without going hungry? In less than a week, we had finished the last of our supplies. Still, Godunov buried some of the weapons.

The next morning we expected to find ourselves completely encircled, but instead the landscape around us was completely empty. They apparently wanted us closer to the city first.

United for the first time, we climbed the hills and explored our surroundings, careful not to stray too far. But the troops had dug in or withdrawn. We had no choice but to break camp and move on, and at once our escorts showed themselves again. We came to a halt once more and waved flags, but they stayed at the same distance or even pulled back a little. As we waited the day passed and we saw we would have to spend the night in an exposed spot on the low edge of a large marsh with a lake in the middle, and when darkness fell we saw campfires blaze up again on the far side. The black herons were back too. When the moon rose we saw dense flocks of them flying over the lake. In our frustration, and to goad the enemy into action – since it seemed likely these birds were regarded as sacred – we started to shoot at them, but the sight was less than awe-inspiring, as we were poor shots. At last, one of the two herdsmen hit a heron's wing. The bird fell into the water far out of reach and spent the rest of the night flapping about in the reeds, thrashing and screeching.

Our shots met with distant, scornful laughter, and when the wounded bird fell, the camp on the far side showed no sign of religious outrage, but a few soldiers did make their way through the reeds to see what had happened, giving us our first close look at them. They were dressed in yellow nankeen with belts around their waists, and some wore shiny black leg guards. All they were missing were modern weapons; they used their spears to clear a path. None of them tried to save the bird; they stood staring for an instant and vanished again. This gave me a similar, but opposite, feeling to seeing the camels on the newly resurfaced dike. Those animals had seemed the epitome of calm and self-control, the weight of their humps pressing them safely against the ground where their flat feet stood, immovable. I had seen myself then as a restless wanderer, driven this way and that. Now I felt pity for the injured bird, because I too had fluttered around an expanse that offered no place to rest, while now I stood on solid ground, calm and decided. Fortunately, the herdsman killed it with a well-aimed shot. The rest of the night was quiet, and the next morning was the first clear one after a string of misty days.

All-But-One and I left the camp. We two were the most indifferent to being taken prisoner, he because nothing in the world concerned him any longer, and I because after concealing the weapon parts, I felt safe enough and had a secret longing to be taken hostage, so that I would enter the city before the others. They would have to release me again anyway, for lack of anything to hold onto. So we wandered out free and easy and were the first two to look up at Chungking. Through a stand of bamboo it looked like a smooth, hard rock and, once we had passed through the grove and were out in the open again, it was menacingly close by. Its walls were duller and blacker than those of any other Chinese city. All-But-One assured me that it was still at least a day's journey away and that with our heavy baggage it would take us two days or more. So we returned to camp, told the others what we had seen, and discussed the situation with the ones who were interested. All-But-One volunteered to go ahead with a letter announcing our arrival and asking permission to enter the city and deliver the weapons. Godunov and the herdsmen were opposed to this plan, of course, since they were the only ones who didn't care about entering the city but wanted to make a clean getaway with their money. So their proposal was for our messenger to say we had the weapons but could only deliver them in a usable condition if we were paid half the price in advance and received guarantees of safe conduct and of our safety and liberty in the city.

Three coolies were sent with a letter to this effect. They were quickly ambushed and sent back by the troops watching over us. That evening, we saw a narrow column heading for the basalt and granite walls on the horizon, which the earth itself seemed to have disgorged in its earliest and most violent convulsions. They left us out on that low plain for days, and the longer we stared at the walls, the higher and more immovable they seemed, until in time we hardly thought of the city within. Our vigilance weakened, and one evening we were not surrounded but flooded by hordes of the same type of soldiers we had seen in small groups all around us and across the lake. They seemed like an aimless swarm, but they had some system, for soon enough each of us was separated from the others, surrounded by a few hundred men. We could see that behind us other troops had closed in on the coolies and their freight, and like a compact mass, this army, without a single shot or blow, victorious by sheer numbers, advanced towards the city gates. These were probably the troops that Godunov and the two Buryats were supposed to train, in which case their authority as commanders had been undermined before they even started. They would show the soldiers how to use the equipment, and once their students were fully trained they would cast off their teachers like tools that had served their purpose.

We marched towards the walls in silence. Only the groups around All-But-One and Fong Shen made any noise. It sounded as if All-But-One was being ridiculed and Fong Shen praised for her beauty; now and then the two groups stopped for a few minutes. Then we saw no more of each other until we reached the moat, which was dry but as deep and wide as a ravine, affording the city more than adequate protection. The bridge was not lowered and the gate did not open. They were as large as the bridge and deck of a great ship. Hours without shade in the scorching afternoon sun left us even weaker. Neither food nor drink was offered, and when darkness fell we were taken inside. We saw many people leaning over the parapets to see us, their yellow faces grinning in the last of the dusk like a wreath of skulls around the city. Inside it was pitch dark in the narrowing streets. We were brought to an abrupt halt in a square on a steep hillside, the top of which was no longer visible in the darkness. There was a large building there with small, sinister windows. Lights burned inside a few of them, revealing the gratings. The herdsmen were gone. Had they escaped, or had they been separated from the rest of us? We were held there, not in cells as the windows suggested, but in a large, dark, low-ceilinged room. We would have to resign ourselves to passing our days there, waiting for Chungking to decide whether it would take us in or cast us out unseen.

Part Two

Chapter 9

Chungking, built before the Han Dynasty came to rule the empire, had for centuries led an independent existence on the margins, its fate almost never bound up or aligned with that of the other cities in the sublime Celestial Empire. Every time the fickle, bad-natured Yellow River had changed its course spontaneously, or to punish a dynasty for misrule, swallowing up regions and churning over cities, Chungking had remained outside the boundaries of the flood. The river, which spread two arms through the city, had crept as far as the walls, carrying away bridges, but had always retreated before the city itself was harmed. In the middle of Ch'in Shih Huang's reign, the Great Wall was built, rising over mountains and valleys, ravines and rivers, twelve fathoms tall and the span of eight guardsmen wide, with watchtowers two *li* apart, to prevent the barbarians and nomads from setting foot on the soil of the empire. Many outlying cities paid rich tributes for the privilege of lying inside that wall, so it curved outward in many places. But Chungking, trusting in its own walls and guardsmen, had no interest in giving up its profitable trade with the barbarians. Choosing to remain the stopping place for caravans that arrived exhausted from the months-long journey across the steppes and through the Gobi, it paid just as high a tribute for the privilege of remaining *outside* the wall. That was why, to the east of Chungking, the wall was indented twenty *li* inward.

As the empire became ever more closed off and the fruits of its once-flourishing civilization ever scantier, as arid tradition and intensive inbreeding drained away its force, as its wise men no longer made the effort to use their will for their country's good, as misrule, revolt, and poor harvests came in turn, Chungking remained outside, savage in the external forms of culture, exposed to influences from Mongolia, Turkestan and the countries beyond. And like a raw but purgative mountain wind from the high peaks of Tibet and the Mongolian steppe, the rivers of nomads and pilgrims came rushing in, camping along the riverbanks in the open, uncultivated areas outside the city walls, bringing their wares to market and spreading their ideas among the people and the priests.

But not only the nomads of Central Asia but also those driven by wanderlust from the plains of Cimmeria and Persia and countries still more distant were drawn to Chungking, the only free city in the great, fossilised empire, and all of them, even those who came empty-handed without beasts of burden, brought the products and customs of their remote western lands. Some settled there, while others merely passed through but later returned, because the cities of Kublai Khan and the Manchus, which drew in Westerners with dreams of greatness, splendour, and religious scholarship, were a disappointment to foreigners who had spent time there. What good was there in walking the perimeter of the high palace walls around the Forbidden City and seeing, not the great worldly and spiritual leaders, but only their henchmen in the markets and the monastery forecourts? The emperor and the Dalai Lama practically never received visitors. Then they would recall that in Chungking the city of Peking had always been spoken of in cool, dismissive, contemptuous terms as a latecomer, which had borrowed and stolen all its glamour and wealth from the older cities deeper in the empire. And many, pleased to be back in Chungking, remained there, daunted by the prospect of repeating their long journey, this time not to the mysterious east, but back to the foggy, familiar west. To think how far behind them it lay – the years, the continents! They would be received there as people presumed dead, for whom there was no place in a changing society.

Chungking had no Tartar or Manchu districts, dominating the lower city like a humiliating memory of its past subjugation, but sometimes in a narrow street, passing through a gate into an unexpected courtyard, you might encounter a house in the Byzantine or Venetian style, because every foreigner, once accepted as a resident of Chungking, could build in whatever manner he liked.

Much later, foreigners no longer came by land, over the steppes and through the mountain passes, but from the south, crossing the sea and the plains to the rivers, and all they wanted to do was buy and pay. But Chungking was already wealthy enough, despised their obvious profiteering, and sent them on their way without buying their products – lacking that desire.

One of the foreigners who came by the new roads was welcomed, and remained. He belonged to the race that in recent years had arrived by sea near Canton, the powerful but degenerate capital in the south, and founded a small settlement on a narrow peninsula at the mouth of the Pearl River. They called it a city, though it had fewer houses and inhabitants than a medium-sized village in one of the central provinces. This man came not to trade, but as an exile. That fact came to light only later, because he made his entry with twenty camels and one hundred porters laden with so many valuables they could scarcely carry them. He had not been banished for any crime, but his will and enterprising spirit were so strong that his country, to protect its monopoly on trade and relations with the Celestial Empire, had driven him out, calling him a danger to the city.

His name was Velho, which meant 'the old one' in his language. He was so different in nature from other Westerners that the people of Chungking almost immediately trusted him as one of their own. He had a large, stout build, like a man of distinction; his countenance was not red and puffy, but yellowish-white and fairly narrow; his nose was not long and purple, but broad and flat; though his eyes were blue, they did not bulge out of their sockets; and his hair was dark blond (nothing to be done about that), but at least it rested smooth and straight on his scalp.

Even so, Velho did not merge with the new race, but remained who he was and later built a house according to his own principles, which astonished both the ancestral inhabitants of Chungking and the more recent arrivals. He was as unconcerned as the latter with the cardinal directions, the day of the year when construction would begin and the composition of the soil. But he did not use the fine slender columns of the Byzantines, nor Venetian walls like vast paintings. Sturdy pillars, encircled by snakes and flowering vines, held up the front gallery. The inner and outer walls were covered with glazed tiles in soft colours, on which he himself painted scenes from an unknown history.

But his own life soon came to resemble those of the people around him. He wore their garments, ate their food, drank their drink and dealt with them as an equal – except that on certain days, which recurred in a regular pattern, he remained indoors, put on old clothes and read his books, books with pages as thick as pigskin. He sold a great deal and bought little. The goods he had brought with him lasted for years, and later, a large caravan brought fresh shipments three more times, sent not by his countrymen, but by other Westerners who had settled on the island of Taiwan. Whenever his descendants built or restored their houses, they were true to the style he had introduced.

A few years after his arrival, the empire was closed once more to Westerners, who had brought not only goods that they traded for other goods, but also their religion, which they hoped would win them power. It was already beginning to undermine ancestor worship in some places, and in some coastal cities the graves were neglected, the stones at the entrance crumbling and bones rising to the surface. Memorial tablets were broken and never replaced, and the funerals were hasty, slipshod affairs; the mourners hummed psalms and litanies to themselves as the professional mourners let out their piercing wails. And even at the exalted court in Peking, the infiltration began with mathematics and astronomy but eventually came round to the gospels. The emissaries introduced themselves as scholars and experts but soon set to work as missionaries. Already hundreds of thousands from the lower classes, as well as mandarins, judges, and public prosecutors, professed the faith that preached gentleness rather than violence, but brought war.

Emperor Yung Cheng, who cared less for science and scholarship than his predecessor, but was also a better, more diligent ruler, obliterated this rising Western influence with a decree that was ruthlessly enforced. Many were tortured and killed, but far fewer than after an ordinary popular uprising or an invasion of the border tribes, and this was said to be a stroke of luck. Those unarmed, defenceless foreigners clutching their bibles to their chests and their crosses in their hands had proved more dangerous than the immense nomad hordes that came charging in with their bows and swords and spears.

This time Chungking went along with the imperial policy. The Velho of that era, the grandson of the first, had warned them incessantly against the influence of the emissaries of Jesus, who came so quietly, did so much good, accepted the state institutions so humbly and never drew attention to themselves until they were ready to seize power. Chungking was ripe for the taking by the time the decree was issued, and it was enforced there more strictly than anywhere else. Only twenty-four hours later, the clerics were shackled, and a guard of six spearmen surrounded them and led them to

Ichang, where they were put on a ship. After a few days, the monastery and the two churches were demolished, and the bricks and stones were used to fill in a pond. No one dared use them in any other buildings. Only the old Byzantine chapels were left in place, and most of those disappeared naturally in time. Meanwhile, by the Western gate, through which the foreigners had been driven out, a temple was erected to the war god, who bore a sword in each of his many arms, frozen in terrifying gestures, barring the return of the hypocrites with their talk of love and peace. And after that, not a single foreigner with a pale face, blue eyes, a long nose and thick red lips was permitted to enter Chungking. Only the descendants of the Byzantines, and of Velho, still lived among the other inhabitants of Chungking, becoming less distinct from them with each generation.

Centuries later came the descendants of the barbarians who had once tried to insinuate themselves through trade and conversion, and the Middle Kingdom was overpowered. The foreigners' mighty weapons, which were mounted on ships of iron and steel and carried deep inland on carts, pushed the gates of the empire ajar in a few port cities, and later blew them wide open in all the ports, as far upriver as Hankow and Ichang. The empire was humiliated, and had a hard time saving its sublime face.

But the inner circles knew that this violent incursion was a mere illusion. The foreigners lived on small strips of land outside the port cities, and their firearms were carried down narrow tracks as far as the borders of Cili and Honan. But millions and millions of subjects of the empire had never heard of the fat foreigners. Only the residents of the coastal cities, or along the main roads and on the narrow strips of land that lay between them, had ever seen them face to face, but they had gone on with their work, indifferent.

And as the empire was wrenched open, Chungking, once so

willing to absorb and integrate outside influences, had closed itself up completely. Now it shut out not only foreign people but also, and even more strictly, foreign products, especially the metals that were not in use in Chungking: steel, nickel, and aluminium. Following their intuition, pure and strong this time, that the metals and what was made from them – engines, machines, weapons, and tools – would inevitably strip them of their power, the magistrates of Chungking remained loyal, as so often in the past, to their ancient tradition of rejecting and resisting the general tendency in the empire. That is, until the old Tuchun was succeeded by his son.

The new warlord shared his father's fanatical hatred of Westerners but did not oppose those who declared it essential to obtain and study their weapons, the better to fight them off later, and to train the people to use such weapons before the enemy was at the gates. Other leaders and the most influential citizens, including the Velho of that era, argued that they should fight in their own time-honoured manner, through force of numbers and fierce resistance, rather than demeaning themselves by wielding the weapons of their inferior adversary, but the Tuchun refused to intervene, and in the end two negotiators were sent to Taihai in secret. But wise men knew what such weapons would bring. The danger came not from the unruly barbarians, but from the silent chasms of the earth from which they hoped to extract metals. It was those metals, far below the surface of Chungking, that would destroy them if they were released.

But there was no longer any stopping it. The opponents of the new weapons gave the appearance of conceding, but they set to work in secret among the people and hired a stray English artilleryman to advise them, not on the arms trade, but on how to render machine guns and cannon inoperable by making a small dent in a certain place on the barrel, and how to spoil ammunition by wetting it. There were plenty of volunteers, and the weapon destroyers formed a secret society that offered its members certain benefits. But more than the weapons themselves, they feared the people accompanying the arms convoy. Suppose they remained in Chungking, sought fertile ground for their expertise, churned up the earth, and built factories, telegraph stations, and those fire-chariots of theirs, which took only a day to cover distances that had traditionally required a months-long journey. Then Chungking's remoteness, the source of its power and freedom, would come to dust. So they decided to let in the weapons and keep the foreigners outside the gates, where they could kill them or drive them back as quickly as possible. This plan was destined to succeed – the first time.

In Taihai, the negotiators found their only option was to go to Hsiu, who controlled almost the entire arms trade in western Szechwan. He prepared a consignment of ten light cannon and many hundreds of machine guns with ammunition. This arrived in Chungking unharmed. The weapons were demonstrated outside the walls, and the quiet valleys and sacred temple halls resounded with cannon fire, which rebounded from the walls of the temples and mountains in cacophonous echoes. The purchase price was paid, and the convoy returned to Taihai. But a day later, not a shot could be fired: the ammunition lay in a pool of water, a few cannon had been rolled into the river, and the machine guns were bent and broken.

Chungking's pro-armament party then demanded that Hsiu should deliver twice the amount of the first consignment and send instructors, who would not be permitted to leave until the weapons had proved their worth over months of use and the city's people had grown accustomed to the sound of the shots and the big guns rolling down the streets, until the weapons had been in place on the walls so long that no one would dare to damage them any longer, any more than they would a monument of venerable age. A hundred men were to be instructed daily in using the weapons, and the instructors would remain prisoners the whole time, locked up at night. Their hosts would have to take responsibility for them and accept the consequences, becoming hostages to their own captives – because if the instructors escaped, their gaolers would pay with their lives.

Few volunteers stepped forward to take in the foreigners. Even the most fervent opponents of Western progress and supporters of the new weapons demurred, so great was the risk, so perilous the months-long measures required to protect their own lives. As difficult as it would be to escape over the high walls around their houses, and then from the city over the ramparts and moat and across the barren plains to the borders of Szechwan, a series of three impossibilities, who could say what routes might be open to the Westerners? Some of them flew through the air; others dug deeper into the ground than any mole, or even any tormentor in the underworld. They sent messages through the sky that remained invisible until they fell to earth in just the right spot, where someone else was waiting to catch them and make them visible with a complicated device.

So the few volunteers to house these unwanted but temporarily indispensable guests saw their offers gratefully accepted, even though they were not well-liked – hated, in fact. The first was Kia So, the priest of the war temple, who could keep his guests in the deep cellars under the altar at night. The second was Lao Yin, an elderly uncle of the Tuchun, who was only allowed to attend the New Year's festival and the autumn festivals. He never left his house and large garden otherwise, and seemed to have no desire to do so. Within his walls, he threw strange parties for his own enjoyment.

Once, before he had been removed from all his posts, he had invited twelve of the oldest and poorest residents of Chungking to dine with him. They dared not refuse. The other twelve guests were the youngest and costliest girls from the city's finest tea house. The banquet took place in utter silence, to the profound disappointment of the many curious onlookers who scaled the walls, braving the nails and glass shards that covered them, crept into the garden, and peered through the windows. By some odd coincidence, nearly all the shutters were open just a crack. The guests sat politely at the table, the courses were served in the prescribed order, and the sing-song girls stood behind the guests' chairs. Many onlookers went home disappointed, and injured in various places, but too early. After Lao Yin himself had passed around the fruit, he asked what else he could do for his guests. Then he pulled a cord that lifted the outer garments of the twelve courtesans into the heights by invisible threads – which must have been connected to them the whole evening. It was their fear of gliding out of their shells too soon that had led them to stand at the table so stiffly, with exaggerated courtesy. Now that this obstacle had been removed, the lamp was put out. It is said that three of the aged guests were brought home dead, and four others passed away a few days later.

After many other lugubrious jokes, which cannot be summed up here, Lao Yin was ultimately expelled by his own nephew from the office of judge, the last post he had retained. He was entrusted with the care of two Westerners, and the only fear was that he would conduct potentially lethal experiments on them before they had completed their work. After that it would no longer matter, and he could use them for any purpose he liked as long as he rendered them harmless.

Another was assigned to a surviving descendant of Velho, much less active in public life than his forefathers, because he had no political ambitions. Even so, he enjoyed a degree of respect, because he was known to be engaged in the long-term study of secret writings, and above all because in desperate cases, when the doctors threw up their hands, he was summoned as a last resort. He had gone away for two years to study at academies of higher learning in Moscow and Berlin and was therefore assumed to be familiar with the medical science of the Westerners. His house was in such a secluded location that escape was impossible, and as he hated Westerners more than the Chinese themselves did, he could reasonably be expected to test one of his poisons on his guest as soon as he heard that the foreigners were no longer welcome in Chungking.

He had no friends in the city, but he must have felt attached to Chungking itself. It was the only place on earth where he could live. In other Chinese cities, his way of life would have given offence, and he would never have been left to his own devices. In the cities of the West, he could not have lived at all, and even less so in the steppe, considering his need for great silence in cool or mild rooms alternating with great noise, for crowds by day and empty squares and streets by night. What other choice did he have but to remain in Chungking, hoping it would remain as it was, and helping to prevent outside influences from causing upheavals that would permanently disrupt the environment on which he depended? That was why Velho took it upon himself to host the barbarian who would be seen by the city authorities as the most disruptive. The others – they didn't know how many were coming – were assigned to Cheng, a mandarin who had strayed far beyond the bounds of the law and could be kept in line by threat of punishment.

Having made these preparations, Chungking awaited the second arms convoy, serene and self-confident. They had agreed to pay Hsiu the full price, but only after the weapons were in full use and the escorts had vanished or returned to Taihai. At last the city would be able to protect itself against aggression of the new variety. Their only remaining concern was to restrict the use of the weapons to members of a new guild, which would remain isolated from the rest of the population by a series of privileges and prohibitions. Chungking's masses had to remain as they were, ignorant of any progress. The guild members were recruited in advance, forbidden to marry, and subject to rules as strict as those of a monastic order. In fact, they were housed in an actual monastery and made a lifelong commitment; once they were no longer fit for military service, to the monastery they would return.

The compulsory hosts were all pleased with their role, in the end – not because they had any desire to serve their community, but because they secretly expected that having the foreigners at their disposal would be most amusing. Only Kia So refused to attend their premature meetings and voiced his contempt for them. They soon fell into the habit of taking an early morning walk on the city walls, after the fog had lifted, and staring out over the plain. The walls were wide enough, and they could easily pass one another as they did in the streets of Chungking. But soon enough they were exchanging greetings, and before long they met in one of the watchtowers, furnished with a wooden bench and a stone table. Of course, they took care to talk about anything but their one point of common interest.

But one morning Cheng leapt up and cried, 'Here they come!' Velho and Lao Yin wanted to stare through the peephole too, but it was too small and Cheng was blocking the way. The others went out onto the wall and, sure enough, could see an advancing dust cloud in the distance. Then a gust of wind cleared the view, the cloud disappeared like a ghost and all they could see was a small flock of sheep on the move. They heaped scorn on Cheng.

After that, the three barbarian-keepers – as they were already described by the city guards and some of their fellow citizens – played mah-jong or chess at the stone table, casting only furtive glances out towards the plain. Each of them anticipated serious disagreement when the time came to distribute the foreigners among the hosts. Only Velho was largely untroubled by this thought. They wasted many hours considering the situation ahead. Otherwise, there was no change whatsoever in the life of the city, except that now and then a bamboo pipe, driven ever deeper over the years by pounding hammers, would hit an aquifer and send water shooting to the surface, so that some additional fraction of the city's people could, if not improve their hygiene, then at least quench their thirst more often and prepare their food more easily. There was nothing to suggest that the city would not remain as it was until it had completed its time on earth, for cities, like their inhabitants, are mortal and must perish someday, even if they usually outlive trees and turtles, and yes, even the personal and collective memory of humanity.

Chapter 10

Letter from Kia So to Wan Chen

It was forty years ago that we left Phodang Monastery, after completing our studies and meditations, and parted ways, you to live in the Land of Snows, in sacred Amdo, and never venture outside its borders, I to become a priest in Chungking.

I myself am amazed to find myself writing this letter, covering paper with characters, which are thin but unmistakable to the touch. But the events and facts I must relate are not suited to the thought-transmission by which we otherwise communicate. Like other men, I must use words now, including some that do not even exist in the language of the initiates.

I must call for help now, but not the help that has always come to me from the sacred halls on the far side of the mountain ranges, that of exalted thoughts. Those will no longer suffice. Demons must be released to battle demons. Perhaps I should ask you to leave Amdo after all. For thirty years I alone have carried out the sublime task of maintaining reverence for tradition, as staunchly as ever. Now the time has come when the invasion of the new can no longer be stopped. The coast of the empire has, as you know, been infected by the barbarians for some time, and a few inland cities, too, have become sources of contagion. The empire will overcome this disease as it has so many others in the past; their towering houses and factories will remain standing and be used by the people until they have crumbled, that is all.

Chungking had remained undefiled until now. In recent centuries, not a single alien had been admitted. But now it seems that this misfortune cannot be undone. Our ancestors always managed to keep Chungking as it was. Now the evil has made its way into our midst. Many people here would like to get their hands on the barbarians' weapons and systems of warfare – the better to keep them out when the time comes, or so they claim. And these are not commoners, but our leading citizens! I have never understood how people of their status and refinement could waste their time on such contemptible things as war. But once they appeared to have made up their minds, I and a few other initiates gave the impression of belonging to the armament party, so that we could neutralise it as effectively as possible, or otherwise find a way to absorb these novelties, as detestable as they are, into our vast system of customs and morals, so that our people are not even aware of the intrusion. The task is daunting, yet who remembers today that fireworks were brought to us by the Byzantines, crystal glass by the Venetians, pepper by the Portuguese, and Buddhism by the Indians? All these things wrought great changes, at first, in our ways of living, celebrating and thinking, but ultimately they changed nothing. Most people do not know these things are foreign in origin, and those who do think twice before calling our Chinese traditions foreign.

And these weapons, however contrary to our customs they may seem, may follow the same pattern. They could be used in some ceremony or other – perhaps to exorcise an unlaid ghost. But now the weapons and the foreigners who can use them to sow destruction have arrived together!

Chungking is so many thousands of *li* from the sea, so much further even than it is from the Land of Snows. The Westerners do not like to stray far from the water, where they truly belong, as we have seen time and again. Almost all of them arrive by ship, and they have a fishy aspect (one might take a good look some time, for instance, at the English consul in Langchow and the German representative of Siemens-Schuckert in Ichang, viewed in profile!). When they walk, they not only move their legs forward, but also row with their arms, even though there is nothing in the air to be rowed. They want ships near them wherever they go, dig canals where none have ever existed just so that their ships can sail there, use far too much salt in their food and must therefore drink to excess, so that at least they have an inner lake, like camels, even (especially!) in the most arid regions. They apply water to their skin countless times a day – no wonder they are covered with red and blue blotches – and all the while they suppose they are cleaning themselves. I could present many other proofs that they do not really belong here on earth, especially not in the Middle Kingdom. They would be better off staying in their own part of the world, which is divided and split by the sea like no other region.

In the old days a few of them, different in nature, came by land with caravans from Samarkand, and many centuries ago some of that sort were allowed to enter Chungking. But we never kept them here for long – a couple of half-mad Venetians were sent on to Peking, where foreigners were in fashion at court back then, a fashion whose dangers only later became apparent. Velho, who first came by river and then by land from the coast, bound his fate to our own, but he and his descendants have never been assimilated, their origins never forgotten. They have always been shunned. Now foreigners have nothing else to offer us. What are we to do with their rifles, cannon, machine guns or grenade launchers?

They will not reach this place, so far from the sea. The bandits who roam the steppes and the envious governors of neighbouring districts can be bought off, or kept at bay if necessary by a well-drilled group of archers and mounted lancers. A short siege is easily withstood – fields, wells for drinking water, supplies, all this we have within our walls

– and there will never be a long one. They lack the patience and tenacity. A siege even has its benefits: more worshippers in the temples, more sacrifices, more children conceived.

But once we have their cannons and machine guns, a siege will no longer proceed peacefully and according to the rules, as it otherwise would. Instead, accidents will always happen. After a few shots some of the weapons will explode, laying waste to their surroundings. Besides, they are loud enough to drown out all the consecrated clarions and cymbals, making our worshippers less receptive to those sacred instruments for a time – even though in the long run, the wail of the mountain horns and the blare of the kanglings, the thighbone trumpets, is more impressive and fearsome by far than the dull boom of cannonballs or the squeal of grenades.

To you, for instance, who no longer dread the thunderous outbreak of avalanches in the spring, you who wage solitary battle with the dead in their thousands on your desolate plateau, the sound would seem feeble and ridiculous. And the threat would not be serious if the weapons went unused for a few years, since they would rust in the meantime. But in most cases, as soon as they are installed – as many forward-looking cities further east have learned – some warmongering general from the penniless, half-starved zone around the city will begin to wonder why Chungking is so well armed. Even if it is known only as a stopping place for silk and tea caravans and a centre of culture, which brings little profit, it must have treasures secreted away. Why else would they be so concerned about defending themselves? If such a general is literate – as he often is – and happens to read that there used to be a lively trade with the realm of Bukhara, then he will grab his elbows in surprise and berate himself for never turning his thoughts before to that treasure chamber in its greyish-red river basin!

The cannon and machine guns will not command his respect in the slightest. He will make inquiries about the barbarians who brought them and installed them, to find out how long ago they left. If enough time has passed, the garrison will undoubtedly have forgotten how to use the weapons properly. And otherwise, some other stretch of the wall is sure to be undefended. That is where he will strike. No one will consider moving the cannon there. The defenders will be much too relieved that the guns are still upright and have not tumbled off their platforms, which are already sagging under their weight, leaving them unbalanced. The battery commander will give a sigh of gratitude after each successful salvo and hope to himself that it wasn't the last one.

Then it will be easy to shoot down the undefended section of the wall, pillage the city, and take hostages. If the secret of where the treasure lies cannot be squeezed out of anyone under torture, then at least a hefty tribute can be exacted.

Many cities have met with this fate; Chungking has thus far avoided it. Now and then we have ordered weapons to appease the armament party, but we have also sent a secret courier to the supplier with a bonus and a request to deliver mainly defective equipment. Most arms dealers would do so anyway, but we like to be certain. Or we bribe one or more members of the expedition to sabotage the weapons during transport by getting water or sand into them (which sometimes happens naturally) or simply by misplacing them.

This time, however, the opponents of armament did not have luck on their side. After a long search, the enthusiasts had found a Mr Hsiu in Taihai who comes from Chungking and has every reason to hate it. He was once flogged out of town for thieving and insulting the Gods; the high price his grandfather paid to the judges was the only thing that saved his life. If only the judges had for once been incorruptible, they could have accepted bribes to their heart's content in so many cases of lesser importance. Hsiu never missed an opportunity to let his acquaintances here know how well he

was faring in the outside world and what a favour Chungking
– which he never called 'The Peerless City', but always 'The
Airless City' — had done him by casting him out as a callow
youth. Otherwise he would never have become a great
merchant in Taihai – the true capital of the empire – but
would have remained an official all his life.

As if the lowest official were not superior to the wealthiest
merchant.

He once had thousands of copies of a magazine distributed
in Chungking in which alongside the Chinese the mongrel
language of the English stood printed in vulgar letters, with
an article in both languages about his generosity, his eminent
qualities, and his love of the nation. Beside it was his preening
portrait. I do not know, Wan Chen, why I am telling you all
this in such detail; it must seem foreign to you, although even
in the Land of Snows some monks stoop to becoming traders.
But no one else in Chungking seems to share my anger and
frustration. Even the Tuchun laughs and does not feel how
gravely Hsiu has insulted the city.

Another time, two street musicians handed out small
packages of sweets to all the children in Chungking, printed
with the words, 'Hsiu's tongue-tempters.' So this young
generation, for as long as they live, will always praise Hsiu's
name and never forget him. For as long as they live – because
soon after that, many children were felled by intestinal
disease. Of course, it was in the sweltering summer heat, and
all the wells were contaminated, but still, the mortality rate
was much higher than usual.

A little later he had two travelling doctors hand out boxes
of pills that were said to cure all ailments. Was this a kind of
peace offering, or were those pills poisoned too, as the sweets
had probably been? As credulous and naive as the people
were, many of them accepted the pills with gratitude, and
Hsiu's name was praised throughout Chungking.

And now Hsiu has been given the chance to supply his natal city with the weapons that may lead to its downfall. We may have fulfilled his greatest, longest-cherished wish!

He wrote a letter, a model of courtesy and convention, expressing his thanks to us for honouring him with the order, promising to supply the finest wares available and expressing his wistful regret that he could not deliver them himself and see Chungking again. (The terms of his banishment forbade him to come within one hundred *li*.) But he was consoled by the thought that he could contribute to the city's security and preservation.

The experts he was sending, Hsiu went on, were the best to be found among the many thousands that the vanquished city of Taihai was forced to accommodate, seeing its ancient outlying districts overshadowed by their powerful concessions. (How proud a place, in contrast, was Chungking, which though impoverished had remained unspoilt.)

He enclosed their portraits and fingerprints, so that the foreign creatures could be recognised and checked for authenticity. At the same time, he explained, he was helping the Chungking police to take a step forward by introducing them to Western criminal methods, which were truly deserving of emulation, as this experiment would prove.

I was the only one – apart from Cheng, perhaps – who could hear the mocking tone of this letter and the others sent by Hsiu, that cunning devil. We two had joined the armament party by necessity, because we had debts to pay (you alone understand that it was not any fault of my own, but a demon who sought to cut off my breath, that drove me to such lamentable acts) and could make ourselves useful to the city leaders by faithfully reporting on the decisions made at the party's secret meetings. Every word Hsiu wrote was taken in earnest by those half-educated folk, to the point of absurdity. The fingerprints were kept in the society's secret storeroom, along with the portraits, after they were viewed by the inner circle.

Considering all this, Hsiu had very sound reasons for looking forward to his vengeance on the city that had cast him out. In truth, the whole transaction must have been nothing but a malicious joke to him. The price of the weapons was so low that his profit cannot have been more than two hundred per cent, and the leaders of the armament party were entitled to a share of that (the fee for the convoy's escorts was not to be taken seriously, of course, and once they had played their part, they could fall prey to some disease or vanish into a well or a house). It must seem to you that I am disturbing your sacred contemplations with reports of insignificant events, but I must tell the whole story so that you will fully understand what follows – and like all men, I must unburden myself sometimes. There is no one here to whom I can speak of this; the Tuchun waves me off, certain that everything will work out for the best, and Cheng, who is in perfect agreement with me, has almost completely given up using words – as you have in Amdo – but for other reasons, of a physical nature.

The first pair of portraits – there were two of each foreigner, one profile and one full face – showed a French naval officer in full dress uniform, with a face like a dead moon. The second man was garbed as a member of the Forest of Brushes – another sinister joke on Hsiu's part, since his sunken features, hollow cheeks, and dull eyes gave ample evidence that his brain no longer functioned, that he was in no state to string characters into a single coherent sentence on paper. Under this portrait, Hsiu wrote, 'He is luckier than I. He has served his time.' Did this refer to a temporary banishment? His face looked familiar. The next man was heavyset with a low forehead, large, bulging eyes and a broad smirk. Below: 'One of the bravest officers of the sadly assassinated Emperor of

All the Russias.' The following pair showed a woman with a classically beautiful face, but the profile view revealed a wart or blemish in the middle of her cheek and a star-shaped scar. The caption: 'I hand over my most precious possession to the city that fathered me.'

Lastly, there was a man ... words cannot begin to describe to you what he was like. His face was narrow, his mouth weak, but the corners of the mouth were drawn back in contempt, his eyes staring as if they saw into the deepest depths. That is how an anchorite looks after three years of seclusion in the darkness of his cell, when he samples earthly life for one last time before turning his back on it and withdrawing for good. Immense contempt for everything human could be read in his face and made it almost beautiful, as if he belonged to the pure race, although the broad lips and oversized nose gave the lie to this resemblance.

None of the city leaders paid any attention to that face. Hsiu had written nothing under the portrait, or under that of the French naval officer, as if those two were of lesser importance. But it seemed to me, as I recall, that this man might be capable of more than building and wielding weapons.

The city leaders were very pleased with this delegation, especially because Hsiu wrote in a separate letter that each had mastered a certain branch of their profession: the French officer knew how to construct artillery, the Russian could use rifles and machine guns and train soldiers and the Chinese scholar could translate Western military terms into Chinese.

A few months later – months in which we met a few more times for no compelling reason – we received word that Hsiu had left Taihai and would lead the transport himself, as far as the law permitted him to go. He couldn't say how long it would take; he had a few things to take care of first, he explained: private matters, so trivial compared to Chungking's interests that he wouldn't care to mention them by name. In other words, opium smuggling and the covert sale of prostitutes from the coast to brothels in the interior, the transmission of messages to far-flung branches of various societies and the sale of rice in famine areas – I knew very well what 'trivial interests' a man like Hsiu might have.

We estimated that the news of the convoy's departure could precede its arrival by as much as half a year. Even so, the city leaders at once began preparing to 'give the weapons a worthy reception', as they put it.

Along the battlements of the city walls, which had collapsed and crumbled in many places, large stones were soon lowered into place, grave-robbed from the resting place of the past Tuchuns, to serve as bases for the cannon. When I protested, I was told that those were the only stones large enough in surface area and sturdy enough in composition.

They also began recruiting soldiers, in a campaign that violated our most cherished principles. For instance, they claimed that the warrior caste was no longer the lowest in status, since they would not be waging war but simply defending their city. Their task was even given a certain aura of sanctity, with the declaration that the defenders of Chungking would not be permitted to marry, and would thus be equivalent in status to monks.

Their pay was shamefully high in view of their social class, and served no good purpose. Since they could not take wives or sire children who would need a larger home, they had nothing to do with their wealth but addle their brains with wine and opium, until the rough quality of character known as valour had degenerated completely – the very quality they needed in their work!

The entire effort to establish this warrior caste, led by Feng and Shu and the members of the yamen, was in fact so ineffectual as to provoke both laughter and tears. After Hsiu's last letter, it seemed the city's fate was sealed, since there was little chance of the caravan meeting with an accident along the way. So the best I could do was to turn this debacle to the benefit of my temple. The populace had long understood – for the private secretaries of the city leaders are usually quick to spill their secrets – that, after so many years, the weapons of the barbarians would soon be welcomed into Chungking. The rumours were confirmed by the premature gatherings of armament party members on the city wall. The result was a tense anticipation of things to come, a sense of impending doom out of all proportion to the matter's true scope and significance.

Many people believed that each watchtower would be armed with a cannon, that the ramparts would be thronged with soldiers night and day, ten or twelve ranks deep, that Genghis Khan had risen from the dead and was approaching with an army of Turcoman, Cimmerian, Kyrgyz and Buryat soldiers. After years – peaceful years – of benign, weather-beaten neglect, the time was ripe to restore the temple to some semblance of its old lustre.

I hired town criers from among the jobless, the invalids, the ex-convicts – one hundred and fifty of them, who plunged into crowded marketplaces, wedding celebrations, funeral services, shouting to each other that it was high time to placate the war gods with sacrifices, that they seemed ill-disposed towards Chungking, which in its long stretch of peace, calm, and prosperity had neglected its old tutelary gods.

I had a painter work all night to give them a fresh coat, and the glaring colours made them look more lively and menacing than ever, after so many years in the half-darkness, dull and mouldering. I had the temple halls brightly lit, strewed herbs, and burned pungent incense.

These measures had no effect at first, but all of a sudden, one night after distant but ceaseless storms – which sounded remarkably like artillery fire on the horizon – after signs such as geese and herons leaving early for the southeast, after beams had fallen from gates and a newly built house had collapsed (and another had been burnt down, on my orders), the fearful crowds came pouring in, and every evening, they brought huge quantities of grain and rice to fill the temple cellars; I received the strangest offerings, some of which made fine new ornaments for the temple. In the process, it became clear to me that there were many more objects in Chungking produced by foreigners than I had ever suspected. In some cases, I did not even understand their purpose.

After all the frustration of the prior months, this gave me great satisfaction, especially as it was the result of my own ingenuity. Yet I knew the reason for these abundant gifts, and my joy faded at the thought that the foreigners were truly on their way and that this time the weapons would remain in working order. And one evening, I saw for certain that the whole matter would end badly.

On one of the first calm days of the month, I went outside the city walls and strolled along the edge of the lake. The weather was clear; the green of the pines, the blue of the drifting clouds, the mountain peaks and the sun shining over them normally lightened my mood when my long residence in the monastery left me gloomy and fearful, but not this time, and the rippling surface of the lake had a strange cast like a purple veil drawn over it, and did not catch the light.

I turned away and went to the nearly empty temple, where I pretended to pray to the gods. The offerings were becoming meagre again; it was taking too long for the danger to arrive, and never before had we experienced such good fortune: no outbreaks of disease, no failed harvests, no new follies perpetrated by the Tuchun, and few crimes. And yet ... our fate was inescapable.

I considered fleeing with the richest offerings, the money, and the seed corn, but it would have caused a stir if I had changed all the money at once, and besides, when I think of preparing for the great journey – for where else could I go but the Land of Snows, where once, in my early life, I knew the peace and joy of non-possession, where the Monastery would take me in spite of the path my life has followed here in the lower lands, especially if I did not arrive empty-handed – when I open my eyes to the dangers I would face, to the chance that robbers would leave me destitute, to the difficulty of crossing the high mountain passes at my advanced age, I who have grown accustomed to the mild climate and the protection of the walls, then the courage and strength to take flight seep out of me. And I sensed I could no longer exist outside Chungking, the city where I had lived my life. If it went to ruin, I would have to go with it. And then I was filled with fresh hate for the gang of pale, uncivilised, malnourished foreigners who, without a shred of wisdom, their brains stuffed with nothing but figures and formulae, were bringing this fate down upon us.

***

And I realised that my doubts had faded, that I feared them, while the others were still curious – I, who despised them as nobody else did.

And I thought of you, Wan Chen. You are capable of more than I. Before it is too late, return one last time in your mortal life to the city where we were born and where I shall be buried, or if you can, ward off disaster from a distance. I could not do it on my own.

Consider this: the venerable Chungking, which you scorn for its corruption, may nonetheless have some value, some reason for existing. Maybe it attracts and captures powers that would otherwise cross the high passes, unstoppable as the thaw winds, to harm and soil the Land of Snows, the fortress of eternity. Do not imagine that the contagion comes only from the south, where the barbarians from the Ganges valley in Nepal and Bhutan have broken through.

Help to preserve Chungking, this outpost defending you from the dangers that lie beyond it. Though the foreigners seem ignorant and inconsequential, what guises would the evil demons *not* take to avoid suspicion on their way to the place they mean to destroy?

So help Chungking from afar, or from close by. Send the most powerful powers, or come and repel this danger yourself.

Chapter 11

When the captive foreigners were about to be brought before the Tuchun, the greatest care was taken to make sure they would see no sign of the intense interest and curiosity that their presence inspired. The people were threatened with severe punishment; in the streets through which the foreigners were led, no one was allowed to step outside, and even so, the captives were blindfolded and surrounded by a dense mob of guardsmen. The plan was to dumbfound them with the sudden sight of the Tuchun's hilltop abode in all its glory and the vast sweep of the city below. There, in front of the red and umber temples and the white palaces behind them, where otherwise only the traveling high lamas, the emissaries of the emperor, and the collectors of the annual tribute were received, their blindfolds would come off. They would feel like the insignificant worms they were.

Covered with sand and dust, exhausted from waiting by the city wall, unwashed and thirsty, they were led forward with both hands bound to a rope in front of them and quick-marched through the city, along a winding path up the steep hill that rose in the centre, with walls at five different levels. Then they had to climb the twelve tall steps to the terrace.

It was still empty. Behind a golden balustrade were three unoccupied thrones, shaded by pine trees and the pagodas behind them, which rose twenty-four storeys high. There the blindfolds were removed.

The shade did not reach beyond the balustrade. The foreigners stood in the fierce sun, which now hurled its fire at them from even nearer. From the white limestone tiles of the terrace, the light and heat splashed back up at them; they were overwhelmed for a moment but then lost all sense of time and place, swaying where they stood like shrivelled, burnt-out branches – then motionless, like dead wood.

Only All-But-One stood there at ease, taking a few occasional steps back and forth. His face expressed gratification, alternating with surprise. He seemed to be comparing the city to the image he had preserved so long in his memory and was happy whenever he saw something he recognised, something he hadn't forgotten in all those years, as if nothing had changed and the years of misery had suddenly withered – more than that, sloughed off completely, leaving him as he had been, ready to start his life afresh. He seemed unconcerned about being punished for defying his banishment, even though the statute of limitations had not quite expired. As he turned his bald head back and forth on his stiff neck, his eyes were searching eagerly. The others were given old straw hats to wear once the guards realised they might otherwise succumb to sunstroke before the Tuchun arrived.

***

Suddenly, two of the seats were occupied. The one in the middle remained empty, suggesting the presence of a higher, infallible power in Chungking. On the right sat the Tuchun, his large figure swathed in an amber yellow robe without a belt or ornaments other than braiding, wearing a crown like an upside-down cone, the tip of which would have reached his chin. His face looked white against the deeper yellow of the gold and silk.

Opposite him was a small elderly man trying to strike an impressive pose, which he couldn't pull off well in the large throne. But his suppressed wrath showed in his eyes, along with disgust and a hint of fear. He had a very dark dull-bronze complexion with bags under his bulging, jaundiced eyes. It was not hard to see which of the two hated foreigners the most, and which was likely to live longest.

Behind the Tuchun was a third man, in a close-fitting Western uniform with a broad belt that held a revolver. So a few firearms had already made their way to Chungking after all. Gazing serenely at the foreigners, as if they were odd, lifeless objects, he played no active role in the gathering.

All-But-One, who had so far been the best able to tolerate the glare of the sun, was the first to be summoned and interrogated, in a long interview. He was first ordered to explain how he, though born in the Middle Kingdom, had fallen into the company of barbarians.

He boasted of his great knowledge and complained that all his life his own people had failed to recognise his talents. He had eventually been left with no choice but to accept an offer from Hsiu, who found him in a third-rate inn in an outlying district of Taihai.

Why had Hsiu chosen him for the expedition? Not for his great strength, surely?

For his great understanding.

Of what? Surely not of the weapons?

No, of the terms used to describe them and of the areas around Chungking.

How had he become so well acquainted with them?

All-But-One said nothing, confused and anxious. Then he broke into a wail: he was an old man, he moaned, but as well acquainted with the classics as a graduate who had passed the final examination. He begged the Tuchun for some menial position, so that he could end his days in peace in Chungking.

The Tuchun and the priest exchanged a look.

'He can come and sweep the temple floor.'

'Aren't his joints too stiff for that? Make him an assistant schoolteacher.'

When All-But-One heard that, he began to feel better.

What an enviable fate it seemed to him: to end his days as a man of letters, after all, even one of the humblest sort. He produced papers from his sleeve: a worn passport and a collection of unpublished essays. The priest took only the passport, and All-But-One, disappointed, slid the essays back into his sleeve.

After the priest studied the passport at length, he presented it to the Tuchun for a brief glance and then handed it to the silent third man, who mumbled a few words and kept it.

Kia So said coolly, 'You fled Chungking to escape punishment for theft? That is why you are so familiar with the surroundings?'

'More than thirty years ago. The statute of limitations has long since expired.'

'You have lost count of the years. One might expect that of a coolie, but not of a scholar. It was twenty-nine years ago. The sentence remains in effect.'

All-But-One's face fell as he saw his fleeting hope of passing his years as an assistant teacher, working with books and children in a classroom of his own, slip away from him, replaced by the prospect of execution. He bewailed himself, crumpling to the ground, crying out that he knew the customs and habits of the barbarians and would tell all. The priest snarled that they had no need of him for that, but the Tuchun made a weary, dismissive gesture.

'Oh, let him be. It's not his fault that he fell in with these people. Give him to Cheng, he'll amuse himself with this fellow, and we can always see what to do with him afterwards, whether to make him an assistant teacher, a temple servant or a forced labourer.'

All-But-One mumbled a few words but without looking up. He seemed crushed by the misfortune that followed him everywhere. Drained of will, he was led away, as Kia So looked on in displeasure.

All-But-One's interrogation had gone on for a long time. Godunov had made one attempt to sneak away to a spot in the shade of one of the closest pine trees, but he had been dragged back. The heat of the sun was apparently a deliberate form of torture.

Then the herdsmen were brought forward. They remained standing as the man behind the seat exchanged inaudible words with them. Their voices were dull and gravelly; their strength, too, had been broken by the hardships, the hot sun, the degrading way they had been brought there. And as meek and helpless as All-But-One, like cattle, they were led away.

Godunov, Sylvain and Cameron remained now, forced against the balustrade together. To their tired eyes blinded by dust and blazing sun, the Tuchun looked enormous, like a looming catastrophe, as he sat with his knees spread wide under the heavy yellow robe, the tall crown on his large head. But fear crept over them at the sight of the small, wizened priest, now behind the Tuchun, pointing at a scroll. 'This says that one of you is capable of training warriors and handling the weapons. Which one?'

Godunov tried to saunter forward with a show of indifference, but failed: his knees shook, his arms swung too far back and forth, and his grin was too broad. When asked for his name, place of origin and occupation, he shrugged, dug in his pocket, and held out Hsiu's letter to the Tuchun, but Kia So snatched it; the exalted one could not take an object directly from a barbarian hand. The priest was about to read the letter aloud, but the Tuchun impatiently demanded it from him and read it at his own pace, folded it, and slipped it into his robes, and when the priest, burning with curiosity, asked what it said, replied only, 'Don't bother reading it. More of the usual vapid courtesies about his boundless love for his city of birth, and a list of all the weapons and parts, and under the heading of "further equipment", the person we see before us.'

Godunov straightened up for a moment, limped forward on his weakened legs, and asked, 'What's that? Doesn't Hsiu say that I'm in charge? He must have forgotten to mention it. I'm the only one who has the right, the only one who can possibly do it.'

And he pointed to the others as if to say, see for yourself the state they're in.

'Here in Chungking, we know nothing of commanders. There is only one question: can you turn coolies into soldiers, so that they can use the modern weapons unsupervised, in one year's time? If so, you may remain in Chungking, and once that year has passed, you may leave with your pay.'

Godunov laughed disdainfully.

'A year is a long time. I agreed with Hsiu that I would stay for six months and receive half the fee in advance.'

The Tuchun and the priest were silent. Encouraged, he continued: 'That's what it will take to get my brains working again. The locks of the rifles, the cogs of the machine guns, the contacts and circuits for the searchlight – we left them all behind, not far from Chungking, but I can't seem to recall quite where. I do know there was a lot of sand blowing about. If too much grit gets into the mechanisms – and it's bound to, eventually – then they'll be unfit for use.'

He had a pitying expression at first, which slowly transformed into his usual broad smirk. But no outburst followed. He looked up to savour the effect of his words. But the Tuchun was staring straight through him, as indifferent as ever, and the priest had a friendly smile on his rat-like face for the first time in the entire audience. The Tuchun, glancing over his shoulder, asked the Chinese general for his opinion.

'The exercises can start with theory. Sticks will do the job if there aren't enough rifles, and old Singer sewing machines can replace machine guns. I've heard that's what the German army has been doing recently, because of a shortage of weapons, and even so, they're still the best in the world.'

Were they really so indifferent to the success of the weapons? Godunov looked back and forth from one to the other in surprise but could see no threat or impatience.

As the general spoke, another man had joined the group, old, tall, thin and even skinnier than All-But-One. He wore an expensive silk robe that was much too wide, and awkward. Holding it shut with one hand, he tugged at his goatee with the other and examined Godunov.

'This foreigner will be your guest, Lao Yin. Don't bother trying to civilise him, it's no use. Just teach him how to eat.

'Lao Yin,' the Tuchun continued, 'has the finest kitchen in Chungking. His cooks can devise infinite variations on the exquisite recipes for which Chungking is known. Some of the dishes served there are beyond the wildest dreams of a barbarian like you. To be honest, I suspect you won't care for them.'

'Of course I will, of course!' Godunov declared with enthusiasm. 'I can live on water and bread for months if I have to, but I know how to appreciate a good meal. I was on the general staff in the war. We spent more time at the table than we did poring over our maps. What a joy to hear I'll be eating well again, with a good host to take care of me, and such important work to do besides. Those things are all I've wanted my whole life long. Sometimes I had one of them, sometimes another. And now, all of them at once. I know Chinese grub is the best on earth once you're used to it. My body is waking up again, my blood is flowing, my mouth is watering. My memory will come back soon too, no doubt. After a couple of good meals, I'm sure to recall where those weapons are buried.'

The Tuchun gestured impatiently. Two meaty hands on Godunov's shoulders staunched the flow of words, and the Russian allowed them to lead him away, not in triumph, but not in humiliation either. Lao Yin walked ahead, looking back often to make sure his guest was still behind him. At the edge of the terrace, Godunov shook off the guards and said farewell to the others still standing there with a broad, generous wave of his arm.

Now it was Sylvain's turn. He made a more battered impression than anyone else in the group. His bones seemed to have turned to jelly; for several days, he had gone without a pipe, living on a little powder that he had saved underneath his vest for dire emergencies.

Aside from that, he comported himself better than the men who had gone before. The mere fact that he remained standing showed that in some corner of his soul he possessed a reservoir of willpower, much like that small supply of opium he had hidden away. The Tuchun and the priest seemed particularly pleased with him, exchanging a look of approval. He was a more familiar type than any of the others. They knew plenty of people in his condition, going through life with pinprick pupils, knocking knees, a weak backbone and a bowed head, despising earthly things, yet still displaying a scrap of human dignity.

The great diseases, the great vices and the great flaws and deficiencies make the people of different races more equal to one another than centuries of missionary work, peaceful penetration or adoption of customs and folkways ever could.

The Tuchun and the cleric had other reasons to be pleased. They could see that this man was not in any great rush to assemble the weapons, any more than they were, and that they had the means to control his pace.

The Tuchun asked if he was Sylvain, ex-naval officer and

mechanical engineer, qualified to run an arsenal. Sylvain confirmed all this with a listless nod.

'Wouldn't you like a pipe or two before we continue this conversation?' the Tuchun asked abruptly. A shiver went through Sylvain's body. He stretched his limbs, looking as desperately eager as a half-drowned castaway who unexpectedly catches sight of the coastline. After a few muttered words to the general, who seemed reluctant, the Tuchun extended his arm and commanded him, 'Take him with you and give him what he can no longer do without.' The general bowed and offered his arm to Sylvain, who stumbled solemnly away with him.

Cameron – the last of the foreigners who had imagined themselves the leaders of the convoy – stood before the ruler of Chungking alone and solitary on the terrace, a confrontation between the spotless blue sky above and the spotless limestone below. They regarded each other. How easy the others had been to recognise, before they had even spoken a word. A scholar gone to seed, a boozy Russian officer, two brainless, warlike nomads and an opium-smoking naval officer, like so many others expelled by way of Toulon to the Far East.

But this one was strange, blank, an everyman, and indefinable as twilight.

He too was having a hard time staying on his feet, he too looked pale, but his attitude was perfectly nonchalant, except that he shivered now and then as if struck by an invisible lightning bolt, and now and then a flush coloured his pale face for a few seconds.

The Tuchun beckoned him closer, closer still, until Cameron was right next to him, as far from the Tuchun as from Kia So, forming an equilateral triangle with the two of them.

Silence, all the wider and deeper for the sunlight shining from above; the tumult of the city around them, down below.

Then the priest broke into a torrent of words, curses and

incantations, while the Tuchun remained quiet, smiling now and then. This seemed to infuriate the priest, who rose from his seat and called out to the guards, but the Tuchun ordered him to return and uttered a few curt words of command. The priest became smaller, seeming to shrink from one moment to the next, and finally crept away, a puny, broken figure. At the edge of the terrace he straightened himself, looked back menacingly and departed with a final curse.

The Tuchun, facing forward with a smile, lifted the heavy flat-topped crown from his head and placed it on the empty throne beside him. He looked youthful now, despite his shaven skull and the fleshy bulk of his face – above all, his eyes looked large and animated, hardly slanting, nestled deep in their sockets under heavy eyebrows. He slid from his throne like a child from a high chair and shook his robe into place.

The thrones were still behind them, but the agonising ceremony seemed to have taken place an eternity ago, in a different century, or perhaps it was merely an episode from the annals. After a gesture that swept away the thrones and the palace hill – the whole threatening, unknown city of Chungking – the Tuchun simply reached out his hand.

Cameron felt his self-confidence drain away. All Sylvain wanted was a large supply of opium, Godunov the semblance of authority – though the promise of gourmet meals was good enough – and All-But-One would be contented with a humble position. His desires and dreams for the future shifted like mirages, promising everything then nothing, combining, almost in one instant, wonderlands bathed in pure light and barren plains in a false light filtered through low mist, where clouds drifted past with a sneer of contempt for the paradise that had led its illusory life below. 'Kia So claims you will bring greater calamity to Chungking than all the other barbarians put together. Is that true?'

Cameron stammered a denial, saying he had but one wish: to be allowed to live in Chungking, in peace and out of sight.

'What Kia So calls calamity is, above all, whatever may be harmful to his temple, leading to fewer offerings to the gods worshipped there. The war god is only one of them. He is quite right to think that modern weapons will impress the people more than the war god's terrible appearance and the noise they make during the prayers. And what sort of calamity could you bring that would be more harmful to the temple than modern weapons? Let's go over there, it's cooler in the shade.'

Under the pine trees in front of the row of temples was a light awning under which a pair of rattan benches faced each other. As they approached, bowls were placed on the table and tea was served.

For the first time, it became clear to Cameron that it was not enough to go further than other mortals. The most difficult thing was to *be* there, to remain and make a life there. In the dim interior of one temple he saw, like a fish in murky water, the old yellow priest, his malevolent features caught in a ray of light as the wind blew aside the branches. Then he was plunged back into darkness. The Tuchun shrugged off his robes of state and stood like an ordinary Chinese nobleman, in a long silk gown with a short black silk waistcoat over it.

But his nearness became more threatening still when it became clear he wanted Cameron to do something for him.

'All the others have boasted of their skills, and Hsiu wrote to us about them. What drove you to journey to our city?'

'I wanted to see all of China, bid farewell to the sea forever, avoid encounters with spirits and leave my old occupation behind.'

'What occupation was that?'

'It's impossible to understand without technical training.'

The Tuchun smiled.

'Can't you impart that higher wisdom to me?'

'It's hard to explain. Once, I sailed a ship along the coasts of China and operated a device that made it possible to hear the voices of other ships, to transmit my own ship's voice over great distances, and to receive warnings of approaching typhoons from stations on land.'

The Tuchun nodded.

'It is not so impossible for me to understand. I have read of such things, but I thought they were fables. If you can build such a device here, then I will be more grateful to you than to all the other foreigners, and let you stay here if you wish. I have always wanted to learn more about Western science, but my office, along with a certain distaste, has always kept me from going there. I could not undertake such a trip without sacrificing my dignity.'

This was Cameron's chance. Yet he hesitated.

'It may be possible to build the device. But what you would learn about Western science and wisdom would greatly disappoint you. You will not like opera or music, propaganda speeches will offend your ears, sermons will bore you. The voices of science cannot be heard with this device. Most European countries are driving out whatever great minds remain to us. It is seen as contrary to the national interest for a handful of individuals to have original, forward-looking thoughts that the masses cannot comprehend. In the national interest, the human masses must remain equal, all thinking the same thoughts if they must think at all. The people with new ideas – even about mathematics and physics, subjects that have nothing to do with statecraft – are not tolerated. There used to be a few countries where they could live; now wherever they go, they are chased away.'

The Tuchun did not answer. He seemed utterly indifferent to affairs in the West; even the fate of the persecuted scholars left him unmoved, since he knew that wiser men had been subjected to greater indignities in China, forced into lifelong exile or hounded from kingdom to kingdom, without ever complaining. All he wanted was to possess the device, as a curiosity. He was bemused to hear that this man, who judging by his appearance and career had long ago transcended earthly cares – or at least was well on the way – could still trouble himself at all over the bad taste and illusory wisdom of the West, which had no real existence here! And this man behaved like all Westerners, as strange and frightened as a trapped animal at first, and then – as soon as he was released and asked to demonstrate his abilities – as if he were a master, indispensable. The Tuchun frowned impatiently.

'I would like to have such a device. But never mind if it's too much trouble. You will be treated well, as well as the others – better, in fact – as long as you stay out of the whole armament affair.'

Cameron lifted his hand.

'I will build the device, if you grant me the freedom to search for the components I need. The unwelcome voices can be fended off and filtered out. Then perhaps, in good time, the enlightened spirits will use that instrument to announce their will and law.'

The Tuchun shook off his listless, guarded attitude.

'Where would you find such components?'

'Here in Chungking – I can start with a few parts from the weapons – and in the countryside around the city. I need freedom of movement, and the services of a few diggers.'

'And can you make it in the east wing of my house?'

'No. I must be at complete liberty to find the spot where the device can operate.'

This final demand dispelled the Tuchun's last shred of doubt. When building a house or tomb, an auspicious location was essential. If the device for receiving and listening to distant voices had similar requirements, then it was not a mere product of artifice, but had at least some slight connection to the eternal, unchanging laws.

'Can it truly capture the voices of the spirits?' he asked. 'And what else do you need for your work?'

Evening had come, the sun was passing behind the western wall, and in front of the wall lay Chungking. Long shadows were climbing the hill, and between them the colours of the city shaded into all the tones from brown to grey. A few temple roofs remained red; rooftop terraces lay like glaring white squares above the windows, which were black holes in the walls. In the centre were the tall, geometrical buildings amid their gardens; around them, the houses fanning out, lower and lower; the huts in the fields beside the city walls; the river winding through the city, invisible save for the gleams of sunset on its surface, its bend skirting the north wall. Darkness fell suddenly, the shadows united, lights winked into view, not many. Cameron gestured at the scene below.

'All I ask is permission to come and go as I please, throughout the city, without being shut up or shut out as a foreigner. I have no use for a name anymore; I want no more recognition than a coolie. And to spend the rest of my life here.'

The Tuchun had new appreciation in his eyes. This was close to what a sage might desire! He had expected a request for money or position.

'Your wish, humble as it sounds, may not be within my power to grant. There is a man in Chungking who was born here and is a foreigner by ancestry alone. His forefather settled here, I don't know how many generations ago, after a murderous vendetta with his own race. Though he and his lineage gave up every tie to their homeland, they have never been accepted here. And the last one remaining has isolated himself completely. After three years in the West, he returned loaded down with knowledge and driven by the desire to make himself useful to his city's people. But he had grown too distant from this place and can no longer bridge the gap. He is still summoned to attend to the sick when all other measures have failed, but that doesn't earn him any gratitude. Many people have tried to be thankful, to offer their friendship – impossible. He is a different creature from us.

'But I don't mean to discourage you. I will send you to live with him, in the beginning. Maybe you will discover why he cannot live in Chungking, and use that knowledge to your advantage. But I'll tell you this beforehand: if you don't give up everything that ties you to your past, it will never work. Even the memory of the past must vanish.'

'I don't know what sort of past you expect me to have. I have no roots or blood relations, and I haven't seen my country in many years.'

The Tuchun looked at him in pity. If this man spoke the truth, how adrift and abandoned he was. For himself, having ancestors and descendants was the essence of life, one's own life a secondary thing. How could a person live in that way? Now, once again, he regarded Cameron as a foreign creature, hardly of this earth, and yet he looked ordinary, too ordinary, pale, blank. Could he be a ghost returned from the underworld? Is that what Kia So had meant when he said this foreigner was more dangerous than all the others put together? As if to persuade himself the man really existed, he extended his hand again as Westerners do and felt the firm pressure of the handshake.

Cameron had grasped the benefits of agreeing to build the radio set. When the Tuchun heard the many conflicting and confused claims about politics and religion, it would confirm his opinion that the Europeans were creatures with a knack for building machines but otherwise inferior in spirit: quarrelsome, inclined to muddy the truth and so arrogant that they tried to take over the work of nature. He would be glad of the opportunity to form such a thorough impression for himself, and the Westerners' shrill, aggressive self-promotion would ensure that Chungking remained closed to them. Then there would be no chance that anyone of Cameron's own race would find him there.

His search for components would give him the freedom of movement he longed for, which the others would have to do without. He could wander freely in and around Chungking, and that deep, intense communion with the earth would make up for what he still experienced as a lack of human contact.

And yet ... hadn't he found some hint of that in his conversation with the Tuchun, who seemed well-intentioned towards him? The man showed signs of inner feelings like derision, joy and curiosity, which the other Chinese did not possess, or kept hidden.

Would he be able to track down all the components he needed? He was thinking it through when the Tuchun asked, 'Are you certain you can build the device?'

He suppressed his doubt. If he was, or seemed, uncertain of himself, this victory would be snatched away from him.

'I can do it, if you give me time and freedom of movement.'

'Not straight away. For the time being, there can be no difference between you and the other captives. After you have spent a month within the walls of Velho's house, you may begin your search. When will the device be ready to receive the voices?'

Again Cameron hesitated, and again the importance of seeming confident forced him to answer. 'A month later.'

The Tuchun rose to his feet.

'Whether you will be granted your wish to stay in

Chungking – or rather, to vanish into it – is not up to me. It will depend on you, and whether you are truly as free of your past as you believe. Are you willing to take a Chinese wife?'

This time Cameron could not conceal his inner hesitation. He was silent a moment, and then said, 'If I meet the right woman.'

'Your answer shows you are not serious. There are no right or wrong women. They are all the same. In the West they have been festooned with virtues and vices not truly theirs. We dress them all the same at weddings, in colourful garments and plenty of jewellery. After the wedding we take it all away again. They dress up only on special occasions. For the rest of their lives they are all the same. We don't practice wife-swapping, but we might just as well. Then again, what would be the point, since they're all the same?'

Cameron replied that he had no wish for descendants and hoped that his line would die with him. The Tuchun stared at him in astonishment.

'A man with no wish for progeny? Then you'd be better off in a monastery with the lamas than settling here in Chungking.'

'I don't want to be alone with myself.'

'So take a wife and father children. And ... pay attention to what sort of life Velho leads. He is truly the last of his line, which he is evidently incapable of extending. See how he bears up.' He took Cameron by the shoulder. 'I think you'll change your mind about this. You are famished and exhausted now. But there's still energy in you, I'm sure of it. Otherwise you would never have made the long trek to Chungking.'

Cameron's eyes widened. What the Tuchun said was true. Didn't the walk prove his point? And the voyage to Taihai? But at that moment, he could scarcely believe it. His ears started to ring, the scene before him flickered, and his head crashed down to the table. The Tuchun, leaning over him, could hear him muttering in a daze, 'Who was that man in the middle?'

His eyes widened in surprise. So the Westerner could see more than he could; the Tuchun had known that the man had been there but had not been able to see him. Kia So had been so worried about the foreigners' arrival that he had convinced Wan Chen to attend the audience invisibly. Kia So had claimed to have seen him there, but the Tuchun had had his doubts, knowing the priest liked to persuade the gullible that he was in contact with higher, secret powers. But it was clear now that the foreigner had seen Wan Chen too, even if he had no conscious memory of it.

The Tuchun tapped Cameron on the shoulder. He was completely motionless, resting against the table like a block of wood. The Tuchun called for a litter and had the carriers put the heavy load inside it. The foreigner seemed lifeless, but when they picked up their poles he awoke with a yelp and nearly tipped the litter over.

'Would you rather walk? It's far away, first downhill and then a long way up.'

'No, no! I thought I was in a sloop and they were rowing me back on board. I'm glad I was wrong. But this is too good for me. I can go on foot.'

'If you wish to remain in Chungking, you must learn to accept both hardship and luxury with the same equanimity. I will summon you in a few days.'

He gave a sign, and the carriers took the litter on their shoulders. Cameron felt a weight lifting, as if a long period of suffering, forbearance, and desperation had ended. He stared eagerly from side to side, drinking in his first impressions of Chungking – the first any Westerner had seen of the city for centuries. After the ramparts, watchtowers, walls and rooftops, he was at last inside the city, in its streets. How much longer before he saw the interiors of the cells, the rooms, the houses? They were moving fast, the lantern-bearer leading the way and the litter-carriers hurrying after. It was then that he first saw the people of Chungking, working through the night. All around him were bare torsos glistening with sweat, blue rolled-up trousers, faces glancing up for an instant, a few grinning at the sight of the foreigner but most so cramped with fatigue and tedium that no twitch of expression remained for amazement or horror. In the outdoor workplaces or behind wooden grates, in the glow of oil-soaked wicks in iron bowls, they slipped in and out of his attention like an army of equals, of forced labourers by night. What did strike him were the changing sounds and smells from one street to the next, from the clang of hammers on iron to the panting and groaning of workers sawing wood; from the whirr of a weaving-mill to the virtual silence of ivory-cutters polishing; from the foul odour of the slaughterhouse to the sour stench of the tanneries and the fug of the fur workshops. Sometimes they transformed as quickly as the change in pitch when a whistling locomotive drives past. They were bewildering, these rapid transitions, after months of the constant smell of space and silence on the plains of water and sand.

Just once, the trip was interrupted. The litter made a sudden turn into a street where the air was filled with sweet perfume, trilling strings and sobbing flutes. Yet even there, hard work was being done, all the more so because it was night.

Still, a few women who had no customers with them and were standing outside under their lanterns, their coats pulled tight, each wearing a flower in her straight, black, shiny hair, surrounded the litter with loud squeals, and a few of them tried to lift the foreigner out. Others, however, ran back into the houses, distraught and shrieking.

After that, the streets became narrower, darker and more deserted. They no longer encountered any passers-by. The only obstacles were posts that had fallen on their sides, piles of coal and metal slag, and rubbish heaps in which a carrier sometimes got stuck. The few labourers – a tailor, a weaver – sat in the gloom working almost by touch.

Suddenly Cameron realised he hadn't been looking around for materials, had given himself over entirely to his attention. And now the litter was passing between walls like sheer cliffs. Now and then he glimpsed a house high above; down at street level, there was no sign of habitation. The litter scraped along the stones projecting from the walls on either side and, after a steep climb, was set down. The lamp-bearer squeezed through an opening, and the carriers forced Cameron to do the same. The lanterns illuminated a snarl of split tree trunks and old broad-leafed trees, the surviving branches growing through the holes in the dead ones. A kind of path led through it, but his guide didn't seem very familiar with it. They kept stepping and groping in the wrong direction. When the lantern was raised, it was as if an army of ghosts, who had stood veiled in the shadows around them, shrank back. Suddenly the light revealed a gate. They had arrived.

It was unlike any other gate in Chungking. No dragons or lions guarded the way through. Two columns, wound with braided cables of stone, held up a pointed arch. Cameron flinched back and tried to twist free. The two carriers grabbed him, the lantern-bearer brought down the knocker, the door opened: on the other side was another man with a lantern – two carriers – a push. Cameron stumbled over the threshold, where the waiting group took charge of him, and the door fell shut again. The carriers outside lingered there for a while, half-expecting the door to open again and the foreigner to be tossed out, beheaded or stabbed in the heart.

But nothing happened. The wind moved the trees inside the wall back and forth, and when the moon broke through the clouds and cast shadows across the forecourt, they hurried off. After all, if he *had* been killed in there, his spirit could use the branches and the shadows to pursue them. He knew how they looked and how they walked. After making a few loops and zigzags through the trees, they felt reassured and moved on together through the slums of Chungking. Even in the craftsmen's workshops the lights were out now – even in the red light district. Only a few lamps still burned, beside smokers or the dying.

The city lay under the night as if under a thick stuffed quilt, on its ancient ground, below which the earth's age-old fire glowed at a safe depth, as if on an enormous kang, large enough and warm enough to support all the thousands of families and millions of dead within the walls. Even so, they huddled together or lay in narrow graves, always – in life and after, by night and by day – cherishing their fear of open spaces, despising and devouring one another yet seeking each other out time after time, like atoms driven by mutual attraction and repulsion.

What could disturb Chungking's ongoing existence? What could bring about its downfall? Only the downfall of the earth itself.

Chapter 12

I saw only the peaked roofs of a few houses, the lintel of a gate arched towards the sky, the tops of a few pagodas like pinecones against a green-and-black mountainside, and then, in the unreachable heights, no longer part of it all – and how distant from me, since I could barely make out any of this – a serene white mountaintop, sometimes moon-bathed, sometimes covered with clouds, sometimes shining with light of its own. Staring at it, I forgot that while craning to look out over the bottom edge of the high window, I was standing on a hard, narrow kang; the best way to forget myself and the threats I faced was not to lie down on it but to stare at that distant white peak. Then it was as though I drifted in cool mountain air, while the demons jumped up and down far below in impotent rage.

But the moment came when my body couldn't bear to stand outstretched any longer, and I collapsed, lay down on my side, and tried to think back to my conversation with the Tuchun and the task before me. Yet my thoughts kept returning to what I had seen. I could not drive it away. It began at the gate, the columns twisted as if cables had been wound around them, the anchors above that reminded me of the sea.

Then the garden. The tangled shrubs, two or three thick plane trees with wedge-shaped, many-sided roots, the ruined well, the garden house with weather-stained windows on the left, the headless, armless idol on the right, and the house beyond them.

It looked so much like what once, when I plied the coasts, had been my only point of contact with Chinese soil. Had I crossed half of China to reach what I used to reach in ten minutes of rowing and five of walking? It was like a gruesome joke, blown out of all proportion.

Who was I, what was I, that such things could happen to me? No, it was impossible, a fantasy, a superficial resemblance. If I'd had the chance to look around longer, I might have discovered differences. But I was marched straight into the house, at which I'd gazed in fascination so many times before, down corridors, across spacious halls, up and down staircases, yet another corridor, and then ... this room. Trapped here, how could I ever build the radio?

No more thinking. Couldn't a head, like a boiler under too much pressure from the steam inside it, burst with dammed-up thoughts? Has it ever happened? If an exploding boiler can destroy a city, couldn't that greater explosion destroy a world?

No more thinking!

I was well-rested again and could stand, staring at the distant mountain top. As long as I could do that, I had nothing to dread. This time I stayed on tiptoe for a long while.

The moon dimmed, the clouds drifted away, doubtless blown by a waking morning wind out there, and below the summit I now saw a soft red zone. Was it the red of dawn, or a red lake? If I could live there, on that white peak on the shores of that lake, I would be safe and have no need to go anywhere else. So it seemed to me now. But didn't I always have second thoughts about everything? Out at sea I saw life on land as superior, after going ashore I sought fulfilment in a long journey, and along the way I imagined I could be happy and free by immersing myself in an unspoilt Chinese city; no sooner had I arrived than I was glued to the window, gazing out at an unreachable summit.

Then again, had I chosen this place? The others were sent to stay with priests and mandarins. And where was I? Back in my own past? Or was there more to come? I had reached my limit, my muscles were starting to cramp, my hands going numb. I had to let go. I held the stretch. It made me dizzy, as if the mountain top were floating free, drifting closer.

Then, just then, I slid back down and saw a jug that had not been there. The door was half-open.

I had a drink of water and went through the doorway. The corridor lay at my feet, its tiles cracked but sturdy. Was this house a city? There was no end to it; I passed through corridors, up and down stairs. Were the passageways alleys, the great halls squares? But then I found myself in another room. Slowly adjusting to the drab half-light, I saw a multitude of objects around me; the fug of books hung in the air; I felt my way along curved objects, figurines, the framed pictures and curled cards that lined the walls. Books, sculptures, paintings, tapestries combined to evoke a long-lost age. This room had to be the cherished retreat of the Velho who could not live in Chungking. But where was he? How long had I been in his house without seeing him?

I was seized with anger at my host, who had confronted me with my past without even deigning to show his face. I pulled a painting off the wall and brought it down on a sculpture, again and again, until I held an empty frame. Then I kicked over the statue. A nymph was near it. I crushed them together into a pile of rubble, it was easy, they were both hollow, plaster casts. Then I sat on the floor in a corner, dropping the shards through the empty frame for a while. A man came in. I was startled, even though I knew the noise had drawn him there. He was portly, concealing his large, slow form in a loose robe. His face was puffy and pale; his voice was worn out and noiseless and seemed to come from far away. There was no way he could have hurt me, more likely the reverse. He too belonged to the past that kept trying to grab hold and strangle me, the great, oppressive past that had begun with such tremendous courage and cruelty and decayed into slow nostalgia and apathetic grief, like silted streams by deserted coasts, collapsed castles on decaying ships that had once changed the course of the country's history. He lived here, where even the past had died, had become an ornament. His voice remained flat as he took me to task for destroying his treasures and abusing his hospitality. He told me he could have me put to death if he reported it to the Tuchun.

'Do it. My life is safe for the time being. I've talked to the Tuchun myself. And I don't care what happens later. But what is all this doing here?' I asked, with a sweep of my arm.

He replied in the same flat tone, 'I cannot live in this city without all this around me. I am officially recognised as a citizen and dignitary, yet I remain a foreigner and need this to keep myself from wasting away into nothingness. In a place where everyone has ancestors, you cannot do without them. My earliest forefather in this country was a barbarian and a pioneer, who lived only for riches and whose only concern was to make trouble for his countrymen, who had cast him out, and to excite their envy. His descendants felt a new sense of ancestral identity; they added architecture to this house that reminded them of the old country, and collected relics, more and more. My feelings for my country of origin run deepest of all, for I have no son. Everything returns to its origin. You'll see.'

I shook my head mockingly. 'Not me. I don't know who my ancestors were and can't even find the exact place I came from on a map.'

His nod was full of pity and superior wisdom. 'And now you're looking for other people to take you in, and a city where you can live. Well ... don't settle here in Chungking ...'

'Why not?'

'If I wasn't able to live here, with all my ancestors, how could you succeed? You are left with no choice but this: to pay homage with me to a past that was great, too great to go on existing.'

'That past is worth nothing at all.'

'Nothing at all? The cruel vandalism you committed tonight proves that it does mean something.'

'I want to leave this place. It stifles me, like bad air.'

'Then I shall have you escorted back to your room.'

It was hazy and cloudy that day, and I couldn't see the mountains. In any case, I hardly had the strength left to pull myself up to the window. Along with the food and the jug, a stack of books and engravings were brought to me. I ignored them, of course. But I did think – too much – about what had happened.

That night, which began in fear, may have brought me further than my entire journey through the Chinese realm. And ... shouldn't I be grateful to Velho, since my final collision with the past had taken place in his home, even if he had intended no such thing? I resolved – out of gratitude or wilfulness – to liberate him too, but to proceed carefully. I knew from experience how attached people are to their chains, their dungeon, their tormentors. I meant to spend the whole time planning my escape, but before I knew it I was engrossed in the books.

When a few days later he came and asked me to join him in his gallery, I was happy to oblige. My room was cramped, and though the weather had improved, I had stopped looking out at the mountain top. I lacked the courage, or the passion, or was I ashamed? My feelings were tangled up again, but even though Velho went to great pains to win me over to his cult with stories and prints, I had no interest. At first I put up with it, then I asked him for books and maps of the country where we really were. He refused. I remained in my cell. Then he handed them over, on the condition that I spend a couple of hours every evening in his gallery of the past. I did so, but with greater reluctance each day, and in my resentment, decided to conquer his private kingdom later, by identifying his gallery as the only suitable place to set up the wireless receiver.

There were times when I had second thoughts about my plan. He was so easily pleased; just spending an evening listening to his stories was enough to delight him. But sometimes his obsession with the past would take abrupt hold of him: he would stare at me with a strange, rigid, ecstatic look in his eyes and slide his chair closer to mine. Then I would stand up at once, and he would meekly bring me back to my room, which I still couldn't find on my own.

The month of isolation ordained for the foreigners was not yet near its end when a message arrived from the Tuchun, summoning me. On the way there, I fretted about how I would accomplish my task. I was nowhere near certain I could find all the components I needed. I could only hope – above all, for the parts we had buried outside the city. Were they still there, or had Godunov succumbed to pressure or overfeeding? The Tuchun greeted me stiffly and went straight to the heart of the matter, without preliminaries. He confessed that he was eager to see the device in operation and had released me early for that reason – since in fact I no longer had anything to do with the armament question.

'If you have promised me too much, now is the time to say so. If you accept this task now, then you must complete it, and guarantee the results with your life. Otherwise you are welcome to spend the rest of your days in Velho's house. Apparently he enjoys your company. He's asked that you be kept there as a favour to him.'

Although the idea of being discharged from my uncertain mission came as a huge relief, the prospect of being at Velho's mercy, forced to pay tribute with him to a past I despised, led me to promise the nearly impossible once again.

The Tuchun looked at me, and his look told me that I must have changed somehow since I had overcome the past. Or was it simply the rest and recuperation that had done me good? I was looking forward to seeing myself, but Velho did not have a single mirror; he seemed frightened of encountering himself.

'Starting tomorrow, you can go wherever you wish in the city and within a radius of twenty *li*. I hope you will not keep me waiting for long.'

Velho welcomed me back with a hopeful look, but when he heard I'd been granted my liberty, he couldn't hide his disappointment. From that moment on, I was determined to show him no mercy, to use his gallery to bring my plan to fruition.

So I was set free, after many days in two narrow rooms connected by corridors, and one morning I stood at a bend in the river, Chungking on the plain below, the mountain I'd gazed up at now standing tall among lower chains on the horizon. Neither one made a great impression on me: the mountain no longer looked unreachable, and Chungking didn't seem so uninhabitable. But neither was it any longer the sole remaining spot for me to live out my days. It was more like my only company in an otherwise empty cosmos, the only city along this river, the rest of which ran through sandy plains, growing ever shallower. To be honest, I now knew once and for all that I could not live among people, but I could live alone on earth.

The mountain and the city in the distance, and nearby, the fields or rice paddies, which were inundated, each stalk and ear precisely mirrored in the clear grey shallows. The peasants, working or wading through the flooded fields, never looked up; in their blue work suits under wide straw hats, they looked more like swamp plants or fungi than like human beings.

The guards who followed me did not disturb me, but kept their distance. Now and then I would pick up a stone, which they would carefully place in a basket. Sometimes I even found something I could actually use, but for the first few days, I didn't trouble myself about it. Then I started to think carefully about everything I was missing. I had to find my former travelling companions; by now there was probably an artillery workshop.

In the old days when, lacking self-confidence, I had sailed on ships and wandered around Taihai, I would no doubt have offered my head to the executioner. Now I waited for some chance event to lead me onto the right path.

I went on roaming the area, enjoying my solitude. Now and then I drove a stick into the ground to serve as a divining rod. In the evening, when I was brought back to Velho's house – sometimes allowed to return to my cell at once after feigning exhaustion, and sometimes forced to sit through a conversation in his gallery – I longed to stay out after dark, in one of those inns where the smoke from the day's cooking hangs in the night air, where the cattle sleep in the courtyard and the guests use bedding they brought with them or lie on the hard wooden floor. But even though the guards allowed me ever greater liberties, they still surrounded me each day at dusk and led me back to the city.

In the city itself, however, I could circulate freely, since everyone knew by now I was the foreigner searching for magical stones in the earth for the Tuchun. I could go wherever I pleased. My escort often lagged behind, as if by chance, to explain to inquisitive people what I was up to. Our paths would meet again later, and over time we reached a tacit agreement that they would pick me up at the end of the day in a market square that was always easy to find, because crowds of people from every corner of the city would make their way there every evening to buy and sell, visit healers and fortune-tellers, swap stories, and amuse themselves in other ways. The beating of the gongs and blowing of the whistles made a ruckus heard far and wide, so I always knew which way to go.

I planned to use this freedom of movement in the city to track down one of my former companions, but I had no idea where to begin. For the first time, I felt the stirrings of desire for a woman, and I received plenty of invitations whenever I passed through the streets of hospitality, but none that appealed to me. I think it was mainly my long hours of sitting with Velho, the heavy meals and conversations, that had roused my desire, rather than any deeper feelings. In truth, the freedom to pass my time wherever I wished in a wide radius around Chungking was more than enough for me.

So time passed and I made no progress. Unfulfilled urges weighed me down, and in the end I could no longer enjoy my wanderings through the quiet rice fields outside Chungking with the mountains in the distance, my unseen passage through the cedar and thuja forests, the fields of sorghum, giant maize and bamboo, where there was no view, where I could see neither the mountains nor the city and liked to imagine I was lost.

Chapter 13

One day I found not my usual escort waiting at the door, but a horse and a small cart. I took this as a sign that I needed to hurry. That evening Velho told me he'd been invited to the autumn festival. The Tuchun was inviting many friends, he said, and planned to treat them to a special attraction.

The look on my face must have betrayed my fear. Velho knew nothing of my situation, but even so, he offered to go to the Tuchun, tell him I was ill, and keep me in his home from then on. But I turned down this tempting offer, and the next day I enjoyed another ride – all the more, in fact, since I knew that without a radio receiver, I would be put to death at the autumn festival to provide the Tuchun's guests with at least some entertainment.

I found myself in a part of Chungking that I'd never visited before. The streets were broad and empty, flanked with rows of heavy old trees, both palms and deciduous varieties in full summer bloom. The houses on either side seemed ancient, weathered and grey. This part of Chungking must have been built when the climate was different and water more abundant. Was I still truly in Chungking? On that dim, humid day, I felt I was riding through a vast greenhouse. Aside from a few textile merchants, who coat the earth like flies and beetles, I did not encounter a single person. Invisible drizzle gave way to heavy rain. It was as if I was no longer riding through Chungking but through some major city in the Indies, somewhere in the wide, wet, flourishing Ganges valley, a city deserted by all its people, who had gone down to the distant riverbanks to immerse themselves. The city had been abandoned to its fate, to the whims of the earth and the water and whoever unexpectedly stumbled upon it.

The horse stopped. I thought it wanted a drink, but a snake was crawling straight across the road, contracting and stretching its long form in slow pulses. In front of the horses' hooves, it lay still. No sooner had I leapt out of the cart to drive it away than it slithered to the side of the road and the horse galloped off. I made no attempt to run after it. The snake crept into a garden; I followed. What if someone was napping on a terrace or veranda, unprotected ... but that wasn't why I followed.

Suddenly I heard faint, distant music, a flute and something like a gamelan, luring the snake from afar. It glided through flowerbeds and foliage, faster and faster; it was hard to keep up now. In front of a raised walkway, it stopped, rolled itself up, and raised its head out of the coils. It lay there like a hawser on a foredeck, so lifeless yet so powerful.

When I came out of the bushes after it, two slender young women – or were they children? – scurried off, and another woman propped herself up on her elbows; over the railing, all I could see were her head, hand and forearm.

'There's a snake on the prowl here. Hand me a stick.'

She flashed me a smile and wriggled closer to the edge, the sharp point of her tongue sticking out between half-open lips.

'They're as harmless as we are. If you leave them alone, they're no danger to anyone.'

'Even this one?'

'I recognise this one. She comes for the music. When it stops, she goes away. See for yourself.'

And the big snake really was slowly slithering away, as if it had no reason to stay now that the instruments had stopped.

'Come closer.'

I went up the low stairs and took a seat beside the daybed. The rain had stopped, but thick clouds made the afternoon even darker, and behind the arabesque folding screens, the light was dim and patchy. Even so, I recognised her, though she bore little resemblance to the scruffy Fong Shen I had known. Her robe was embroidered with flowers and herons, rows of bracelets encircled her now-pale arms, her eyebrows were thin arches, and the blemish on her cheek was gone; never before had I seen her in this guise. She had borne all the hardships and squalor of the journey with stubborn indifference, doing just as she pleased, spending her time with the people she liked best, or the ones likely to do the most for her. She had apparently remained true to that principle, but otherwise changed completely. She was the first of my old companions I rediscovered in Chungking. Did she know more about the others than I did? I thought back to a night in Taihai; then too, after a period of adversity, expulsion and complete solitude, I had unexpectedly stumbled into the luxury of a different sort of life – side by side with all those lives on the brink of hunger, despair and death – where teasing conversation in a languorous, oversaturated atmosphere had paved the way to a strange reality.

We did not speak of the journey there, or of the others, but only about her life in that place. The once indifferent Fong Shen seemed proud of her newfound prosperity. Was that her true feeling, or just an act? Besides the jewels she wore, she showed me many others, and told me the Tuchun visited her from time to time. That interested me more, of course, than all those fine things made by human hands from jade and gemstones. But I didn't press for answers. The sun was setting; the weather grew colder but clammier. Now and then a gust of wind ruffled the limp leaves, and at some point the sun sank beneath the low clouds, shining sideways through the leaves. She looked tired and disappointed. Was Chungking too backward and insignificant for her after all? Did she dream of the imperial palaces and gardens, or of Taihai's Bund and Palace Hotel?

In her case, both were possible. What other creature could so easily accept the extremes of the two lives between which the earth is more and more divided?

I don't know what we talked about, for a long time. She seemed not the least bit curious about the life I led there, so I couldn't expect her to volunteer information about the others either. I would have to ask.

'The others? Godunov sometimes comes in secret.'

'Can I meet him here?'

'I don't think so; it's too dangerous. He only comes at night, when you're both under guard.'

'What's he up to these days?'

'Oh, he's doing very well. He's started training cadets. They've established an elite corps of young men from distinguished families – all very hush hush. They train in a courtyard with high walls. He drills them and teaches them to read maps. It must be terribly amusing. Sometimes he's still chuckling when he gets here.'

'Can you find out where Sylvain is too?'

'He still sees Cheng every evening, and sleeps there, but his host is no longer so impressed with him. He's practically stopped eating. Sylvain is entertaining enough at first, with his slow, grumpy ways, but he soon becomes tiresome. Well, what doesn't?' She sighed and stretched. 'I believe they've cut his opium rations too. During the day, he works in a big old broken-down building they call the arsenal. If you need something from him, you should visit him there and bring opium. But if I were you, I'd give up this whole fool's errand; if you fail, they'll have your head.' Evidently the Tuchun had told her everything.

'I can't put it off any longer; I've promised too much. I have to speak to Sylvain. But where will I find opium? That's the only reason Sylvain would ever do anything for me.'

She clapped her hands, and one of the girls who had slunk

away when I arrived came over to us. Fong Shen whispered something, and the girl left, returning with a couple of tins.

'That's all I have now. But come back in a few days, in the afternoon. Then I'm always alone. But now it's time for you to leave. Visitors will be arriving soon, and the streets are filling up with carriages again.'

I hurried back through the garden and found my horse and cart in almost the same place I'd lost them. I clutched the tins tight; maybe they would lead to a solution. Velho was in a dreamy mood that evening, and each of us sat sunk in our own musings at the dining table, the books, engravings and sculptures seeming to absorb all the light of the many candles, leaving the centre nearly dark. The whole evening Velho made no effort to engage me in conversation.

***

The next morning, I went out early again. To reach the arsenal, I had to cross the bridge, which started out broad and heavy on either bank and narrowed towards the middle. Now and then one of the piers would drift away, or the members of the ferry guild would undermine them. No more was left of the structure than a framework of planks in constant motion, forever bumped about by passing boats, yet considerable numbers of people, balancing heavy loads on their heads, attempted this dangerous crossing, sometimes forced to give up and slide or jump through onto the boats below, which were always waiting. That was how the bridge and ferry coexisted.

The two ends of the bridge served as public promenades, and the crowds there sometimes blocked the way on and off. It was especially cool there in the evening; you could lean out over the sides and look down at the fishing villages, where the fishermen lived as if they were deep in Siberia in prehistoric times and not within the walls of a venerable city. Covered in grime, mud and scales, with strings of fish and copper coins slung over their shoulders – they sometimes used the coins to lash their wives and children, who would wail for mercy – on the slimy banks, their territory, they trudged back and forth between huts and boats as if there were no city, and probably never went there.

On the banks underneath the bridge, a medicine market was in progress. Many substances came from the river: molluscs, shells and plants. Hunters supplied a share: the skulls of small animals and dried organs. Parts of larger animals, like bears and lions, fetched the highest prices.

I made my way through the masses with difficulty; no one here knew my story. The crossing over the wobbling planks was treacherous, and when I reached the crowd on the other side, I spotted nothing resembling an arsenal. At one point I caused a commotion by stepping on a small child that crawled under my feet as I looked up to search for a wall higher than the houses.

But when I could go no further, there it was in front of me. The windows were sunk a full metre into the brick, and I could see no sign of panes through the rusted, bent bars, which were thick and so close together that no cats or birds, but only bats and insects could pass through. It had to be dark and musty in there. There was no door to be found, but I was caught by surprise by Sylvain's shadowy form in one of the windows, dressed in a blue smock, thin, with dull eyes and fallen cheeks, in a more advanced state of decay than I'd ever seen him in before. When I rapped on the iron with a stone, he shuffled over and, showing no sign of surprise, asked what I wanted.

'Let me in first.'

'What for?'

Our time together before Chungking meant nothing to him. All the reasons I gave made no impression, and I could see him fading away again, dissolving back into the jumble of collapsed beams, cobwebs, nettles and rubble. Then I held up one of the tins and called out, 'Look at this! Do you want it?'

He returned to the window and snatched at it, but I held it out of reach. 'Let me in first.'

'Come around the left side. Four metres from the corner, there's a hole large enough to crawl through.'

The inner walls had collapsed or been pulled or knocked over. One space that had once been a room was cluttered with tools, and a bellows hung over a coal fire. About six Chinese men were at work, looking apathetic.

He led me past them to a corner, had me squat down, and held out his hand, refusing to answer my questions until I gave him the tin. From a hole between the bricks, he took out a bamboo stem with a large stone bowl and lit a charcoal stove in a pit. He clawed the tin open and took a sniff. 'It's good,' he said. He used a nail to fill his pipe and smoked greedily. I could see I wouldn't get anything more out of him until he had taken the edge off his physical cravings, so I waited.

'Haven't they given you any?'

'I bought some from the fishermen and ferrymen, or traded iron for it, but I could hardly smoke the stuff – even pipe scrapings would be preferable. You were just in time; I wouldn't have lasted another day. And on top of that, I had to find food.'

After six pipes he looked somewhat recovered. His sideburns had overgrown his whole face, and his hands were still trembling, but there was a faint spark of attention in his eyes; he seemed to truly see me now.

'You're doing well.'

'I found a good host.'

'If the opium's as good as that … Could you bring me more?'

'There are a few things I need more than you need opium.

If you give them to me, I'll give you a tin a day. Look, don't you have a roof here?'

The rain had started again. The stove was hissing; Sylvain covered it with his hands.

'Those villains say the sky should see everything we do, so they took the roof off this house, which had been abandoned long ago – because someone who lived here was torn to pieces by ghosts, if I'm not mistaken. There's a little awning over the oven in the workshop. We can go there if the rain bothers you. I don't mind anymore. We just stop working for a while, that's all.'

'Is it coming along nicely?'

Sylvain's frustration suddenly made him talkative.

'After performing my specialised duties for twenty years, do you think it's pleasant to have to start all over, practicing every aspect of my field? Do you think a doctor who's worked only with madmen for twenty-eight years is ready to start doing surgery again?'

'The consequences don't seem as serious in this case.'

'Still, I have to make them work somehow. If these things won't shoot, it's curtains for me.'

'I thought that hardly mattered to you.'

'That's true, but I'll go my way, not theirs, and I'll bet no conceivable dose is strong enough to kill me anymore. But maybe you can help me.'

There in the workshop were a couple of machine guns, a few rifles, a flamethrower, and a howitzer, all the latest models as far as I could tell.

'That doesn't look too shabby. And if they explode, it's sure to be blamed on the guards who were handling them. And a lot of people will be happier that way. And besides, maybe this job is good for you, and you'll soon be in better shape than you ever were. If you taper it off ...'

Sylvain rounded on me with a contemptuous glare.

'Did you come here to give me hope and then try to convert me? I have only one thing to say to you: if you have the nerve to come back without a fresh supply, I'll kick you out of here.' He was shouting, a new experience for me, but apparently not for the workmen, who went on undisturbed.

Then I showed him another tin. He leapt for it, but I put it away again.

'I repeat: there are things I need more than you need opium, and I expect you to find them for me.'

He stared at me in bewilderment, and I told him the task I'd accepted.

'You're out of your mind. If you want your head chopped off, there are easier ways.'

'I've made good progress already. But how can I get my hands on wire and arc lamps?'

'Don't ask me. That's your business.'

'I'm counting on you. No lamps, no opium.'

Sylvain looked at me in hatred, full of reproach.

'Try the market out back first. That's where they sell whatever they've plundered from caravans.'

'I'm counting on you. I have to go.' And without giving him time to respond, I left.

'Come back tomorrow,' he called out after me.

I felt certain that once Sylvain had smoked enough, he would start searching, but I decided to keep at it myself as well. The next day, I looked everywhere and of course found nothing. It was an absolutely hopeless task. Discouraged, I returned to Fong Shen and told her the trouble I was in. She offered to speak to the Tuchun, but when I turned her down, she didn't insist. She did give me all the opium she had, twelve tins of it. At least I could make Sylvain do his best for me. She kept me with her and embraced me passionately. It seems a doomed man holds a singular attraction for women.

I had the feeling she wanted to bestow one last favour on

a man condemned, to let him savour the pleasures of earthly life for as long as he could. When it was time for other visitors to arrive, she gave me Ngan Tse and left me alone with her. She was charming and bashful – pure pretence, of course – sang a few songs, all with the same subtlety, and brought me to her own room, where among the silk cushions and the satin screens – and later, on the fragile bed – I did not feel altogether at ease.

The afternoon passed as it must, and by evening I was on my way again, feeling more or less the same way I might following a visit to a flower garden or aviary after a tiring journey: soothed by the colours and soft warbling. But I also felt cheated and wished I'd continued my journey without that unnecessary stop, frivolous yet exhausting because of the contrast with the real world, to which I'd already returned. I could hardly believe this was the first time I'd been with women after a year of solitude, so unmoved was I by my encounters.

But I'd already been living in a world of my own, receiving only weak impressions from the outer world, just enough sound and light to find my way. I hoped it would fade away entirely before my execution; by that stage, I was certain my scheme would fail. In spite of all this, I was freshly impressed by Chungking's masses that evening; the bridge was as full as a branch on which a swarm of bees had landed, as a Moscow or Tokyo tram at nightfall, and more and more people poured onto it from the banks; the sunset no longer gave much light, the faces were deathly pale blotches in the teeming throng under the mist that rose from the river, and I felt as if I was walking among those people for the last time in my life, as if they were already far away and the scene no longer had anything to do with me. That evening Velho did not disturb me; I climbed up to the window, as I had the first day, and although the distant mountain was visible again, the sight failed to lift me above my predicament; I longed for a quick end and envied Sylvain, who at least had a way of escaping time's slow passage. Why hadn't I made the same choice he had, he and so many others, when I had even less to lose?

Chapter 14

The next morning I didn't have the chance to visit Sylvain. He couldn't have had the time to find the parts, of course, but I was worried he'd do nothing but smoke as long as he had a supply. Instead, I was brought to the Tuchun's palace again.

After a long wait I was admitted to his presence. He did not welcome me or ask me to sit down. All he said was that the receiver would have to be ready in ten days, and he asked if I was nearly done. He suspected I was not, since I hadn't even identified where it was to be built. I told him that, as fate would have it, my host's great gallery was the only suitable place.

He was startled but replied that such things could happen.

'And there's one more thing I need before I can finish it. I need arc lamps.'

I tried to explain their purpose to him, but of course it was hopeless. He thought it would be much better to ring the device with torches, the only light to which underworld spirits were accustomed. That was sure to attract them by the hundreds, or thousands if necessary.

So I stopped trying to explain and was brought back to Velho's house. 'In ten days,' the Tuchun had repeated.

That afternoon I returned to the arsenal, already less hopeful. I found Sylvain sleeping next to the stove against his piece of wall, and with some difficulty, I woke him up. He didn't seem to remember what I was looking for and asked only if I had a fresh supply for him. Livid and desperate, I stormed out of the arsenal again, at a loss about what to do next. Too dispirited to search the markets when I was bound to find nothing there, I roamed the fields along the river where I'd gone in search of minerals earlier.

It was a deserted place, as silent as the grave, with a solitary house here and there and, in one spot, a large team of workmen driving bamboo rods into the earth to find a natural spring. Chungking was thirsty, because its broad river emptied into a nearby lake, and the water was becoming more and more saturated with alum, lime and rock salt. They were constantly drilling wells, on which the city depended for its survival, as other countries depend on building and maintaining dikes.

The rows of coolies advanced like tugboats exiled to the interior. Then the block fell with a dull thud and the bamboo drilled a few inches deeper into the soil. They returned to the platform and began straining at their ropes again, pulling away from the centre.

I sat by the edge of a pool and watched, splashing my hand absent-mindedly in the water. At some point I had a sip. It tasted like oil. I took a closer look and was startled by the dingy yellow colour. Petroleum.

For another man, this discovery might have meant immeasurable wealth. My only thought was whether it could distract the Tuchun from my failing venture. But no sooner had this idea come to me than I dismissed it. He would see it only as an impurity, spoiling his wells, and could not be expected to grasp how it would ever lead to wealth. And even if he could understand, he would oppose the plan. Permit Chungking to fill up with derricks, oil tanks, refineries and factories? Never. And I too hated the idea.

But even though I would soon have nothing more to do with Chungking, the petroleum industry or any other earthly affairs, still I hoped, for no good reason, that this new element in a place unchanged for centuries would bring distraction, delay – though I couldn't imagine how.

On impulse, I went to the foreman and ordered him to drill in the place where I'd been sitting. My quest for underground materials gave me some authority in the eyes of these men;

he obeyed promptly, telling his crew to erect a platform there. The primitive approach has its advantages; although it takes a long time to achieve any results, the structure was in place an hour later: a few poles tied together at the top, a few crossbeams to guide the falling block in the right direction, a long beam with a pulley high above the others, and a hundred men standing ready to usher in the age of energy.

It lifted my spirits when the block began to fall, at irregular intervals at first. Being obeyed is one of the things that gives a man in a tight position the greatest faith in his own value. In a better mood, I went to see Ngan Tse. She did her best to match my high spirits, straining to be cheerful, but in the middle of the ceremonial that precedes an embrace, she burst into tears. I seemed to have struck a well there too. I asked what was wrong; she refused to answer. Finally, between sobs: 'Kia So was here.'

'What does that matter? Who is Kia So?'

I discovered with effort that Kia So was a priest of the war god, who wanted to expel them from the city. 'Kia So is powerful. He hates all forms of joy and, of course, all people who bring joy and receive wealth, garments and jewels in return. But the women of joy in Chungking have been protected by law for ages. Not Fong Shen, however – she comes from far away. The Tuchun wants to keep her; Kia So keeps threatening to drive her out. So the Tuchun invited Kia So to make use of her without asking her consent. He came here, and she laughed in his face. Then he showed her the warrant, and her laughter stopped. Ma and I offered ourselves, but he doesn't like children or very young women – strange, for such an old man. So she had no choice. The first time, she prayed for hours afterwards, drank herself into a stupor, and swore never to entertain the Tuchun again. But she went on doing so, all the same, and Kia So still visits too, once in a while. She doesn't seem to mind anymore and says he's not much bother. The last time he was here, he said we would have to leave the city.'

'Can't you put him in a good mood, win his favour?'

'He doesn't even glance at us. And the Tuchun always gives in to his demands. There's only one solution: an offering at his temple. And even that won't work anymore. A few days ago he announced that the temple will no longer accept grain, rice or valuables – it already has too much. The only thing he wants now is money.'

She had stopped crying and looked at me with expectation in her eyes. Was this convoluted story no more than an elaborate request for the one thing that even the sweetest and most unexpected adventure boils down to in the end: namely, money? I was sceptical about the priest. Supposing he existed, why would he take an interest in whether the Tuchun's favourite had a couple of servant girls from outside Chungking? But she insisted.

I still had a few banknotes. One came from Hsiu, for keeping silent about his opium smuggling. Why not give her everything? In a couple of days I would have no use for any of it. Even so, I didn't give her everything – I gave her fifty dollars. She appeared to think it wasn't enough, the way she kept staring at it and turning it over and over.

'Still won't do?' I said, embittered to see that this young creature who had seemed so tender and guileless could be so grasping.

'Oh yes, it's a lot of money, but I don't dare go there on my own. It's so dark there, with human bones all over the walls, and Kia So is horrible. Couldn't you come with me?'

'Fine, I'll meet you in front of the temple. Tell me where it is.'

She looked relieved and, in an onrush of words, described where to find it. I agreed to wait there the next afternoon, though I half-expected she wouldn't turn up. Maybe she'd heard from Fong Shen that my days were numbered and decided it was time for me to settle my debt.

***

I went to the arsenal one last time, though I no longer had any hope. To my astonishment, Sylvain was not muddled and groggy, as he had been both times before. He strode up to me and held out his hand in something like fellowship.

'What's happened to you?'

'The opium was good. I'm back in form. But I had the greatest shock of my life today.'

'That put new life into you?'

'No, but it made me think of you. Look at this.' He opened a little box. I saw a couple of dry electrical components, metal wire twisted into thick hemp ropes, and a couple of primitive coils.

'Did you find any lamps?'

'No, no lamps.'

'Then what use is all this?'

'I thought maybe you could find the lamps yourself.'

We were both speaking frankly. I felt I couldn't blame him for failing to find the lamps, but neither could I bring myself to thank him for everything that he had found. 'What was it that gave you such a shock?'

'Oh, I'd rather not say.'

'Did you read somewhere that they're planning to execute me?'

'No. It's Godunov. Godunov is dead.'

'How do you know?'

'They bring me here through the east gate. I usually can't see what's going on around me, because I'm right behind the front guardsman, but this morning I stumbled, looked up, and saw Godunov's fat head in a cage, the curls matted with blood, but the same old grin still on his face.'

'It could be worse, really. Beheading is an easy death, and it sounds like he saw the funny side, as always. Who knows what's ahead for me.' (I didn't want to say 'what's ahead for *us*', but we were both thinking that now our whole group would soon be dispensed with.)

Sylvain stared out ahead of him. Then he said, 'I'll smoke myself to death. Did you bring me anything?'

I had three tins in my bag. But I gave him nothing. 'I don't believe you're still capable of it.'

'Then I'll eat it.'

'Your stomach won't tolerate that amount.'

I could see his mind was made up, and I wanted him to stay alive as long as I did. We had travelled there together, we were both lost in Chungking, and although I'd become better acquainted with the city than he, it was still an alien world with strange inhabitants: the Tuchun, the judges, the mandarins and the people living and dying in the streets.

'Don't do it. Let's get out of here together. I can bring enough opium to keep you going for a long time.'

'It'll never work. We're not allowed to leave, and they'd spot us passing through the open fields outside the walls. Where did you think we could hide? The whole area around the city is exposed.'

'Let's ride a raft downriver.'

'And end up in the salt flats and die of thirst? Let's make ourselves comfortable here!'

He looked around as if the arsenal were a palace of delights – and to him, maybe it was. There was nothing I could do; each of us would have to submit to his own fate.

***

On my way to the temple, I wanted to pay my last respects to Godunov but didn't dare. As it turned out, the temple and its grounds were more than enough to fill my mind with morbid thoughts. Not from a distance – it stood ponderously on top of a hill like an ark, surrounded by low pines. But along the path that ran through the complex, there were garlands of human bones strung between the trees, and poles topped with half-skulls.

The temple itself was painted in garish colours and surrounded with sculptures with gleaming eyes of glass and stone, but inside it was dark. It was crammed as full as the studio of a sculptor doomed to remain undiscovered until his death. But instead of heads with a bit of shoulder or torsos without arms, these sculptures had many heads, more arms than squid and octopi, and more eyes and wings than the dragons of the Apocalypse; they seemed inspired not by the Venus de Milo, but by Laocoön. I went deeper into the deserted temple, curious what I might find. Just as elsewhere in the city I had occasionally run into a remnant of a mosque or a chunk of Doric or Byzantine architecture, there I discovered a few Greek influences among the monstrous idols.

What might lie beyond Chungking to the west, beyond the mountaintops? Now and then I had to hunch down to avoid all the objects hanging from cords, probably votive offerings: bones, jewellery, pottery, bronzes, weapons, small cloths and axes of silver, furs, bridles, bracelets, and predators' teeth. I could see why the priest had decided to stop accepting anything but money.

At the end of a straight and slightly less cluttered path, I saw torches and incense sticks burning and a priest on a dais, seated in prayer. The light blazed up and I flinched; this was the same priest who had sat on the throne beside the Tuchun! Fortunately, he hadn't noticed me. I crept back towards the exit but lost my way; the darkness grew deeper. Thinking I heard steps, I ducked behind an idol. There I saw something gleaming ... Lamps, dangling from cords. An insane thought went through me: what if these were the lamps I was searching for? The steps kept coming and going, but I had to know for certain, so I lit a match. They were looped around the sculpture's neck and hung from its cheeks like big earrings. If I stole them, they could save my life. They were the kind I needed!

So the caravan robber had not brought his loot to the market, but to the temple. I owed him my gratitude; I even wanted to go to Kia So and thank him, to praise him for making possible what he'd hoped to prevent at all costs. His temple had given me what I needed.

Squatting in the dark, I pondered whether to take them with me straight away. It was risky, but so was leaving them there, since I might not have a chance to return. But what if my theft were discovered?

I took six, hiding them under my robe, and left the rest of them there. From a distance, the gleaming necklace still looked complete. I would have preferred to leave at once, but I waited for Ngan Tse at the bottom of the hill. When she arrived, I pressed the money into her hands and told her to hurry. She was back five minutes later.

She had burnt incense. Kia So had accepted the money, murmured to himself, turned away and said they could stay another month. That was the longest the gods would tolerate their presence. She shook with sobs.

'A month? But that's plenty of time.'

She misunderstood me; her sorrow doubled in intensity, and she accused me of not caring about her. She inflated her true feelings into a charade with almost European skill. I comforted her and told her I had something that would permit them to stay longer.

She didn't believe me at first. Where had I found it? she asked. Why hadn't I said so right away? Then she wouldn't have wasted the money. Eventually, still far from persuaded, she left.

Once she was some distance away, I went off in a different direction, cautiously, my hands in my pockets, still full of dread as I moved through the packed streets. Along the way, it occurred to me that Ngan Tse was in such agony, and so scared of being expelled from Chungking, because she feared she'd miss me. But what did I care? She didn't know me. She knew nothing of the dangers I'd faced, my isolation and my fear of human contact. What she loved was not me but the way I treated her; I was gentler, less demanding than the others, seeing her less as a mere tool, or as prey. But what did it matter? Now I hoped my plan would succeed and I'd be free to travel to the mountains. Ngan Tse was certain to forget me.

Once I'd put away the lamps with the other parts and knew I had everything I needed, that my life was saved for the moment, what arose was not joy or relief, but only a strange, airy feeling as if the whole business no longer had anything to do with me and everything was over. It was also as if there was someone in Chungking I didn't know, whose bodily form I'd never seen, whose language and ways of thinking were worlds apart from mine, but who'd nonetheless taken an interest in my fate. Had he led me to the temple? I didn't want to think about it, in fear that this unknown presence would be another threat to my existence, would soon lay claim to me and make demands.

I went to Ngan Tse to forget, and this time it worked. She did her best to please me, and her devotion brought a series of erotic sensations that left me inwardly indifferent but nonetheless surprised me in a way. It was as if she could duplicate herself somehow, as if several ghostly Ngan Tses surrounded me, first flattering me, then taunting me and, in the end, tormenting me.

I had sent word to the Tuchun that I would be ready in three days, two days before the time limit. Velho's great hall had to be cleared out; to me, this was like sweeping away the last shards of the past.

That afternoon I also saw Fong Shen for the last time. She and her two attendants were in the laborious process of packing all her things. I told her I was grateful to her for letting Ngan Tse spend so much time with me. She told me the Tuchun was sending her away to a pleasure villa in the mountains, many days' travel from Chungking. Was it exile? She didn't know. She wasn't allowed to bring either of her women; the Tuchun's own servants would accompany her. 'Will you visit again?' she asked, half teasing, half wistful.

'Life must be monotonous there.'

She shrugged her shoulders in disdain. 'It's the same wherever you go. You dull your mind with wine and opium and hope other people will live up to your expectations, but they never do. Taihai's the only place I'd like to see again. Now and then you find people there who will stop at nothing. But even they disappoint you eventually ... So, how's that famous device of yours coming along?'

'I hope the spirits will be contented with my work.'

'Oh, don't be so secretive. I've known for some time now it will be the highlight of the autumn festival. Well, I know what that's like. I wish I could be there this time and see the wise and venerable whitebeards gawking. But women aren't allowed to see it. Besides, I'll be on my way by then.'

'Do you know about Godunov?'

'Yes,' said Fong Shen, folding up her silk garment. 'It's his own fault. He never learned when to stop grinning.' I heard regret in her voice. He had probably made her some lovesick proposal while wearing that same smirk.

'And All-But-One?'

'Oh, he's fine. They've made him a teacher, he's very grateful. Always behaves himself, doesn't notice the children making fun of him or shouting names, and only gets drunk once in a great while. None of us have accomplished much here. You still have a chance.' She looked as tired and downhearted as I was; her mouth drooped; for the first time, she seemed worried about her own future.

The process was almost complete; Chungking had sapped a few outsiders of their life force and was about to spit them out. Only All-But-One, who belonged here, would be allowed to remain, in an almost vegetable state, along with Sylvain, whose inner and outer worlds were sustained by opium.

The threat of armament had been staved off once again. A small band of social outcasts would go on working with the weapons for a while; once banished, they would join irregular armies; and if any of them ever returned to the city, they would keep out of sight. Should one of them become a mercenary commander, he would never attack, not because he feared the guns rusting on the walls, but in profound respect for the city itself, which defied time and eternity.

I bade farewell to Fong Shen and did not cross paths with Ngan Tse again. I went home and locked myself in my room. Even when I heard Velho's insistent knocking – he must have heard about the order to clear out the great hall and hoped I would show mercy – I refused to open the door. The moon was bright that night. I didn't try to look up at the mountains, but stayed awake half the night retrieving the components from their hiding place under the kang, checking if they were all there and putting them back in place, finding a safer spot for the lamps each time.

But the prospect of success weighed on me as much as ever. The Tuchun would keep me in Chungking, and my fondest wish was to leave, now that I knew I would be the only remaining foreigner – at least, once Sylvain had achieved his purpose of smoking himself to death, which would not take much longer.

Chapter 15

Velho watched passively at first, slumped in his deep chair. His books and furniture had been heaped in a corner, the paintings and embroideries removed, and holes drilled in the walls and roof. He looked at me reproachfully, but I avoided his eyes. With a sudden shiver, he rose, summoned his servants, and had everything carried away. Would he try to reconstruct the same atmosphere, on which he was so dependent, with the same arrangement in a different room? I didn't much care what he did, but I regretted the spitefulness that had driven me to disturb something of value to him, from which he would never be able to free himself even if it was burnt and destroyed. The dull hate I felt for him transformed into pity, though still mingled with faint revulsion.

I made an effort: 'Wouldn't it be better to box it all up, or else burn it? Your life would be the better for it.'

His only answer was another reproachful look, and he went on giving instructions to his servants, who were removing things as my assistants went on with their work. The two groups acted as if they didn't see each other, but as the day went on and the first wires were strung, they grew uneasy and would sometimes let out a loud cry or suddenly drop something, as if to scare off invisible intruders.

I had to set up the antenna on the roof myself. No one could be persuaded to help me. I thought of sending for Sylvain, but maybe he was in his final fog, and in any case, he wouldn't be steady on his feet. So I clambered about the roof on my own, installing poles and attaching wires. It was a misty day; beyond the surrounding mass of roofs, walls, and treetops, nothing was visible; only the top of the hill at the heart of the city, where we had stood the first day, was drifting on a cloud.

After three days of hard work and countless unsuccessful attempts that led to nothing but screeching and rumbling, during which my frustration at my repeated failures was not leavened by any relief from the mortal fear that held me in its constant grip, I managed for the first time, deep in the night, to tune the receiver to a clear signal. But ... could I bring myself to do it? To open the gates to the life I had come so far to escape, even if only in the form of sound?

How long ago had I left the sea that confined me to the company of peers I shunned, ended my battered banishment in Taihai, and put the coast behind me? And now I would let that life pour into this secluded part of the earth to save my own isolated self.

Come on, nothing else to be done.

I switched it on: voices and music, a squawking march that ended with a few booms of the kettledrum, a silence that opened the way to a harsh, arrogant voice. Here in the middle, in remote China, far from the coast with the high mountain ranges looming up like another world on earth, here I could hear, in the middle of the night, the words others heard in the afternoon or evening in an echoing, brightly lit room full of people, smoke and breath. I heard a man boasting of the victory of common sense under his leadership over a madness fatal to law and order that had swept the Western world, glorifying the material and ideal benefits that a chosen people had won under his leadership and would go on winning as long as they put their complete and blind faith in him, seeking only to follow and never to think for themselves. Then thunderous applause, stamping feet, roaring voices, more music, another march, party songs, shouted slogans, thudding drums, a wailing that raised the suspicion that opponents were being tied to stakes.

So this – aside from the weapons, which didn't really

count – was the first manifestation of Western life in this secluded part of the earth. I shut it off. After a while I found a Siberian border station transmitting Communist propaganda in Chinese. Then dance music. That was enough for now. I could supply the Tuchun and his guests with plenty of new sensations – too many, perhaps. There was not much atmospheric disturbance. And once I was gone, both the receiver and the weapons would go the way of decay. It would irritate Kia So and make the dignitaries of the ancient race more wary of Western civilisation.

The day had come. The hall was packed with all the chairs and seats that Velho owned. In the front row were the Tuchun, Kia So, Cheng and the chief justices, and behind them the magistrates of the city government, four or five prominent merchants, a few priests, lower-ranking mandarins and people whose rank and status were unclear to me. Three clerks from the yamen squatted in the corners, their brushes bolt upright over the outspread paper, poised to make an official record of the event. Every spectator strove to maintain a dignified attitude, cool and contemptuous. Only the Tuchun, Kia So and a few of the eldest judges succeeded in giving no sign whatsoever of the fear and nervous anticipation in their hearts. The others kept shooting each other glances, shuffling and kicking their unseen feet under their floor-sweeping robes; some excused themselves for a moment and never returned, while others stayed close to the door for safety's sake, sliding their hands in and out of their sleeves as they chattered, loud and excited, all talking at once. The air was filled with the scraping of throats, and the mahogany floorboards, always polished to a shine on Velho's instructions, were losing their original purity.

To my astonishment, Velho himself was present. He sat by a window that opened onto a narrow terrace bordered with flowers, as if prepared to leave at the first sign of trouble, but also as if he had not yet given up hope that the experiment would fail and the hall would be evacuated. Maybe he even hoped to become my rescuer and bind me to him forever with chains of gratitude. Well, that was an idle hope, as he would soon see. Still, I was concerned about disturbances in the atmosphere of this unfamiliar region, and who could tell what influences my enemies might bring to bear on that.

Velho's presence disturbed me more than Kia So's. But I suspected the priest had noticed the missing lamps, knew what had become of them and was waiting until the end of the demonstration to declare that the sacrosanct nature of temple offerings outweighed the importance of the magical device, and to claim the whole thing for himself.

Tea was served to everyone except the clerks and me. It was a slow, decorous proceeding, as if they were playing for time. But then at last the Tuchun beckoned me and commanded me to explain the workings of the device. He seemed to wish to temper the audience's superstitions with sober facts, so that the demonstration would have the least possible impact. My response disappointed him. A detailed technical explanation would have had to include the lamps, and I was determined to avoid drawing attention to them, so that any suspicions would not become certainties. Instead, I held forth about the elements required for the formation of a receptive organism most comparable to Yin, the passive female force, and the current in the ether that engendered the sound as soon as it came into contact with this receiving element and was therefore equivalent to Yang, the seminal male power.

Like so many earthly things, I continued, this device was based on nothing other than the union of the creative, active principle and its passive, receptive counterpart.

The Tuchun gave me a reproving frown, but Kia So, who had come to see me as a rival whose magical powers outshone his, fixed me with a look of fury. All the others had listened with their eyes closed, perhaps peeping out at me through invisible slits.

But a man towards the front, dressed in a white robe around which a golden yellow cloth had been wound twice, with a two-horned hat on his head, a chain of small bones around his neck, and a plump red face with large eyes, looked at me mockingly: 'He blustered his way out of that one: that sounded an awful lot like higher wisdom. He doesn't want to give away his secret, but that story would never have worked on us.'

True, amid a ring of men like him, I would have held my tongue in shame, offered up the receiver to them with a wave of my hand and continued on my way. He sat alone in the multitude. Was this the man whose invisible presence I'd felt at that first audience? Could he be the one I had sensed, faint and distant at first, then ever stronger, over the past few days, until now he had finally made himself visible to me (though not nearly to everyone) in an earthly guise?

My shame gave way to confidence. He was the first person I'd met who was not dependent on Chungking like a part or function of an urban organism, the first who had an autonomous existence. All of a sudden, it was as if I could see straight past Chungking to where the mountain rose from the mists to show that the distances beyond were within my reach.

I cut the lecture short. The Tuchun made an impatient gesture, and I twisted the dials, hoping for a beginning. The silence was complete. Gradually, the throat-scraping and shuffling grew louder. I didn't dare to look behind me.

Suddenly it burst loose, dance music, probably from one of the Taihai hotels. It made little impression. Maybe their eardrums were insensitive to those vibrations. In haste, I searched for something else, a human voice ...

Thank goodness, a Siberian border station, Soviet

propaganda in Chinese, though a kind of Chinese very different from their own, and almost certainly incomprehensible. The impression it made was all the stronger. This, yes, this must be the voice of a spirit of the air, uttering supernatural truths in words akin to their own.

Another speaker, still another, then a chorus of chanting voices.

The silence in the auditorium deepened. I felt the anxiety and dread that held them in its grip; some trembled in their seats, now and then one slipped away, but most remained, solely out of fear of the Tuchun and Kia So. And those two remained out of fear of losing their authority over the others.

That was their only defence against the overwhelming urge to flee.

Why could I no longer enjoy my success, which felt like a victory over Chungking, the immovable city? In spite of my hopeless clutching at everything that made it strong: its solitary location along the river in the middle of the steppe, its age, its stony paralysis, it was a dream in the past and I myself was travelling over the plains again – no, drifting vacantly in space. And to root myself in the earth again, I reached for the radio. Chinese music this time: drums, cymbals, gongs, flutes. It calmed the crowd, even though its source remained a mystery. Then came another human voice, a woman singing, tinny and distant, heart-wrenching, an outcry against all the insults she had endured. I shivered, but they relaxed in their seats; this reassured them!

And out of nowhere, a man came between me and the audience, waving his arms wildly. His robe clung to his skin, his slippers were worn and muddy, and his eyes bulged out of his head. He was shouting, but no one seemed to know what he was saying. The Tuchun barked an order and the messenger was grabbed and set down in front of him. Then he asked me to restore the silence. But I had an urge to compound the confusion, and chance was on my side; after only a brief search, the massive strains of a German symphony came crashing into the hall, an inundation of sound. The Tuchun approached me and asked again for silence, almost pleading; he pointed to the man and told me a disaster was in the making. I switched the receiver off with a brisk wave of my hand, and the sudden silence seemed more ominous still. I stood with my hand on the switch, like a gunner at the fuse of his cannon.

The man, still unable to speak, pointed to the corner, wailing. Next to the clerks were two men with broad, short swords. If I had failed, they would have dealt with me; the bearer of bad news thought they were there for him. Once the Tuchun had sent them away, his story spilled out, still rushed and choppy: 'The yellow flood from the underworld has burst loose, where the men were drilling the latest well. The plain has turned into a lake. The Tsong Fu Han district is flooding. The people are fleeing; the yellow flood is rising faster and faster.'

Then he kowtowed to the Tuchun and remained prostrate. Most of the audience was leaving the room. The Tuchun and Kia So rose to their feet; the remaining spectators gathered around them. Only the man with the mocking expression was still sitting quietly.

Kia So screeched, 'The spirits of the underworld have been disturbed! They will not tolerate the air spirits manifesting here on earth, walking on their roof. They have broken through the vault that separates their world from ours. Chungking will be the battlefield in the war between the spirits of the air and the spirits of the underworld. Destroy the device. Sacrifice him at once! Perhaps we can still appease their wrath!'

A couple of mandarins dutifully grabbed me, and the swordsmen approached. If the Tuchun had looked on passively, that would have been the end of me. But his presence of mind did not fail him.

'Stop this, Kia So! You know very well the two events have nothing to do with each other.'

'Nothing to do with each other!' Kia So cried. 'Surely it's clear to us all there can be no other explanation!' A murmur of support rose from the crowd; Kia So was right.

Now the Tuchun tried to buy time for me. 'We can always sacrifice him later. Go on and promise him to your spirits. But first, let's see what he can do for us alive. He knows more than we do about some things between heaven and earth.'

Furious, searching for allies, Kia So looked around. But the mandarins, who had no ideas of their own, had thrown their support behind the Tuchun again and met the priest's gaze with cold stares.

'Wan Chen!' Kia So screeched, turning to the man who'd been sitting so calmly, 'will you stand idly by as Chungking is destroyed? Then why did you come all this way? You know better than I that these foreigners are the ones who have thrown off the balance of ground and air under and around Chungking. My premonition, my certainty ... One night I saw the yellow-violet hue of the underworld shine through. Why didn't we kill them at once?'

He turned back to the Tuchun. 'Because you were not satisfied with your duties: protecting Chungking and preserving the sacred rites for our ancestors and the gods! In your boredom and hunger for novelty, you let them go their way, and even encouraged them! Curse him, Wan Chen, and have this foreigner killed.'

At one word from the seated man, I would have been executed and the Tuchun seized. But he made no reply, merely meeting Kia So's eyes with a smile on his face. And Wan Chen did not move, as if he had no part in this scene. No one moved. Only a mandarin bent down, laid some fireworks on the ground, and set them off. They'd been intended for the festival and now, he hoped, would ward off evil spirits. Maybe it helped for a moment. Kia So was working himself up into a frenzy. 'Then I will fight this battle alone! Carve up that device!' he ordered the swordsmen.

But they didn't obey him either. Kia So snatched a sword from one of them and started chopping, but the wooden case was hard and slow to splinter.

Wan Chen was gone; the rest of us were waiting to see what the Tuchun would do. He turned to me and asked me to accompany him to the well from the underworld to see what could be done. He seemed to believe, even now, that it was a false alarm, or a natural phenomenon blown out of proportion by the priest for his own purposes. Behind us, packed together like a frightened herd, the crowd was leaving the hall.

Only Kia So and Velho stayed behind, the latter sweeping up the splinters chopped off the device by the former, two old men, one half-senile, the other seething with powerless rage.

'It's no use trying to stop him,' the Tuchun said, as we sauntered through the garden. 'He has to vent his anger one way or another. Too bad, after all your trouble, but I'm sure it will be easier now to build another device. Although, come to think of it, perhaps I've heard enough.'

Chapter 16

At first, the master drillers had not planned to keep the crew at work for long in the spot the foreigner had pointed out. They had selected a thin, flimsy stalk of bamboo, which bent easily, even though the block was light, the drop was short, and the coolies pulling the ropes were slow and sleepy, sensing that this job was unimportant. They did not form a tight row or pull the ropes as far as they could before letting them go, but stayed close to the platform, paying them out and pulling them in again without leaving their places, except when they stopped to smoke and gamble. They spent three-quarters of the afternoon sleeping, like punkah-wallahs who nod off in their corners but go on pulling the cords of their fans to create a breeze.

But after a few days, in spite of all this, the hole had reached a greater depth than the others, which were being drilled by the book, with a sturdy drill, a heavy block and a whipped-up work crew. The water had already come fairly far up the shaft and shimmered with strange colours. But the foreigner did not return. He had probably been taken captive. Maybe the master drillers could keep this secret to themselves. That strange-looking fluid must have unusual properties. Maybe it had healing powers. Maybe it could soften stones, making it possible to build huge structures, like the ancients who had erected the great walls that no one could demolish, even now.

The flimsy platform was replaced by a strong one with a heavier block, and the coolies no longer had time for naps and stealthy games, not even in the afternoons. Back and forth they went in a long, straight row of a hundred men, as strong a team as the one that pulls the heaviest junks through the fastest-moving waterfalls outside Ichang. One of the masters was always present to make sure that the rope did not go slack for an instant, that the block crashed down at regular intervals on the bamboo shaft crowned with a brass band, whether in the hot sun or on moonless nights, lit by glowing fires or, in the rain, by covered torches.

Why such haste, when they'd been drilling wells all their lives and never worried about whether it took them a month more or less? They didn't know. Did they hope this unusual well would free them from the menial life in which the guild kept them trapped and bring them closer to the sublime? When it happened, they ran away as fast as the coolies and hid among the masses; only one of them had the courage to report the incident to the Tuchun. It was too soon, too unexpected. It should have taken many weeks more before the new well sent its slow, stately jet rising to the sky ...

But one afternoon, during one of the coolies' ever-rarer and shorter breaks, it happened. The earth heaved, and everyone fell to the ground. A subterranean rumble was heard, still subdued at that stage. A large crack ran straight across the plain; in the spot where the platform had stood was a deep, crater-like ulcer in the earth – the platform had vanished into it. And from it came gushing, not merely a jet, but a rain of stones and sludge high into the air. A few people were injured; everyone was covered in muck. Then the ulcer filled with the strange fluid, no longer violet and purple now but a muddy yellow, spilling over the edges and spreading over the plain. By the time they'd recovered their wits, they found themselves beside a lake whose edge was advancing towards their feet. Now and then fountains of mud and gravel spouted up in the middle.

For the people of the underworld, it may have been a day of celebration; for them, it was a disaster – not the usual variety, like a flood, fire, or epidemic, but a kind they could not yet understand. But they did understand that they had unleashed great misfortune on Chungking, that the city authorities would hold them responsible, and that their lives were in danger.

When the lake rose even higher, a couple of them ran to the city to warn the magistrates and plead their own innocence; others went into hiding; a few scaled the walls and waited nearby to see what would happen.

***

The residents of the nearby district came in droves, some carrying their belongings, others still carefree and simply curious. As soon as they caught sight of the strange yellow lake, and saw the stones surging into the air and crashing down, they fled for the ramparts.

When the Tuchun arrived, many people turned to him expectantly, but he went straight into one of the low, broad stone watchtowers, took his place beneath a hastily erected canopy, and did nothing to stop the flood.

He did emerge once to walk along the inside of the wall, accompanied by the foreigner whose reckless prying and poking in the earth and summoning of voices from thin air had no doubt disturbed the balance, and who remained at the Tuchun's side. He kept pointing to a lower-lying spot; the Tuchun shook his head in refusal. Then they entered the watchtower together as the yellow lake continued to rise and the people kept pouring out of the city and scaling the walls. By the time Kia So arrived with a procession of masked priests, to the strains of woeful chanting and the drone of sacred music, their bodyguards had to clear a path through the crowd for them with the traditional weapons: staff, sword and spear. A few people stood too close to the edge and fell in, and a cannon – one of the first installed – slid off its base and plopped into the liquid.

These first victims were not enough to appease the underworld; the lake went on rising. Kia So ranged his followers along the inner edge of the wall and brought the music to a stop, while he remained below and implored the Tuchun to sacrifice the foreigner, who was standing quietly at his side, and deliver him to the priests, insisting that until he did, the evil that had come over Chungking would never cease.

'On the contrary, the foreigner is the only one who may have the power to ward off this catastrophe. He has just supplied a method. But I'm happy to give you and your band of priests the opportunity to test your powers first.'

In despair, Kia So turned to Wan Chen once more. 'Why did you come to Chungking, if you weren't planning to defend the city from destruction? Why give us hope if it must remain unfulfilled? Must you too protect the foreigner who is guilty of all this? Am I the only one who wishes to save Chungking?'

The Tuchun gave him a haughty stare. Wan Chen explained, again, that his appearance in the city had nothing to do with the letter Kia So had sent him earlier and did not signify that he had come to save Chungking. He warned Kia So not to meddle in affairs he did not understand, not to resist, not to struggle.

This advice went unheeded. Kia So turned away from the watchtower and called out to the people, 'The foreigner must die, lest Chungking go to its doom!'

The priests took up the cry, and the people joined in and pressed forward. The watchtower was not heavily guarded, and for a moment it seemed it would be captured and the foreigner dragged away, but before that point was reached, a body toppled from the wall; it was Kia So. He let out shrill cries and floated on the oil for a little while, but soon drowned. Some people said a couple of the Tuchun's bodyguards had pushed him off; others claimed to have seen two women shoot out of the crowd, one slapping his face while the other dived at his feet, throwing him off balance.

The lesser priests, fearing the same fate, quickly scattered into the crowd; another one fell, while the others hurried to strip off their vestments and toss them into the yellow flood with their appurtenances. These drifted on the surface for a moment and then were all sucked in at once. The abrupt death of the powerful, malevolent keeper of the war god's temple and the rapid disintegration of the priestly class caused a panic among the people – they no longer expected the Tuchun to save them, since he refused to sacrifice the foreigner. His bodyguards just barely managed to keep the angry, fearful mob at bay; in the chaos, many more people fell from the wall. Arrows were shot from a distance, and voices cried out for the foreigner. Finally, after many deaths, a calm descended. The Tuchun turned to Cameron and asked what good it would do to tear down a section of the wall. The fountain from the underworld would just keep gushing. Couldn't he build a structure to divert the flow?

The foreigner repeated that a section of the wall had to be demolished so that the oil could run off into the dry moat and, from there, out into the surrounding landscape. That would ensure the safety of the city.

'But the lake will keep rising and rising until it covers the whole world, and if I have the wall pulled down, the people will think we are aiding in Chungking's destruction. That would certainly be the end of us all. Already we can hardly hold them back.'

'If you'll let me go to the arsenal, I can find a way to blow up a section of the wall without any digging beforehand, so that the oil will run off quickly. That sight will reassure the people. You can have soldiers escort me there. The crowd will think they're taking me to be executed, and let us through.'

The Tuchun hesitated, but Wan Chen told him that was how it had to be. They walked along the ramparts, a great distance, to find a place where the ground on the inside was dry and they could enter the city. There they saw districts where life went on as usual. Although criers ran through the streets warning everyone to evacuate, and in some places soldiers were putting out lamps and fires over fierce protests, no one was leaving the place where he lived. It was surprising to see people there, so close to the lake of oil, eating, working, quarrelling and having long conversations.

The river was low; it was easy to understand why no one believed in the flood without having seen or smelled the yellow lake for themselves.

***

It was quiet inside the arsenal. The work there had ended once and for all. Sylvain lay in his corner, his pipe still in his hand, next to an extinguished stove and a half-full tin, a worn-out, happy expression on his face. He had done it – smoked his way into the afterlife. Cameron felt a yearning to lie down next to him; maybe his vital spirits would simply cease to flow. The arsenal, ruined and deserted, now seemed alluring, the only quiet place on earth, a fitting mausoleum for someone whose life had been equally ruined and broken.

But he had to return to the ramparts. Why? For the Tuchun and Wan Chen. The downfall of Chungking, the city that had once fascinated him, now left him indifferent. After a brief search, he found the packets of dynamite that had been intended for the grenades. There was enough to spring a mine, or to bring down a dilapidated old wall. The soldiers each took a package, and they headed back.

Before they reached the walls, they loaded everything into a litter to avoid attracting attention. During their absence, the lake had not risen; if anything, the level had dropped. Even so, they proceeded with the plan to blow up the wall.

Though the people were constantly being ordered off the ramparts, few of them left. Most felt safer near the Tuchun. But in the distance, all the junks and sampans that usually formed thick double swarms by the bend in the river were now floating downstream like one large, crude black raft. The boat dwellers did not have so much trouble throwing off their ties to Chungking. Where the lake lapped at the wall, the crowd was thickest. Everyone wanted to see the fountain from the underworld. Again and again, a rain of stones and mud would send them scurrying away, but they'd return at once, the way flies swatted by a horse's tail keep coming back to the same spot on the flank.

After one such shower, the Tuchun's guards managed to keep that section of the wall unoccupied. The foreigner, who had stepped out of the litter in disguise, and a few forced labourers had themselves lowered to just above the surface of the oil. It was not hard to chip away a few stones to make a space and attach a string of match cords from old muskets. The resulting fuse was so short that he hardly had time to climb back to the safe zone by the watchtower.

But the silence dragged on, and the noise of the crowd died down to a murmur. The Tuchun and his attendants looked pale, even more fearful than at the radio demonstration. The oil had started welling up faster again; rising high above it, as if scattered across a large beige table, were various parts of the city that had come adrift, as well as an empty sampan, washed back and forth against the wall by an undercurrent like a wandering ghost ship. The oil was slowly creeping, smooth and slippery, up the inner wall and would soon spill over the mine. Cameron felt the same dread he had at the thought that the radio might fail, but this time compressed and accelerated into the seconds that remained. Abruptly, like a forerunner of death, total indifference settled over him as to his fate. Only the will to complete this final act remained.

He went to the middle of the cleared section of the wall and stood there, alone, planning to climb back down to light the fuse again. Then, with a series of dull, muffled booms, the middle of the wall lit up, rose into a low arch for an instant, and fell, partly into the moat and partly into the lake of oil. A cloud of rubble and a splashing wave of oil rose side by side and mixed as they descended.

It took a long time for everything to clear. Then the gap came into sight, wide at the top, narrow at the bottom, but more of the wall kept crumbling away. Broader, higher, and faster, the stream of oil into the moat continued. Chungking appeared to have escaped the greatest danger to threaten it in all its history.

And what was almost as good, the foreigner – who had staved off the disaster but perhaps brought it down on them too – had disappeared. Did he lie buried under the fallen stones? Had he drowned in the oil, or been flung across the moat and run away?

Now they wouldn't have to make him a magistrate or refer to him as Saviour of the City, Conqueror of the Underworld – a title that would have courted new danger, and caused new disturbances in the city's otherwise peaceful existence. All the foreigners had been driven out now, their work destroyed, and strict decrees would prevent any others from entering the city in the future.

***

Some people were now venturing closer by. The Tuchun and his retinue stood almost at the edge of the gap, watching as the oil – bubbling and murky at first, dragging along huge clods of earth and waste, but ever smoother as they looked on – ran through the ramparts into the dry moat, sinking into the sludge at first but gradually coating the ground like thick sewage.

Then it seemed that the underworld had discovered the scheme. From the centre of the lake, a fountain of mud shot into the air, this one falling back over the edges of the walls, spattering and scorching the people. Many fled across the moat to the far side; some got stuck in the middle.

When the rain of mud was over, the lake began rising again. The oil ran through the wall at the speed of a shallow mountain stream, filling the moat. It was now impossible to leave the city, except from a few upland areas on the far side, or by bridge or raft.

And then the people, who'd been so sure they'd averted calamity, gave in to a greater urge than ever to flee. They didn't realise that at some point the well would run dry, the oil in the moat would sink, and the ancient, eternal life of the city would return to its usual pattern. The sky grew dark. Heavy cloudbanks had massed on the horizon, as if the heavens and underworld had formed an alliance to blockade Chungking from the remainder of the earth.

The sun sank away into the clouds, and in the city not a lamp was lit. The news of the hastily proclaimed death penalty had apparently reached everyone's ears. The Tuchun wondered what to do; some of his attendants wanted to spend the night in a summer palace at the edge of the surrounding hills, others to set an example for the people by going back into the city. He, who had once been so resolute, was now indecisive, turning to Wan Chen. No one had seen the monk go, but he must have left the wall soon after the explosion. The Tuchun almost regretted the loss of the foreigner, who had been more accustomed to those unknown forces. He felt a strange hesitancy to return to Chungking, as if a place touched by the underworld can never again belong to the living.

Then the sun emerged under the edge of the clouds to cross the small blue channel below. Its rays touched the city, lighting it up one last time, but not in the usual grey and red evening colours; everything was covered in a pale purple film.

And that *was* the last time. A thick, dirty-yellow cloud surged in, cloaking the ramparts. No fire at first, then it flared up in the darkness, here and there, until the flames had climbed to the top. The lake inside the walls was still free of fire; the oil was mixed with too much water there.

The Tuchun hesitated no longer. He dismissed his retinue, his guard cleared a bridge, and horses and sedan chairs awaited them on the other side. They fled into the plains, not stopping at the summer palace when the smoke pursued them. He himself remained on the watchtower, staring in at his city like a captain in the corner of the bridge, surveying the sinking, blazing ship that he cannot abandon. He remained conscious for a long while, mostly pondering whether Wan Chen and the foreigner had died before him or escaped. He was no better able than other mortals to resign himself to the thought of a solitary death.

The foreigner had to be dead. For a moment, he suspected Wan Chen of having used supernatural powers to remove himself from the scene, but he had seen that priestly magic was useless against the underworld. If the foreigner was dead, then Wan Chen was too, he could be certain of that. And of himself. The ruler of the underworld would understand that he had done everything he could to save his city.

It looked as if Chungking would be consumed whole and therefore reach the underworld intact, the image of its original self. There he could go on governing it. The fearful cries of the people burning in the city, drowning in the moat, and choking on the plains had almost ceased. One final explosion hurled mud at the watchtower, and the Tuchun died in complete confidence that after his audience with the king of darkness he could continue his reign in the underworld.

***

But he'd been wrong about Wan Chen and the foreigner. Wan Chen was already far away, on the slopes of the mountain range visible from Chungking. In the distance, he saw a small, dirty-yellow cloud slowly spreading across the wrinkled landscape like the stain made by a drop of spattered oil. On this unusual occasion, he had broken into the breathtaking high-speed run that is the fastest means of transport in the Land of Snows. The explosion had thrown the foreigner to the far side of the moat, dazed and battered, and when he'd come to, he'd decided to lie still until he finished dying. There was nothing more for him on earth. But as he lay there, so ready to die, he saw the mountain top in front of him at which he'd stared earlier, now bathed in a red glow – not the red of sunset. He thought of Wan Chen, who seemed to have orchestrated this last stage of his life, and remembered that he came from the Land of Snows, which was said to lie beyond that peak. Thinking of it brought a coolness. He stood up, and motion came easily, as if he were walking not uphill but down. He took his time, certain Wan Chen would wait for him.

Epilogue

One old summer day, so long ago, a steamship, coming from a plantation-rich archipelago in the southern seas, approached the weathered coast of China with part of the country on board, returning home.

Didn't I trickle out over the land with them? Otherwise, would I ever have reached this dreaded, foreign element?

And one day as evening fell – I've forgotten what season, what year, for in the silence after disasters all years are equal, as are the days in this part of the mountains in the Chinese hinterland – I reached the mountain top I'd seen through the high, narrow window in my days of captivity in Velho's house, and again later, when I wandered freely in and around Chungking.

It was strange to stand on those sturdy chunks of stone and think that this was the sight that had so often hovered before me, under the moon and above the clouds in the azure of a sunny day, in the black of a storm-tossed night. Yet however immovable the ground seemed, I felt it was drifting in space, and so was I. Now that I had finally come to a halt, couldn't I take in the passing parade of life on earth before it was over, enjoying the bodily sensations for which others live? The summit that had seemed so unattainable when I looked up at it from the city was now a low hill against the mountain ranges on the horizon – one after another, how many? – that lifted, hollowed and held up the heavens at all once. But in front of me, under me, the earth was so far below that from where I stood I could not see the bottom of the valley.

But on the far side, in the heights, I saw, in as much detail as if he were next to me, Wan Chen, with his coarse yellow leather shoes, the cord around his waist, a chain of beads from human skulls around his neck, his thin mouth and deep-set eyes in his bronzed, red face, even his expression of good-natured mockery. He beckoned me cheerfully, as if waiting just across the street. In a couple of steps, no more, I could wipe out the distance between us, and travel with him to the Land of Snows. How long my journey through China had taken me; this distance was just as great, but how swiftly I would cross it!

I hesitated; the slopes on the far side were formidably bleak and lifeless, although Wan Chen seemed very happy there. Why must I always visit the barren, inhospitable places of the earth, go through the most harrowing adventures, without ever savouring its beauties or staying in its agreeable climes? But if that was my fate ... I closed my eyes and took the step, expecting to be drawn towards Wan Chen in a rapid fall and find myself at his side. And I fell, but not far, and instead of the howling wind of the void on my face and falling body, I felt something warm against my cheeks and the texture of wool and silk in my hands.

I opened my eyes; through a curtain of crimson leaves above the dark red beginning of dusk, I saw the blue sky and, when I stood, the bare mountain range, towering still higher now but endlessly distant, and Wan Chen was no longer in sight.

A sense of grief and abandonment overcame me, and did not fade when I saw where I was: in a lake of poppies, wide, deep and uninhabited. But along the edge was a row of small, graceful pagodas with steep roofs on slender columns, light and airy, not temples but pavilions in the pleasure gardens of a six-sided house that looked closed and vacant – except that a thin line of smoke rose from the roof, never dwindling.

The very moment that – dizzy, the last of my will to live ebbing away – I'd imagined I would enter the Land of Snows from which no one returns in human form, I had chanced or tumbled into the western paradise of legend, never seen by mortal eyes. I had almost stepped over it, drawn by ascetic delusions. Or ... was it Wan Chen's will for me to come here, so that later I would feel his land's hardships all the more keenly?

No, my own willpower had failed me, thank goodness; I would have the chance to enjoy life for a while.

Forever! I would never leave this place. Others were welcome to the pale outlines of pleasure, which I'd never known. I had stumbled upon their source. It was mine now, the original enjoyment.

The poppies waved in the breeze, lush, warm and red. Among them grew all the other flowers. I could not yet tease apart their fragrances, since the only air I had known was over water or inside walls. In the distance I saw the forms of those who, even after the pleasure the poppy brings, still delight the senses as no earthly woman does.

I waded through the poppies. One of them came to greet me; in the middle, where the lake was deepest, we met. We spent the whole rest of the day stretched out on the fragrant ground blanketed with red petals, which was warmed through and through with sun and gave off the faint fragrance of seed. When darkness fell she brought me to her sanctuary. She was more than all who preceded her. She had no name, but a gesture, a word, expressed more than a profound conversation, more than a whole night's coupling with the women before her.

***

As I lay with her on the soft mats, surrounded by poppies – close by in vases like red snowflakes, in the distance like the surface of one great lake – rarely smoking, more often making love, but still more often gazing up in silence at the far-off mountains, my past experiences were gradually lifted from me. At first they hung in the rooms like seldom-worn garments; then they floated through the air like stray cobwebs or gossamer; then they whirled out towards the horizon like the loose sheets of a book, snatched out of a walled garden, unbound and chased off by the wind.

Sometimes we read a page together. She would laugh or look at me in disbelief and run her hand over my head. Now and then I couldn't resist the urge to write on empty pages, no matter how much she – nameless, thoughtless one – advised against it. She made fun of my clumsy handwriting and showed me how to write with a fine-haired brush, stroking a taut sheet of rice paper. It was a pleasure to watch, but she never left any words on the page. I knew better than to mention it.

She grabbed my pages playfully and released them at the edge of the valley. Wasn't she afraid, I asked, that the wind would carry one of them to the inhabited world and betray the location of the western paradise? But she scoffed at me, constant contriver of worries: the pages would never blow that far, the writing would not remain legible, and if anyone ever did read it, and manage to decipher it, this place would have moved on by then, or would remain overlooked anyway.

'What about me, then?'

'You? If Wan Chen hadn't held you back and I hadn't drawn you in, you'd be freezing to death on snow-covered heights by this time, or else you'd have been torn to shreds by ravenous vultures or maniacal monks at some sacrificial festival. But instead ...'

She stretched out, had me lie down next to her, and captivated me. But now and then I looked beyond her silhouette, the slopes of her shoulders and swells of her bosom, at the mountains, melting white under grey skies again. Now and then, despite her warnings, I would write about the western paradise, the longing to share in it and yet to cross the mountains – the only two desires I still felt, apart from those tied to her.

***

A person standing at the top of Dapsang and staring northwest sometimes sees, when he is tired and longs to rest, through a fissure in the rocks, as the mists unexpectedly clear, nestled between two summits, a red lake. A lake of blood, or is it the red of sunset, lingering in the middle of the mountains?

The warm red of the lake is usually unruffled, except when a mild breeze swoops down from the skies and sets it gently rolling. Almost all year round, the lake is left to itself, swaying and flowering in the dead silence of the mountains.

Only in the early autumn do women and children wade through it in indigo robes. With razor-sharp knives, they slash the pods to make them bleed white. Others collect the liquid in little bowls, in which it hardens and turns brown.

Later, when winter approaches, the seer on Dapsang – if he has stayed there, or climbed to the summit again – can make out a black snake slithering slowly away from the lake and across the mountain ranges, sometimes cut into pieces that reunite in the plains. It grows longer and thinner as it nears the populous cities and the valleys of the yellow, blue and pearl rivers, and eventually breaks apart. In small groups the carriers travel on, not groaning under the weight of heavy burdens on poles that chafe their shoulders, but carrying only what they can strap around their waists, or perhaps hanging from one arm another part of their invisible load, which gives them no trouble. They walk with a light, nimble step, even as they bring humanity greater bliss and misfortune than the heaviest-laden caravan. They move fast, sometimes stopping in the woods for a couple of hours to sleep, avoiding the inns and the main roads, crossing the crumbling slopes, riding the swollen rivers on light bamboo rafts; and when they arrive in the cities along the rivers and the coast, their packets are passed from hand to hand and vanish into the vast warehouses of rice and grain.

From there, the brown sap shares the holds with other cargo and finds its way. On dark nights, it's picked up by low junks with their lights out. It stows away on ships whose commanders regard the substance – the sacred unguent that can make the stiff hinges of the gates of bliss swing open – as a dangerous, defiling poison, because the ones who possess and enjoy it refuse to perform slave labour for their profit, and because it brings serenity, and because they sense how the silent ones mock their rowdy drunkenness.

But has anyone ever reached the highest summit of Dapsang? In recent years, he would not have seen the snake slither away; they have blocked the passes and cut off the roads, the sap is no longer harvested, the soil and the stems are saturated with it. The red lake, though swelling to an overwhelming size, is unapproachable. Those who make the drops of bliss go up in smoke sometimes see, on the outermost edges of their dreams, that distant lake, the rolling red among the immovable mountains.

I live alone there and sometimes wish that others could share this fulfilment with me. I used to dream that once I achieved perfect intoxication, it would never end. Now I wish, not that it would end, but that this red lake would spill down the great blue current to the ocean and merge with a distant coral island, floating into a circular reef of gleaming sand, filling that atoll with its round, red, generous glow, and then coming adrift like a great raft of flowers, bringing its joy and opulence everywhere. This dream is impossible; I must take my pleasure in the sight of the immovable mountains of the Land of Snows.

I see them only when I wake up too early, bleak and lifeless in the morning. And Wan Chen no longer beckons me.

By night she sleeps beside me; by day she watches over me, taking my experiences and memories away. I do not know her name, her thoughts or, in truth, even her face; I would not recognise her if I met her anywhere but here. But I know her at night, when she takes the form of every dream, so that I can bear the changeless surroundings of the western paradise. And then her fragrance drowns out all flowers combined, consoling me.

***

There were only two things that troubled me.

The first was the view of the mountains on the far side, not on misty days, but when in the distance the icy wind from the tundra blew over them and their peaks jutted into the sky.

And the bells. The assembly pavilion lay on the outermost edge, nearly suspended over the ravine. Such a charming building could never spring up in the lowlands, but only there, where – on all sides but one – the graceful contours of the mountains stood out against the empty air. The roof was red and gilded; the inscriptions were not admonitions from the wise, but sprightly lines from poets' songs of debauchery and love. From the twelve finials hung small bells in the shape of poppies – everything there came back to poppies – but they were blue, a menacing cobalt blue. Why? And when the evening breeze sprang up – the most pleasurable hour of the day – they would swing and sound, harmoniously enough, but their tones pained me. They reminded me of the time when I, in a disastrous city, at the end of an inhuman life, made a device that captured voices from the air. And they captured the voices, the cries, from the other side, from the Land of Snows with its life-threatening cold, where each must feed his internal fire with utmost concentration, reserving nothing for physical pleasure.

I asked her to take away the bells, but she refused, and laughed at me.

'They've been there for so long, and they sound so lovely. They scare away the ghosts.'

'No, they draw them in. The demons, driven to the edge by the tulkus' potent prayers and incantations, take advantage of the sound waves to cross the ravine. They wait there; sometimes I see them, blue and purple, perched on the black and sulphur cliffs. And the colour of the bells heightens the effect; that colour doesn't belong here, but on the other side.'

'What are you talking about? I can't see them, or the high mountains you describe.'

'You can't even see the mountains?'

No, she saw no mountains. Her world ended there; all around was nothing but a vague mist. If only I could have been like her! Being able to see them only put me in greater danger.

At my repeated request, she silenced the bells. She wouldn't take them down; she tied them in place. But then the ropes whipped back and forth, and the voices grew more numerous and shrill.

The western paradise had been disturbed; it hadn't taken much.

Under the beating sun and wind, the poppies withered fast; their silky petals became wrinkled and limp. Likewise the skin and faces of the sweet fairies. Noxious vapours rose from the valley; strange trees grew at frightening speed on the edges of the western paradise.

And one night, all the woe I thought I'd escaped came rushing back. Together with her and the smoke, I tried to fend off sleep, but it washed over me like a fast-rising flood, with low crashing and thin hissing. My dreams were breakers rolling me over and over like a shell, dragging me from the softest of beaches to the seething heart of a cyclone, where the greatest ships are torn to planks and splinters. But the shell that whirls in the storm cannot break, and when the tumult subsides, it slowly sinks to greater depths.

***

Again, I see Wan Chen ahead of me, this time on a gently sloping, dark yellow plain that, further along, tips steeply upward into a massive column, its curve almost as straight as the arm of a statue, its torso the mountains on the far side, its head disappearing into the clouds, its legs tightly crossed somewhere deep in the valley. Does this statue watch over the entrance to his temple, or the entire Land of Snows? A continuous dust storm blasts over it but leaves not a grain on the polished armour.

The western paradise has vanished. My stay there, which I thought would last forever, which seemed to go on for so long – was it really no more than an instant?

Wan Chen comes towards me. He is bound to set me some inescapable task, but I will no longer shy away. I have never seen him at such close quarters. Even more than before, he looks slow and kind, not like a general from the country where endless battles are fought against demons and human corpses are kept for everyday use.

He says, 'Paradises do not last long. You must find another refuge now; you cannot die, any more than I can. My good fortune, your misfortune, but why shouldn't you find the good in it too? You are too tired and too sated to search for the pleasures of paradise again; you will return there only if you're sure you know the way. So come with me to my post. From there I can show you what lies in each direction.'

And we go to the summit on the far side, where I now see his home for the winter, a sheepskin tent beside a field of withered grey grass.

'There's a good view here, and enough time has passed now. First take a quick look at how things have been going in Chungking since we escaped.'

He gestures at the panorama, sweeps open the flap of his tent, and leaves me alone. I look. At first I cannot find the ruins of Chungking. But in the middle of the red river basin, I do see a network of lines – five by five? six by six? – connecting squat round towers. Those are the pipelines and drilling rigs. Where the city once was is now a patch of large, low, white houses and next to them, as dull and brown as bone ash, a group of hovels. Those are, respectively, new European and Chinese Chungking.

Further out, the Yangtze has changed its course. Taihai has disappeared, and vast marshes have taken the place of the old estuaries. But still further south, there are new cities alongside the old, towering high above them. I watch as one of them shudders and collapses, struck by an earthquake.

In the south, at the edge of Kwantung, the Macao peninsula remains, like a broken brown bottle on an empty beach.

Wan Chen asks if I still want to go back, but before I can answer, he tells me to turn around. The statue is gone, and ahead of me the endless plateau that fills the interior of the Land of Snows lies open. The fields of snow are broken by red and brown mountain ridges; between them are fields of grey grass around lakes as vast as seas. Sandstorms and snowstorms pass over this panorama like delicate eddies, the night falls fast, the stars are large and close, as red as pomegranates, as yellow as blonde heads, the moon is not a heavenly body but a round complex of mountains; the sun clings to the high ridges for one final moment to hold off the witchcraft of the night and its landscapes of death.

This world is not deserted. Wan Chen points out several monasteries in the distance, far out on the plateau, home to thousands of monks, sometimes pouring into the prayer halls, then returning to the cells around them, reciting hymns for days on end, doing ritual exercises, in their ceaseless efforts to keep the demons at bay, apparently leading idle lives, but in fact never flagging for a second in the defence of their country.

Then he brings me to the small cloister high in the mountains, where ten or twelve hermits live together, fearless, invulnerable, devoting all their time to higher meditations and nothing else, providing the instant telegraph service of mind-transference. They do not clothe themselves, staying warm not through exercise but through the friction of thoughts. Their prayers are as short and thin and clear as the sound of bells over mountain streams, as orders passed on from nearby gods.

Higher still are the tents of the ascetics, who live naked in the snow, the cells of those who have retreated into the enveloping darkness once and for all, saying farewell to light and open air to live in the company of their own thoughts.

I see the demons advancing over the desolate fields of snow, now and then seizing some unwitting creature, a stray shepherd or a monk less diligent in prayer. And in this seemingly desolate country, fit only for natural disasters, the most fierce and grievous of battles is being waged without truce. Time and again, the demons strike, and time and again, the spiritual armies drive them back.

***

Nowhere else on earth are the demon armies so powerful and well commanded; nowhere else do the people have so much power to resist and courage to fight, so much that it makes them inhuman in appearance and almost their opponents' equals. You have to have lived here a long time to tell friend from enemy, fellow human from attacker. Without experience, you might try to defend yourself from both and soon fall exhausted to the barren ground.

I understood that without Wan Chen as my escort, I would fall prey to the demons as soon as I entered the country, torn to shreds in an instant. I turned to him and told him I was ready to enter with him and remain there.

But Wan Chen said to me, 'The only reason I'm showing you this is so that, when you long for it later, you won't think it was kept from you. You can see you aren't strong enough to make your way there alone, and I can't look after you the whole time. You couldn't even stand up to one of the foot soldiers in the spirit army. It takes years of prayer and practice.

'You will often wish you could be in one of the fortresses in the Land of Snows, under permanent siege, where the kanglings sound in the furious winter's rages and the prayers are maintained like rapid fire. Nowhere on earth is such an astonishing battle waged and the emptiness of existence forgotten so deeply, or populated so densely.

'But it is too late for you to adopt this life. You have dissipated your powers. Just after the fall of Chungking, I thought for a moment that it might work, but no sooner did I loosen my grip on you for a moment than you fell into the western paradise between here and there. Go on with your life now in the Middle Kingdom. The multitudes of people there, always struggling with each other and with natural disasters, are your surest distraction and strongest protection against the emptiness and the demons.

'There is no better place on earth to live for a man tormented by his fate and threatened by those demons, like you. Try never to stay in one place; move from city to city, resting your weary body in the inns and your weary soul in the monasteries. Wherever you go, you will be recognised as my kin and given shelter.'

***

And I returned to the kingdom where I would go on wandering without ever stopping, until the end, avoiding Europeans, no longer hoping for closer contact with the Chinese, until I found myself somewhere between the two of them, spending a while in the steppes, then a while in the cities, sometimes travelling with a caravan, sometimes sailing the rivers on a broad junk.

And I took no further part in life on earth. For those who do, it can have only one meaning: conceiving or bringing forth other lives, as many as possible, or exterminating other lives by the throng, yet merely making way for new arrivals. The people of the Middle Kingdom have learned and remembered this lesson: they bring forth and exterminate; they watch dispassionately as children are born and landscapes devastated, as armies obliterate each other and blood relatives die, and they celebrate at funerals and weddings.

I had fulfilled life's meaning, largely in spite of myself, through the twists and turns of my fate, liberating myself from the conspiracy of lineage and menacing spirits, and conceiving the narrow remainder of my days. I would not have to destroy myself before my time.

A long, low mountain ridge led back to the Land of Snows. At the end was the curve of the mountain at which I'd gazed up, with the sun beside it. It was not great and overwhelming, any more than a long-stemmed pipe or the lamp that glows beside it. And the clouds drifted above like the fumes inhaled by fortunate smokers.

Even that no longer tempted me.

I would sometimes yearn to be back with Wan Chen, sunk in year-long meditations or combating the spirit army. Once my years of wandering the kingdom were done, wouldn't he be waiting for me somewhere? No, there would be no point. Against the creatures he battled, I was powerless. Still, I longed to see him again, my final companion.

But maybe the kingdom is haunted by many phantoms like me, and we will greet each other like humans, sit together in smoky inns drinking bad but warm wine, sharing our thoughts and reading the inscriptions scratched in the walls there by earlier passers-by, which can never be erased by time nor marred by the living. Then I won't be so lonely anymore, and I'll eventually forget not only Taihai and Chungking but also the western paradise, not even regretting that I found no meaning but myself for my life on earth.

I only hope that when I cross over, I will not be sitting in some great hall or on the edge of a ravine, squinting at some distant mountaintop under motionless clouds like the spineless sages, but on my way, marching through the mountains or floating down a river. Maybe then, after all, the current will carry me to Wan Chen's country to continue the battle of a man who can neither die nor share in the careless, formless life of the true immortals.

Notes

BY KATE MACDONALD

Part One

Chapter 1

Amoy: a city in south-eastern China, now called Xiamen.

junk: traditional Chinese sailing vessel.

Malacca: now a state in Malaysia.

Dutch East Indies: now called Indonesia.

Middle Kingdom: Zhongguo, the Chinese name for their country, among other elements of the Chinese nation, was translated into Western languages from the sixteenth century as 'Middle Kingdom'.

quicklime: calcium oxide, a common chemical compound used to preserve bodies before burial, by taking advantage of its rapid dessicating action.

Gulangyu Island: a small island off Amoy (Xiamen), the site of an international settlement in the period of the novel.

the great famine: China has experienced many famines; the famine referred to here would be the 1920–21 famine in North China, which killed half a million people.

Natuna: a group of islands between south-east China and the Dutch East Indies (Indonesia).

sampan: a low-lying shore-going boat capable of holding only a few people, also used for floating market stalls.

coal trimmer: the crewman responsible for handling the coal in a coal-fuelled ship, from loading and storage to shovelling into the furnace.

Taihai: Slauerhoff's invented name for Shanghai, one of the five international treaty ports in China and a haven for millions of Russian refugees in the 1920s. When Slauerhoff was writing the novel Shanghai was the fifth-largest city in the world.

Hankow: Hankou, now part of Wuhan city at the confluence of the Han and Yangtze rivers, north-west of Amoy (Xiamen) and due west from 'Taihai' (Shanghai).

Ichang: another large trading city and port, due west of Hankow (now Wuhan city).

the Canton–Hong Kong boycott: a strike by Chinese workers protesting at the killing of nine Chinese demonstrators by British imperial police on 30 May 1925 in Shanghai. It lasted from June 1925 to October 1926, and gives a precise date for the novel , if the reader accepts it as a strictly factual account.

Ningpo: Ningbo, large trading city south of Shanghai.

Chapter 2

Mecca, Memphis and Atlantis: Mecca is forbidden to non-Muslims, Memphis is a lost city of the ancient Egyptian civilisations, and Atlantis is a fabled city lost under the sea.

the inescapable misery of the old days: a reference to Cameron's struggles in Slauerhoff's earlier novel, *The Forbidden Kingdom*.

black-toothed grin: painting the teeth of older women black to prevent tooth decay was practised in some parts of China, though was disappearing due to Western influences in the modern era.

rictus: the stiffening of the body after death.

Woosung forts: these fortifications guarded entry along the Yangtze River to Shanghai, formerly a tidal port.

green isle of Erin: this novel was written not long after the romanticisation of Ireland by the artists and authors of the Celtic Twilight.

the Bund: a central Shanghai waterfront area, formerly the heart of international trading and relaxation.

flagrant juvenility: the girls are children, well below the accepted age of marriage or concubinage in Chinese culture.

camphor: bark product used to ward off textile-eating moth larvae.

the ruler of Mongolia, the living Buddha: the Bogd Khan (1862–1924), born as Agvaanl Uvsanchoijinyam Danzan Vanchüg, was the ruler of Outer Mongolia and the third most important figure of spiritual authority for Tibetan Buddhists. His reputation for loose living has been attributed to early twentieth century Chinese propaganda. After his death Outer Mongolia was contested by both Soviet and Chinese Communist forces.

the Whangpoo: the Huangpu River flows through Shanghai.

Chapter 3

the long pipe: opium is traditionally smoked using a long-stemmed pipe.

Tonkinese opium: from a region in Vietnam.

the Shantung variety: from a region in north-east coastal China.

the Wing On department store: this was one of the four largest department stores in Shanghai and opened in 1918.

a Sikh constable: many British police officers in the international concessions came from the British colonial forces.

Chapter 4

fan-tan: a traditional Chinese gambling game, similar to roulette.

the victorious armies in the south: (note by David McKay)
Until 1927, Shanghai was ruled by a local warlord in cooperation
with the international powers. In early 1927, the southern nationalist
armies captured the city, and there was a brief interim period in which
revolutionaries (mostly communist) within Shanghai controlled the city.
In April 1927, the nationalists carried out a violent purge of communists
in Shanghai but Slauerhoff doesn't seem to refer to that, and it seems
reasonable to assume that Cameron is unaware of the full political
backdrop to the chaos around him.

It's likely that the Japanese felt threatened by both the northern
and the southern armies. Elements of the southern forces, especially
the communists, were more hostile to foreign settlements than the
warlords, but the nationalists were more open to alliances with the
foreign powers and capitalists in China. At the same time, Japanese
expansionism and occupation of parts of Shandong created friction
with almost all other parties.

As soon as the northern armies arrive there are skirmishes,
probably with local revolutionary (nationalist and communist)
forces from Shanghai and perhaps also with foreign troops
defending the concessions. A band of local revolutionaries attacks
the Japanese concession. It's also possible that the band attacking
the Japanese settlement is made up of soldiers from the fleeing
northern armies or other refugees, because of rivalries between
warlords, or the 'race hatred' that Cameron describes, or the desire
to loot, or because they had defected to the south. The Japanese
residents of the outlying streets of the concession are massacred,
but many others remain alive.

Not long after that, Cameron sees Japanese soldiers inside their
country's concession (and inside the barbed wire fence), defending
it from within. Cameron is outside the city gates and the barbed

wire fences, in his undefended outlying district, looking in at the foreign soldiers, revolutionaries, and militiamen defending the city and the concessions. The idea of city gates and a city wall is obviously important to Slauerhoff, but may here be a fictional conceit.

Lilliput and Brobdingnag: references to *Gulliver's Travels* (1726) by Jonathan Swift. Lilliputians are tiny, and Brobdingnagians are giants.

Nanking, the old capital: Nanjing, the former capital city of several Ming dynasty emperors, was selected by Sun Yat-Sen as the new capital for the Republic of China in 1912, though it did not function as such until Chiang Kai-Shek's leadership, from 1927.

Chapter 5

Hupeh, Szechwan: Hubei and Sichuan provinces, west of Shanghai.

carry that disease in your blood: Hsiu is joking that Europeans are inveterate roamers.

Lao Tzu: also known as Laosi and Lao-Tze, a Chinese philosopher thought to have lived between the fourth and sixth centuries BCE.

Chusan archipelago: islands south of Shanghai.

the Thames and the Elbe: the two large rivers in north-western Europe with which presumably Cameron was most familiar.

Chapter 6

Minyang: Mianyang, large city in Sichuan, in the centre of China.

laudanum: a sedative and opiate made from opium.

Chapter 7

Hunan and Shantung: Hunan is an inland province in south-east

China, Shandong is a coastal province on the north-east coast.

Lake Baikal: the largest freshwater lake in the world, and the deepest, in southern Siberia.

a poem: to appreciate and compose poetry was a mark of civilised values in Chinese culture.

Lanchow: Lanzhou is in Gansu in north-central China, a very large city on the Yellow River.

Chapter 8

cogon grass: a grass, growing to three metres high, used widely across south-east Asia for thatching and soil stabilisation.

the lowest rank of scholar-officials: until 1912 the Emperor appointed scholar-officials or 'literati' to run the government and attend to all aspects of civil and political life in China. They were examined on the basis of their knowledge of the Confucian classics and other philosophical texts.

nankeen: a pale yellow cotton cloth, originally made in Nanjing, and eventually exported worldwide as a basic fabric for clothes, particularly trousers.

Part Two

Chapter 9

before the Han Dynasty: that is, before 206 BCE.

Celestial Empire: a literary translation of Tianchao, an old name for China.

Yellow River: the second longest river in China and the sixth-longest river system in the world.

Ch'in Shih Huang: the first Emperor of a unified China, which he achieved in 221 BCE.

li: the Chinese unit of measurement of distance, and of weight. As a distance it is now standardised at about 500m, or a third of a Western mile.

Cimmeria: the reach of the Cimmerian peoples was widespread and scattered across Central and Eastern Asia, and they settled in the area occupied by modern Anatolia.

the Forbidden City: the royal palace complex in Peking (Beijing).

the cities of Kublai Khan and the Manchus: Kublai Khan ruled in the thirteenth century CE, and the Manchu Qing dynasty ruled China from the seventeenth century to 1912.

one of the foreigners: this refers to events in Slauerhoff's earlier novel, *The Forbidden Kingdom*.

Canton: Guangzhou, capital city of Guandong, in southern China.

Velho: the descendant of a character in *The Forbidden Kingdom*.

glazed tiles in soft colours: these suggest the Portuguese tastes of Velho's ancestor, the original settler in Chungking.

Emperor Yung Cheng: Yinzhen, the Yongzheng Emperor, who ruled China in the eighteenth century.

the Tuchun: the warlord ruler of Chungking.

Chapter 10

Phodang Monastery: a Buddhist monastery in Sikkim, northern India.

Amdo: the northernmost of the three regions of Tibet, bordering China.

Siemens-Schuckert: German electrical engineering company, known for their military aeroplane engines in the First World War.

a member of the Forest of Brushes: the Hanlin Academy, the Oxbridge of pre-revolutionary China.

yamen: the office and sometimes also the residence of a Chinese imperial official. Here it refers to the city's bureaucracy.

Chapter 11

kang: a raised platform built at one end of a traditional Chinese house, heated underneath, and furnished with mats or cushions, used for most domestic activities included sleeping.

Chapter 12

so many times before: refers to the plot of *The Forbidden Kingdom*.

Chapter 14

Laocoön: character from Greek myth, a Trojan priest, who was strangled along with his two sons by giant snakes sent by Zeus. Slauerhoff refers to the famous marble statue in the Vatican Museums.

Chapter 15

a man boasting: this could be a reference to broadcast speeches by Hitler, or Mussolini, who could have been heard on the radio when this novel was being written.

Chapter 16

breathtaking high-speed run: this may be a reference to the Chinese mythical character the Monkey King, Sun Wukong. One of his attributes was a magical high-speed run, and he was incorporated into Buddhist traditions. High-speed running was one of the special faculties Tibetan monks acquired through mental training, together with thought-transmission/mind-transference.

Epilogue

Dapsang: K2, or Chhogori, the second-highest mountain in the world, located on the border of China and Pakistan.

tulkus: reincarnated Buddhist teachers of particular traditions in Buddhist thought.

kanglings: ceremonial trumpets made and used by Buddhist monks, made from wood, or a human femur.